Charles John Hyne

Adventures of Captain Kettle

Charles John Hyne

Adventures of Captain Kettle

ISBN/EAN: 9783337076078

Printed in Europe, USA, Canada, Australia, Japan

Cover: Foto ©Andreas Hilbeck / pixelio.de

More available books at **www.hansebooks.com**

ADVENTURES OF CAPTAIN KETTLE

BY CUTCLIFFE HYNE

AUTHOR OF "A MASTER OF FORTUNE," ETC.

M. A. DONOHUE & COMPANY

CHICAGO   NEW YORK

CONTENTS

CHAP.		PAGE
I.	The Guns for Cuba	1
II.	Crown and Garotte	27
III.	The War Steamer of Donna Clotilde	54
IV.	The Pilgrim Ship	77
V.	Fortunes Adrift	100
VI.	The Escape	124
VII.	The Pearl Poachers	147
VIII.	The Liner and the Iceberg	175
IX.	The Raiding of Donna Clotilde	199
X.	Mr. Gedge's Catspaw	225
XI.	The Salving of the Duncansby Head	255
XII.	The Wreck of the Cattle-Boat	280

ADVENTURES OF
CAPTAIN KETTLE.

CHAPTER I.

THE GUNS FOR CUBA.

"THE shore part must lie entirely with you, sir," said Captain Kettle. "It's mixed up with the Foreign Enlistment Act, and the *Alabama* case, and a dozen other things which may mean anything between gaol and confiscation, and my head isn't big enough to hold it. If you'll be advised by me, sir, you'll see a real first-class solicitor, and stand him a drink, and pay him down what he asks right there on the bar counter, and get to know exactly how the law of this business stands before you stir foot in it.

"The law here in England," said the little man with a reminiscent sigh, "is a beastly thing to fall foul of: it's just wickedly officious and interfering; it's never done kicking you, once it's got a fair start; and you never know where it will shove out its ugly hoof from next. No, Mr. Gedge, give me the States for nice comfortable law, where a man can buy it by the yard for paper money down, and straight pistol shooting is always remembered in his favour."

The young man who owned the SS. *Sultan of Borneo* tapped his blotting paper impatiently. "Stick to the point, Kettle. We're in England now, and have nothing whatever to do with legal matters in America. As for your advice, I am not a fool: you can lay your ticket on it I know to an inch how I stand. And I may tell you this: the shipment is arranged for."

"I'd like to see us cleared," said Captain Kettle doubtfully.

"No one will interfere with the clearance. The *Sultan of Borneo* will leave here in coal, consigned to the Havana. A private yacht will meet her at sea, and tranship the arms out of sight of land."

"Tyne coal for Cuba? They'd get their coal there from Norfolk, Virginia, or else Welsh steam coal from Cardiff or Newport."

"It seems not. This contract was placed long before a ship was asked for to smuggle out the arms."

"Well, it looks fishy, anyway."

"I can't help that," said Gedge irritably. "I'm telling you the naked truth, and if truth as usual looks unlikely, it's not my fault. Now have you got any more objections to make?"

"No, sir," said Captain Kettle, "none that I can see at present."

"Very well, then," said Gedge. "Do you care to sign on as master for this cruise, or are you going to cry off?"

"They'll hang me if I'm caught," said Kettle.

"Not they. They'll only talk big, and the British Consul will get you clear. You bet they daren't hang an Englishman for mere smuggling in Cuba. And besides, aren't I offering to raise your screw from twelve pound a month to fourteen so as to cover the risk? However, you won't get caught. You'll find everything ready for you; you'll slip the rifles ashore; and then you'll steam on to Havana and discharge your coal in the ordinary humdrum way of business, And there's a ten pound bonus if you pull the thing off successfully. Now then, Captain, quick: you go or you don't?"

"I go," said Kettle gloomily. "I'm a poor man with a wife and family, Mr. Gedge, and I can't afford to lose a berth. But it's that coal I can't swallow. I quite believe what you say about the contract; only it doesn't look natural. And it's my belief the coal will trip us up somewhere before we've done, and bring about trouble."

"Which of course you are quite a stranger to?" said Gedge slily.

"Don't taunt me with it, sir," said Captain Kettle. "I quite well know the kind of brute I am; trouble with a crew or any other set of living men at sea is just meat and drink to me, and I'm bitterly ashamed of the taste. Every time I sit underneath our minister in the chapel here in South Shields I grow more ashamed. And if you heard the beautiful poetical way that man talks of peace, and green fields, and golden harps, you'd understand."

"Yes, yes," said Gedge; "but I don't want any of your excellent minister's sermons at second hand just now, Captain, or any of your own poetry, thanks.

I'm very busy. Good morning. Help yourself to a cigar. You haul alongside the coal shoots to get your cargo at two o'clock, and I'll be on board to see you at six. Good morning." And Mr. Gedge rang for the clerk and was busily dictating letters before Kettle **was clear of** the office.

The little sailor went down the grimy stairs and into the street, and made towards the smelling **Tyne.** The black cigar rested unlit in an angle of his mouth, and he gnawed savagely **at** the butt with his eye-teeth. He cursed the Fates as he walked. Why did they use him **so evilly** that he was forced into berths like these? As a bachelor, he told himself with a sneer, he would have jumped at the excitement of it. As the partner **of** Mrs. Kettle, and the father of her children, he could have shuddered when he threw his eyes over the future.

For a week or so she could draw his half-pay and live sumptuously **at** the rate of seven pounds a month. But afterwards, if he got caught by some angry Spanish war-steamer with the smuggled rifles under his hatches, and shot, or hanged, or imprisoned, or otherwise debarred from earning income **at his** craft, where would Mrs. Kettle be then? Would Gedge do anything for her? He drew the cigar from his lips, and spat contemptuously at the bare idea. With the morality of the affair he troubled not one jot. The Spanish Government and the Cuban rebels were two rival firms who **offered** different rates of freight according **to the** risk, and he was employed as carrier by those who paid the higher price. If there was any right or wrong about the question, it **was** a purely private matter between Mr. Gedge and his God. He, Owen Kettle, was as impersonal in the business as the ancient *Sultan of Borneo* herself; he was a mere cog in some complex machinery; and if he was earning heaven, it was by piety inside the chapel ashore, and not by professional exertions (in the interests of an earthly employer) elsewhere.

He took ferry across the filthy Tyne, and walked down alleys and squalid streets where coal dust formed the mud, and the air was sour with foreign vapours. And as he walked he champed still at the unlit cigar, and brooded over the angularity of his fate. But when he passed between the gates of the dock company's premises, and exchanged words with the policeman on guard, a change came over him. He threw away the cigar stump, tightened his lips, and left all thoughts of personal matters outside the door-sill. He was Mr. Gedge's hired servant; his brain was devoted to furthering Gedge's interests; and all the acid of his tongue was ready to spur on those who did the manual work on Gedge's ship.

Within a minute of his arrival on her deck, the *Sultan of Borneo* was being unmoored from the bollards on the quay; within ten, her winches were clattering and bucking as they warped her across to the black, straddling coal-shoots at the other side of the dock; and within half an hour the cargo was roaring down her hatches as fast as the railway waggons on the grimy trestle overhead could disgorge.

The halo of coal dust made day into dusk; the grit of it filled every cranny, and settled as an amorphous scum on the water of the dock; and labourers hired by the hour toiled at piece-work pace through sheer terror at their employer.

If his other failings could have been eliminated, this little skipper, with the red peaked beard, would certainly have been, from an owner's point of view, the best commander sailing out of any English port. No man ever wrenched such a magnificent amount of work from his hands.   But it was those other failings which kept him what he was, the pitiful knockabout ship-master, living from hand to mouth, never certain of his berth from one month's end to another.

That afternoon Captain Kettle signed on his crew, got them on board, and with the help of his two mates kicked the majority of them into sobriety; he received a visit and final instructions from Mr. Gedge at six o'clock; and by nightfall he had filled in his papers, warped out of dock, and stood anxiously on the bridge watching the pilot as he took the steamboat down through the crowded shipping of the river.   His wife stood under the glow of an arc lamp on the dockhead and waved him good-bye through the gloom.

Captain Kettle received his first fright as he dropped his pilot just outside the Tyne pierheads. A man-of-war's launch steamed up out of the night, and the boarding officer examined his papers and asked questions. The little captain, conscious of having no contraband of war on board just then, was brutally rude; but the naval officer remained stolid, and refused to see the insults which were pitched at him.   He had an unpalatable duty to perform; he quite sympathised with Kettle's feelings over the matter; and he got back to his launch thanking many stars that the affair had ended so easily.

But Kettle rang on his engines again with very

unpleasant feelings. It was clear to him that the secret was oozing out somewhere; that the *Sultan of Borneo* was suspected; that his course to Cuba would be beset with many well-armed obstacles; and he forthwith made his first ruse out of the long succession which were to follow.

He had been instructed by Gedge to steam off straight from the Tyne to a point deep in the North Sea, where a yacht would meet him to hand over the consignment of smuggled arms. But he felt the night to be full of eyes, and for a Havana-bound ship to leave the usual steam-lane which leads to the English Channel was equivalent to a confession of her purpose from the outset. So he took the parallel rulers and pencilled off on his chart the stereotyped course, which just clears Whitby Rock and Flamboro' Head; and the *Sultan of Borneo* was held steadily along this, steaming at her normal nine knots; and it was not till she was out of sight of land off Humber mouth, and the sea chanced to be desolate, that he starboarded his helm and stood off for the ocean rendezvous.

A hand on the foretopsail yard picked up the yacht out of the grey mists of dawn, and by eight bells they were lying hove-to in the trough, with a hundred yards of cold grey water tumbling between them. The transhipment was made in two lifeboats, and Kettle went across and enjoyed an extravagant breakfast in the yacht's cabin. The talk was all upon the Cuban revolution. Carnforth, the yacht's owner, brimmed with it.

"If you can run the blockade, Captain," said he, "and land these rifles, and the Maxims, and the cartridges, they'll be grateful enough to put up a statue to you. The revolution will end in a snap. The Spanish troops are half of them fever-ridden, and all of them discouraged. With these guns you are carrying, the patriots can shoot their enemies over the edges of the island into the Caribbean Sea. And there is no reason why you should get stopped. There are filibustering expeditions fitted out every week from Key West, and Tampa, and the other Florida ports, and one or two have even started from New York itself."

"But they haven't got through?" suggested Captain Kettle.

"Not all of them," Mr. Carnforth admitted. "But then you see they sailed in schooners, and you have got steam. Besides, they started from the States, where the newspapers knew all about them, and so their arrival was cabled on to Cuba ahead; and you have the advantage of sailing from an English port."

"I don't see where the pull comes in," said Kettle gloomily. "There isn't a blessed country on the face of the globe more interfering with her own people than England. A Yankee can do as he darn well pleases in the filibustering line; but if a Britisher makes a move that way, the blessed law here stretches out twenty hands and plucks him back by the tail before he's half started. No, Mr. Carnforth, I'm not sweet on the chances. I'm a poor man, and this means a lot to me: that's why I'm anxious. You're rich; you only stand to lose the cost of the consignment; and if that gets confiscated it won't mean much to you."

Carnforth grinned. "You **pay** my business qualities a poor compliment, Captain. You can **bet**
your life I had money down in hard cash before I
stirred foot in the matter. The weapons and **the**
ammunition were paid for at fifty per cent. above
list prices, so as to cover the trouble of secrecy, and
I got a charter for the yacht to bring the stuff **out**
here which would astonish you **if** you saw the
figures. No, I'm **clear** on the matter from this
moment, Captain, **but I'll** not deny that I shall take
an interest in your future adventures with the cargo.
Help yourself to a cigarette."

"Then it seems **to me**," said Kettle **acidly, "that**
you'll look at me **just as a** hare **set on to run for**
your amusement?"

The yacht-owner laughed. "You put it brutally,"
he said, "but that's about the size of it. And if
you want further **truths,** here's one: I shouldn't
particularly mind if you were caught."

"How's that?"

"Because, my dear skipper, **if** the Spanish
captured this consignment, **the** patriots would want
another, and I should get the **order.** Whereas, if
you land the stuff safely, it will see them through
to the end of the war, and **my** chance of making
further profit will be at an end."

"You have **a very clear** way of putting it," said
Captain Kettle.

"Haven't I? **Which will** you take, green char-
treuse or yellow?"

"And Mr. Gedge? **Can** you tell me, sir, how he
stands over this business?"

"Oh, you bet, Gedge knows when to come in out

of the wet.   He's got the old *Sultan* underwritten by the insurance and by the Cuban agents up to double her value, and nothing would suit his books better than for a Spanish cruiser to drop upon you."

Captain Kettle got up, reached for his cap, and swung it aggressively on to one side of his head.

"Very well," he said, "that's your side of the question.   Now hear mine.   That cargo's going through, and those rebels or patriots, or whatever they are, shall have their guns if half the Spanish navy was there to try and stop me.   You and Mr. Gedge have started about this business the wrong way.   Treat me on the square, and I'm a man a child might handle ; but I'd not be driven by the Queen of England, no, not with the Emperor of Germany to help her."

"Oh, look here, Captain," said Carnforth, "don't get your back up."

"I'll not trade with you," replied Kettle.

"You're a fool to your own interests."

"I know it," said the sailor grimly.   "I've known it all my life.   If I'd not been that, I'd not have found myself in such shady company as there is here now."

"Look here, you ruffian, if you insult me I'll kick you out of this cabin, and over the side into your own boat."

"All right," said Kettle ; "start in."

Carnforth half rose from his seat and measured Captain Kettle with his eye.   Apparently the scrutiny impressed him, for he sank back to his seat again with an embarrassed laugh.   "You're an ugly little devil," he said.

"I'm all that," said Kettle.

" And I'm not going to play at rough and tumble with you here. We've neither of us anything to gain by it, and I've a lot to lose. I believe you'll run that cargo through now that you're put on your mettle, but I guess there'll be trouble for somebody before it's dealt out to the patriot troops. Gad, I'd like to be somewhere on hand to watch you do it."

" I don't object to an audience," said Kettle.

" By Jove, I've half a mind to come with you."

" You'd better not," said the little sailor with glib contempt. " You're not the sort that cares to risk his skin, and I can't be bothered with dead-head passengers."

" That settles it," said Carnforth. " I'm coming with you to run that blockade ; and if the chance comes, my cantankerous friend, I'll show you I can be useful. Always supposing, that is, we don't murder one another before we get there."

A white mist shut the Channel sea into a ring, and the air was noisy with the grunts and screams of steamers' syrens. Captain Kettle was standing on the *Sultan of Borneo's* upper bridge, with his hand on the engine-room telegraph, which was pointed at " Full speed astern ;" Carnforth and the old second mate stood with their chins over the top of the starboard dodger ; and all three of them peered into the opalescent banks of the fog.

They had reason for their anxiety. Not five minutes before, a long lean torpedo-catcher had raced up out of the thickness, and slowed down alongside with the Channel spindrift blowing over her low superstructure in white hail-storms. An officer on the upper bridge in glistening oilskins had sent across a sharp authoritative hail, and had been answered: " *Sultan of Borneo;* Kettle, master; from South Shields to the Havana."

" What cargo?" came the next question.

" Coal."

" What?"

" Coal."

" Then Mr. Tyne Coal for the Havana, just heave to whilst I send away a boat to look at you. I fancy you will be the steamboat I'm sent to find and fetch back."

The decks of the uncomfortable warship had hummed with men, a pair of boat davits had swung outboard, and the boat had been armed and manned with naval noise and quickness. But just then a billow of the fog had driven down upon them, blanket-like in its thickness, which closed all human vision beyond the range of a dozen yards, and Captain Kettle jumped like a terrier on his opportunity. He sent his steamer hard astern with a slightly ported helm, and whilst the torpedo-catcher's boat was searching for him towards the French shore, and sending vain hails into the white banks of the mist, he was circling slowly and silently round towards the English coast.

So long as the mist held, the *Sultan of Borneo* was as hard to find as a needle in a cargo of hay. Did the air clear for so much as a single instant, she would be noticed and stand self-confessed by her attempt to escape; and as a result, the suspense

was vivid enough to make Carnforth feel physical
nausea. He had not reckoned on this complication.
He was quite prepared to risk capture in Cuban
waters, where the glamour of distance and the dazzle
of helping insurrectionists would cast a glow of
romance over whatever occurred. But to be caught
in the English Channel as a vulgar smuggler for the
sake of commercial profit, and to be haled back for
hard labour in an English gaol, was a different matter.
He was a member of Parliament, and he understood
these details in all their niceties.

But Captain Kettle took the situation differently.
The sight of the torpedo-catcher stiffened all the
doubt and limpness out of his composition ; his eye
brightened and his lips grew stiff ; the scheming to
escape acted on him like a tonic ; and when an hour
later the *Sultan of Borneo* was steaming merrily
down Channel at top speed through the same impenetrable fog, the little skipper whistled dance
music on the upper bridge, and caught the notion
for a most pleasing sonnet. That evening the crew
came aft in a state of mild mutiny, and Kettle
attended to their needs with gusto.

He prefaced his remarks by a slight exhibition
of marksmanship. He cut away the vane which
showed dimly on the fore-topmast truck with a
single bullet, and then, after dexterously reloading
his revolver, lounged over the white rail of the upper
bridge with the weapon in his hand.

He told the malcontents he was glad of the opportunity to give them his views on matters generally.
He informed them genially that for their personal
wishes he cared not one decimal of a jot. He stated

plainly that he had got them on board, and intended by their help to carry out his owner's instructions whether they hated them or not. And finally he gave them his candid assurance that if any cur amongst them presumed to disobey the least of his orders, he would shoot that man neatly through the head without further preamble.

This elegant harangue did not go home to all hands at once, because being a British ship, the *Sultan of Borneo's* crew naturally spoke in five different languages, and few of them had even a working knowledge of English. But the look of Kettle's savage little face as he talked, and the red torpedo beard which wagged beneath it, conveyed to them the tone of his speech, and for the time they did not require a more accurate translation. They had come off big with the intention of forcing him (if necessary with violence) to run the steamer there and then into an English port; they went forward again like a pack of sheep, merely because one man had let them hear the virulence of his bark, and had shown them with what accuracy he could bite if necessary. "And that's the beauty of a mongrel crew," said Kettle complacently. "If they'd been English, I'd have had to shoot at least two of the beasts to keep my end up like that."

"You're a marvel," Carnforth admitted. "I'm a bit of a speaker myself, but I never heard a man with a gift of tongue like you have got."

"I am poisonous when I spread myself," said Kettle.

"I wish I was clear of you," said Carnforth, with an awkward laugh. "Whatever possessed me to leave the yacht and come on this cruise I can't think."

"Some people never do know when they're well off," said Kettle. "Well, sir, you're in for it now, and you may see things which will be of service to you afterwards. You ought to make your mark in Parliament if you do get back from this trip. You'll have something to talk about that men will like to listen to, instead of merely chattering wind, which is what most of them are put to, so far as I can see from the papers. And now, sir, here's the steward come to tell us tea's ready. You go below and tuck in. I'll take mine on the bridge here. It won't do for me to turn my back yet awhile, or else those beasts forrard will jump on us from behind and murder the whole lot whilst we aren't looking."

The voyage from that time onwards was for Captain Kettle a period of constant watchfulness. It would not be true to say that he never took off his clothes or never slept; but whether he was in pyjamas in the chart-house, or whether he was sitting on an upturned ginger-beer case under the shelter of one of the upper bridge canvas dodgers, with his tired eyes shut and the red peaked beard upon his chest, it was always the same, he was ever ready to spring instantly upon the alert.

One dark night an iron belaying-pin flew out of the blackness of the forecastle and whizzed within an inch of his sleeping head; but he roused so quickly that he was able to shoot the thrower through the shoulder before he could dive back again through the forecastle door. And another time when a powdering gale had kept him on the bridge for forty-eight consecutive hours, and a deputation of the deck hands raided him in the charthouse on the supposition that exhaustion would have laid him out in a dead sleep, he woke before their fingers touched him, broke the jaw of one with a camp-stool, and so maltreated the others with the same weapon, that they were glad enough to run away even with the exasperating knowledge that they left their taskmaster undamaged behind them.

So, although this all-nation crew of the *Sultan of Borneo* dreaded the Spaniards much, they feared Captain Kettle far more, and by the time the steamer had closed up with the island of Cuba, they had concluded to follow out their skipper's orders, as being the least of the two evils which lay before them.

Carnforth's way of looking at the matter was peculiar. He had all a healthy man's appetite for adventure, and all a prosperous man's distaste for being wrecked. He had taken a strong personal liking for the truculent little skipper, and, other things being equal, would have cheerfully helped him; but on the other hand, he could not avoid seeing that it was to his own interests that the crew should get their way, and keep the steamer out of dangerous waters. And so, when finally he decided to stand by non-interferent, he prided himself a good deal on his forbearance, and said so to Kettle in as many words.

That worthy mariner quite agreed with him. "It's the very best thing you could do, sir," he answered. "It would have annoyed me terribly to have had to shoot you out of mischief's way, because you've been kind enough to say you like my poetry, and because I've come to see, sir, you're a gentleman."

They came to this arrangement on the morning of the day they opened out the secluded bay in the southern Cuban shore where the contraband of war was to be run. Kettle calculated his whereabouts with niceness, and, after the midday observation, lay the steamer to for a couple of hours, and himself supervised his engineers whilst they gave a good overhaul to the machinery. Then he gave her steam again, and made his landfall four hours after the sunset.

They saw the coast first as a black line running across the dim grey of the night. It rose as they neared it, and showed a crest fringed with trees, and a foot steeped in white mist, from out of which came the faint bellow of surf. Captain Kettle, after a cast or two, picked up his marks and steamed in confidently, with his side-lights dowsed, and three red lanterns in a triangle at his foremast head. He was feeling pleasantly surprised with the easiness of it all.

But when the steamer had got well into the bight of the bay, and all the glasses on the bridge were peering at the shore in search of answering lights, a blaze of radiance suddenly flickered on to her from astern, and was as suddenly eclipsed, leaving them for a moment blinded by its dazzle. It was a long truncheon of light which sprouted from a glowing centre away between the heads of the bay, and they watched it sweep past them over the surface of the water, and then sweep back again. Finally, after a little more dalliance, it settled on the steamer and lit her, and the ring of water on which she swam, like a ship in a lantern picture.

Carnforth swore aloud, and Captain Kettle lit a fresh cigar. Those of the mongrel crew who were on the deck went below to pack their bags.

"Well, sir," said Kettle cheerfully, " here we are. That's a Spanish gunboat with searchlight, all complete "—he screwed up his eyes and gazed astern meditatively. "She's got the heels of us too ; by about five knots I should say. Just look at the flames coming out of her funnels. Aren't they just giving her ginger down in the stokehold? Shooting will begin directly, and the other blackguards ashore have apparently forgotten all about us. There isn't a light anywhere."

"What are you going to do?" asked Carnforth.

"Follow out Mr. Gedge's instructions, sir, and put this cargo on the beach. Whether the old *Sultan* goes there too, remains to be seen."

"That gunboat will cut you off in a quarter of an hour if you keep on this course."

"With that extra five knots she can do as she likes with us, so I sha'n't shift my helm. It would only look suspicious."

"Good Lord!" said Carnforth, "as if our being here at all isn't suspicion itself."

But Kettle did not answer. He had, to use his own expression, " got his wits working under forced draught," and he could not afford time for idle speculation and chatter. It was the want of the answering signal ashore which upset him. Had that showed against the black background of hills, he would have known what to do.

Meanwhile the Spanish warship was closing up with him hand over fist, and decision was necessary. Anyway, the choice was a poor one. If he surrendered he would be searched, and with that damning cargo of rifles and machine guns and ammunition under his hatches, it was not at all improbable that his captors might string him up out of hand. They would have right on their side for doing so.

The insurrectionists were not " recognised belligerents "; he would stand as a filibuster confessed ; and as such would be due to suffer under that rough and ready martial law which cannot spare time to feed and gaol prisoners.

On the other hand, if he refused to heave to the result would be equally simple ; the warship would sink him with her guns inside a dozen minutes; and reckless dare-devil though he might be, Kettle knew quite well there was no chance of avoiding this.

With another crew he might have been tempted to lay his old steamer alongside the other, and try to carry her by boarding and sheer hand-to-hand fighting; but, excepting for those on watch in the stokehold, his present set of men were all below packing their belongings into portable shape, and he knew quite well that nothing would please them better than to see him discomfited. Carnforth was neutral ; he had only his three mates and the engineer officers to depend upon in all the available world ; and he recognised between deep draughts at his cigar that he was in a very tight place.

Still the dark shore ahead remained unbeaconed, and the Spaniard was racing up astern, lit for battle, with her crew at quarters, and guns run out and loaded.   She leapt nearer by fathoms to the second, till Kettle could hear the panting of her engines as she chased him down.   His teeth chewed on the cigar butt, and dark rings grew under his eyes.   He could have raged aloud at his impotence.

The war steamer ranged up alongside, slowed to some forty revolutions so as to keep her place, and an officer on the top of her chart-house hailed in Spanish.

"Gunboat ahoy," Kettle bawled back ; "you must speak English or I can't be civil to you."

"What ship is that ?"

"*Sultan of Borneo*, Kettle, master. Out of Shields."

"Where for?"

"The Havana."

Promptly the query came back : "Then what are you doing in here ?"

Carnforth whispered a suggestion.   "Fresh water run out ; condenser water given all hands dysentery ; put in here to fill up tanks."

"I thank you, sir," said Kettle in the same under-tone, "I'm no hand at lying myself, or I might have thought of that before."   And he shouted the excuse across to the spokesman on the chart-house roof.

To his surprise they seemed to give weight to it. There was a short consultation, and the steamers slipped along over the smooth black waters of the bay on parallel courses.

"Have you got dysentery bad aboard?" came the next question.

Once more Carnforth prompted, and Kettle repeated his words : "Look at my decks," said he. "All my crew are below. I've hardly a man to stand by me."

There was more consultation among the gunboat's officers, and then came the fatal inquiry : "What's your cargo, Captain?"

"Oh, coals," said Kettle resignedly.

"What? You're bringing Tyne coal to the Havana?"

"Just coals," said Captain Kettle with a bitter laugh.

The tone of the Spaniard changed. "Heave to at once," he ordered, "whilst I send a boat to search you. Refuse, and I'll blow you out of water."

On the *Sultan of Borneo's* upper bridge Carnforth swore. "Eh-ho, Skipper," he said, "the game's up, and there's no way out of it. You won't be a fool, will you, and sacrifice the ship and the whole lot of us? Come, I say, man, ring off your engines, or that fellow will shoot, and we shall all be murdered uselessly. I tell you, the game's up."

"By James!" said Kettle, "is it? Look there" —and he pointed with outstretched arm to the hills on the shore ahead. "Three fires!" he cried. "Two above one in a triangle, burning like Elswick furnaces amongst the trees. They're ready for us over yonder, Mr. Carnforth, and that's their welcome. Do you think I'm going to let my cargo be stopped after getting it this far?" He turned to the Danish quarter-master at the wheel, with his savage face close to the man's ear.

"Starboard," he said. "Hard over, you bung-eyed Dutchman. Starboard as far as she'll go."

The wheel engines clattered briskly in the house underneath, and the *Sultan of Borneo's* head swung off quickly to port. For eight seconds the officer commanding the gunboat did not see what was happening, and that eight seconds was fatal to his vessel. When the inspiration came, he bubbled with orders, he starboarded his own helm, he rang " full speed ahead " to his engines, and ordered every rifle and machine gun on his ship to sweep the British steamer's bridge. But the space of time was too small. The gunboat could not turn with enough quickness; on so short a notice the engines could not get her into her stride again; and the shooting, though well intentioned and prodigious in quantity, was poor in aim. The bullets *whisped* through the air, and pelted on the plating like a hailstorm, and one of them flicked out the brains of the Danish quarter-master on the bridge; but Kettle took the wheel from his hands, and a moment later the *Sultan of Borneo's* stem crashed into the gunboat's unprotected side just abaft the sponson of her starboard quarter gun.

The steamers thrilled like kicked biscuit-boxes, and a noise went up into the hot night sky as of ten thousand boiler makers, all heading up their rivets at once.

On both ships the propellers stopped as if by instinct, and then in answer to the telegraph, the grimy collier backed astern. But the war-steamer did not move. Her machinery was broken down. She had already got a heavy list towards her wounded side, and every second the list was increasing as the sea water poured in through the shattered plates. Her crew was buzzing with disorder. It was evident that the vessel had but a short time longer to swim, and their lives were sweet to them. They had no thought of vengeance. Their weapons lay deserted on the sloping decks. The grimy crews from the stokeholds poured up from below, and one and all they clustered about the boats with frenzied haste to see them floating in the water.

There was no more to be feared at their hands for the present.

Carnforth clapped Kettle on the shoulder in involuntary admiration. "By George," he cried, "what a daring little scoundrel you are! Look here. I'm on your side now if I can be of any help. Can you give me a job?"

"I'm afraid, sir," said Captain Kettle, "that the old *Sultan's* work is about done. She's settling down by the head already. Didn't you see those rats of men scuttling up from forrard directly after we'd rammed the Don? I guess that was a bit of a surprise packet for them anyway. They thought they'd get down there to be clear of the shooting, and they found themselves in the most ticklish part of the ship."

"There's humour in the situation," said Carnforth. "But that will keep. For the present, it strikes me that this old steamboat is swamping fast."

"She's doing that," Kettle admitted. "She'll have a lot of plates started forrard, I guess. But I think she's come out of it very creditably, sir. I didn't spare her, and she's not exactly built for a ram."

"I suppose it's a case of putting her on the beach?"

"There's nothing else for it," said Kettle with a sigh. "I should like to have carried those blessed coals in to the Havana if it could have been done, just to show people ours was a *bond fide* contract, as Mr. Gedge said, in spite of its fishy look. But this old steamboat's done her whack, and that's the square truth. It will take her all she can manage to reach shore with dry decks. Look, she's in now nearly to her forecastle head. Lucky the shore's not steep-to here, or else——"

From beneath there came a bump and a rattle, and the steamer for a moment halted in her progress, and a white-crested wave surged past her rusty flanks. Then she lifted again and swooped further in, with the propeller still squattering astern ; and then once more she thundered down again into the sand ; and so lifting and striking, made her way in through the surf.

More than one of the hands was swept from her decks, and reached the shore by swimming ; but as the ebb made, the hungry seas left her stranded dry under the morning's light, and a crowd of insurrectionists waded out and climbed on board by ropes which were thrown to them.

They were men of every tint, from the grey black of the pure negro to the sallow lemon tint of the blue-blooded Spaniard. They were streaked with wounds, thin as skeletons, and clad more with nakedness than with rags ; and so wolfish did they look that even Kettle, callous little ruffian though he was, half regretted bringing arms for such a crew to wreak vengeance on their neighbours.

But they gave him small time for sentiment of

this brand. They clustered round him with leaping hands, till the morning sea-fowl fled affrighted from the beach. El Señor Capitan Inglese was the saviour of Cuba, and let every one remember it. Alone, with his unarmed vessel, he had sunk a warship of their hated enemies; and they prayed him (in their florid compliment) to stay on the island and rule over them as king.

But the little sailor took them literally. "What's this?" he said; "you want me to be your blooming king?"

"El rey!" they shouted. "El rey de los Cubaños!"

"By James," said Kettle, "I'll do it. I was never asked to be a king before, and the chance may never come again. Besides, I'm out of a berth just now, and England will be too hot to hold me yet awhile. Yes, I'll stay and boss you, and if you can act half as ugly as you look, we'll give the Dons a lively time. Only remember there's no tomfoolery about me. If I'm king of this show, I'm going to carry a full king's ticket, and if there's any man tries to meddle without being invited, that man will go to his own funeral before he can think twice. And now we'll just begin business at once. Off with those hatches and break out that cargo. I've been at some pains to run these guns out here, so be careful in carrying them up the beach. Jump lively now, you black-faced scum."

Carnforth listened with staring eyes. What sort of broil was this truculent little scamp going to mix in next? He knew enough of Spanish character to understand clearly that the offer of the crown was merely an empty civility ; he understood enough of Kettle to be sure that he had not taken it as such, and would assert his rights to the bitter end. And when he thought of what that end must inevitably be, he sighed over Owen Kettle's fate.

CHAPTER II.

"WE will garotte el Señor Kettle with due form and ceremony," said the mulatto, with an ugly smile. "The saints must have sent us this machine on purpose."

He threw away the cigarette stump from his yellow fingers, and began to knot a running bowline on the end of a rawhide rope. "I will do myself the honour of capturing him. He covered me with that revolver of his this morning, and put me to shame before the men. I have not forgotten."

"And the other Englishman?" said the ex-priest. "He fought well for us in the morning. He is brave."

"And so is far too dangerous to be left alive, padre, after we garotte the sailor."

"My dear Cuchillo," said the ecclesiastic, "you are so abominably bloodthirsty. But I suppose you are right. I will come with you, and if the man shows trouble, I will shoot him where he sits." He and the mulatto got up as he spoke, and the other men rose also, and the six of them left the *ingenio* silently on the side away from the camp. The jungle growths of the ruined plantation swallowed them out of sight. They held along their way silently and confidently, like men well skilled in wood-craft. With primitive cunning they had arranged to make their attack from the rear.

The noise of their chatter ceased, and from the distance there went up into the hot, tropical night faint snatches of the " Swanee River," sung by a Louisiana negro, who had grown delirious from a wound.

In the meanwhile the two Englishmen were taking their tobacco barely a couple of hundred yards away. They had built a small fire of green wood, and were sitting in the alley of smoke as some refuge from the swarming mosquitos, and the conversation ran upon themselves and their own prospects.

" I don't want to mess about with a crown," Captain Kettle was saying. " A cheese-cutter cap's good enough for me; or, seeing that Cuba's hot, a pith helmet might be preferable, if we are going in for luxury." He peered through the smoke wreaths at the camp of the revolutionists, a naked bivouac chopped from amongst the canes, and strewn with sleeping men who moaned in their dreams. The ruined *ingenio* at the further side had its white walls smeared with smoke. The place ached with poverty and squalor.

"Not that there seems much luxury here," he went on. " These beauties haven't a sound pair of breeches amongst them, and if it wasn't for the rifles and ammunition we brought ashore from the poor old *Sultan*, sir, I'd say they'd just starve to death before they kicked the Spaniards out of the island. But if ugliness means pluck, there should be none better as fighting men ; and when we get to bossing them properly, you'll see we shall just make this revolutionary business hum. You are going to stay on and help, Mr. Carnforth?"

The big man in the shooting coat gave a rueful laugh. "You've got my promise, Kettle. I don't see any way of backing out of it."

"I thank you for that, sir," said the sailor with a bow. "When I come to be formally made King of these Cubans, you shall find I am not ungrateful. I am not a man to neglect either my friends or my enemies.

"You shall sign on as Prime Minister, Mr. Carnforth, when we get the show regularly in commission, and I'll see you make a good thing out of it. Don't you get the notion it'll be a bit like the dreary business you were used to in Parliament in England. Empty talk is not to my taste, and I'll not set up a Parliament here to encourage it. I'm going to hold a full King's ticket myself, and it won't do for anyone to forget it."

"You seem very anxious for power, Captain."

"It's a fact, sir," said the other with a sigh, "I do like to have the ordering of men. But don't you think that's the only reason I'm taking on with this racket. I'm a man with an income to make, and I'm out of a berth elsewhere. I'm a man with a family, sir."

"I am a bachelor," said Carnforth, "and I'm thanking heaven for it this minute. Doesn't it strike you, Captain, that this is no sort of job for a married man? Can't you see it's far too risky?"

"Big pay, big risk; that's always the way, sir, and

as I've faced ugly places before and come out top side, there's no reason why I shouldn't do it again here. Indeed, it's the thought of my wife that's principally pushing me on. During all the time we've been together, Mr. Carnforth, I've never been able to give Mrs. Kettle the place I'd wish.

"She was brought up, sir, as the daughter of a minister of religion, and splendidly educated; she can play the harmonium and do crewel-work; and, though I'll not deny I married her from behind a bar, I may tell you she only took to business from a liking to see society." He looked out dreamily through the smoke at the fireflies which were winking across the black rim of the forest.

"I'd like to see her, Mr. Carnforth, with gold brooches and chains, and a black satin dress, and a bonnet that cost 20s., sitting in Government House, with the British Consul on the mat before her, waiting till she chose to ask him to take a chair and talk. She'd fill the position splendidly, and I've just got to wade in and get it for her."

The little man broke off and stared out at the fireflies, and Carnforth coughed the wood-smoke from his lungs and rammed fresh tobacco into his pipe. He was a man with a fine sense of humour, and he appreciated to the full the ludicrousness of Kettle's pretensions. The sailor had run a cargo of much wanted contraband of war on to the Cuban beach, had sunk a Spanish cruiser in the process, and had received effusive thanks.

But he had taken the florid metaphor of the country to mean a literal offer, and when in their complimentary phrase they shouted that he should be

king, a king from **that** moment he intended **to be.**
The comedy of the situation was irresistible.

But at **the same** time **Mr.** Martin Carnforth **was**
a man of wealth, **and a man (in** England) **of assured**
position ; **and he could not** avoid seeing **that by his**
present association with **Captain Owen Kettle he**
was flirting with ugly tragedy every **moment that**
he lived. **Yet here** he was pinned, not only **to keep**
in the man's society, but **to help him in his mad en-**
deavours.

He would gladly have **forfeited half his fortune**
to be snugly back in **St.** Stephen's, Westminster,
clear of the mess ; but escape was out **of the ques-**
ion ; **and, moreover, he knew** quite well **that trying**
to make Kettle appreciate **his true** position would
be like an attempt **to reason** with the **winds** or the
surf on an ocean beach. **So he** held his tongue, and
did as he was bidden. **He was** a man of physical
bravery, and the rush **of actual** fighting that morning had come pleasantly to **him.**

It was **only when he thought of** the certain and
treacherous dangers **of the future, and the** cosy
niche that awaited him **at home in** England, that
his throat tickled with apprehension, and he caressed
with affectionate fingers **the region of** his carotids.
And if he had known that at that precise moment
the ex-priest, and the mulatto they called el Cuchillo,
and the others of the insurgent leaders, were stalk-
ing him with a view to capture and execution, it is
probable that he **would have felt even still** more
disturbed.

"We did well in that **fight** this morning," said
Kettle presently, as he drew his eyes away from the

light-snaps of the fireflies, and shut them to keep out the sting of the wood-smoke. "You've been shot at before, sir?"

"Never," said Carnforth.

"You couldn't have been cooler, sir, if you'd been at sea all your life, and seen pins flying every watch. Do you know, I've been thinking it over, and I'm beginning to fancy that perhaps our black and yellow mongrels weren't quite such cowards as I said. I know they did scuttle to the bushes like rabbits so soon as ever a gun was fired; but then their business is to shoot these Spanish soldiers and not get shot back, and so, perhaps, they were right to keep to their own way.

"Anyway, we licked them, and that means getting on towards Mrs. Kettle's being a queen. But that murdering the wounded afterwards was more than I can stand, and it has got to be put a stop to."

"You didn't make yourself popular over it."

"I am not usually liked when I am captain," said Kettle grimly.

"Well, Skipper, I don't, as a rule, agree with your methods, as you know, but here I'm with you all the way. Your excellent subjects are a great deal too barbarous for my taste."

"They are wholly brutes, and that's a fact," said Captain Kettle, "and I expect a good many of them will be hurt whilst I'm teaching them manners. But they've got to learn this lesson first of all: they're to treat their prisoners decently, or else let them go, or else shoot them clean and dead in the first instance whilst they're still on the run. I'm a man myself, Mr. Carnforth, that can do a deal in hot blood; but afterwards, when the poor brutes are on the ground, I want to go round with sticking plaster, and not a knife to slit their throats."

"It will take a tolerable amount of trouble to drum that into this crew. A Spaniard on the war-path is not merciful; an African is a barbarian; but make a cross of the two (as you get here) and you turn out the most unutterable savage on the face of the earth."

"They will not be taught by kindness alone," said Captain Kettle suggestively. "I've got heavy hands, and I sha'n't be afraid to use them. It's a job," he added with a sigh, "which will not come new to me. I've put to sea with some of the worst toughs that ever wrote their crosses before a ship-ping master, and none of them can ever say they got the top side of me yet."

He was about to say more, but at that moment speech was taken from him. A long rawhide rope suddenly flicked out into the air like a slim, black snake; the noose at its end for an instant poised open-mouthed above him; and then it descended around his elbows, and was as simultaneously plucked taut by unseen hands behind the shelter of the jungle. Captain Kettle struggled like a wild-cat to release himself, but four lithe, bony men threw themselves upon him, twisted his arms behind his back, and made them fast there with other thongs of rawhide.

Carnforth did nothing to help. At the first alarm that burly gentleman had looked up and dis-covered a rifle muzzle, not ten feet off, pointed squarely at his breast. The voice of the ex-priest came from behind the rifle, and assured him in mild, unctuous tones that the least movement would secure him a quick and instant passage to one or other of the next worlds. And Martin Carnforth surrendered without terms. When the four men had finished their other business, they came and roped him up also.

The mulatto strode out from the cover and flicked the ashes of a cigarette into Kettle's face. "El rey," he said, "de los Cubaños must have his power limited. He has come where he was not wanted, he has done what was forbidden, and shortly he will taste the consequences."

"You ginger-bread coloured beast," retorted Captain Kettle, "you shame of your mother, I made a big mistake when I did not shoot you in the morning."

The mulatto pressed the lighted end of his cigarette against Kettle's forehead. "I will trouble you," he said, " to keep silence for the present. At dawn you will be put upon trial, and then you may speak. But till then (and the sun will not rise for another three hours yet), if you talk, you will earn a painful burn for each sentence.

"You are a man accustomed to having your own way, Señor; I am another; and as at present I possess the upper hand, your will has got to bend to mine. The process, I can well imagine, will be distasteful to you. It was distasteful to me when I looked down your revolver muzzle over the affair of those prisoners. But I do not think you will be foolish enough to earn torture uselessly."

Kettle glared, but with an effort held his tongue.

He understood he was in a very tight place. And for the present the only thing remaining for him was to bide his time. He quite recognised that he was in dangerous hands. The mulatto **was a** man **of** education, who had been brought **up in** an American college, and who had learned **in** the States **to** hate his white father and loathe his black mother with a ferocity which nothing but that atmosphere could foster.

He was a fellow living on the borderland of the two primitive colours, and his whole **life** was soured by the pigment in his skin. As **a white** man he would have been a genius; as a black he would have become a star; but as **a** mulatto he was merely **a** suave and brilliant savage, thirsting for vengeance against the whole of the human race. He had entered this Cuban revolution through no taint of patriotism, but merely from the lust for cruelty. By sheer daring and ability he had raised himself from the ranks to supreme command of the revolutionists, and he was not likely to let so appetising a situation slip from his fingers for even a few short hours without exacting a bitter retribution when the chance was put in his way.

Carnforth lifted up his voice in expostulation, but **was** quickly silenced by the promise of branding from the cigarette end if he did not choose to hold his tongue. Quiet fell over the group. The only sounds were scraps of the " Swanee River "sung by the wounded negro in his delirium from somewhere **in** the distance—

> " Still longing for the old plantation,
>   And for the old folks at home,"

came the words in a thin quavering tenor, and Carnforth, with a sigh, thought how well he could en-
dorse them.

The first glow of morning saw the camp aroused,
and half an hour later the Court was ranged. The
self-styled judges sat under the whitewashed piazza
of the ruined house ; the motley troops faced them
in an irregular ring twenty yards away ; and the
two prisoners, with an armed man to guard each,
stood on the open ground between.

El Cuchillo was himself principal spokesman, and
proceedings were carried on in Spanish and English
alternately. The crime of Captain Kettle was set
forth in a dozen words. He had stopped the right-
ful execution of prisoners, and had let them go
free.

"You had no place to gaol them," said Carnforth
in defence.

The mulatto pointed a thin yellow finger at the
sun-baked ground in front of the piazza. "We have
the earth," he said. "Give them to the earth, and
she will keep them gaoled so fast that they will never
fight against us more. It is a war here to the knife
on both sides. The Spanish troops kill us when
they catch, and we do the like by them. It is right
that it should be so. We do not want quarter at
their hands; neither do we wish them to remain
alive upon Cuba. Three Spanish soldiers were ours
a few hours ago. Our cause demanded that their
lives should have been taken away. And yet they
were set free."

"Yes," broke in Kettle, "and, by James, that's a

thing you ought to sing small about. Here's you:
six officers and a hundred and fifty men, all armed.
Here's me: a common low-down, foul-of-his-luck
Britisher, with a vinegar tongue and a **thirty-shilling**
pistol. You said the beggars should be hanged,
I said they shouldn't; **and,** by James, I scared the
whole caboodle of you with just one-half an ugly
look, and **got** my own blessed way. Oh, I do say
you are a holy crowd."

Carnforth stamped **in** anger. It seemed to him
that this truculent little sailor was deliberately in-
viting their captors to murder the pair **of** them out
of hand. He understood that Kettle was bitterly
disappointed at having his bubble about the kingship so ruthlessly pricked, but with this recklessness
which was snatching away their only chance of escape, he could have no sympathy. He was unpre-
pared, however, for his comrade's next remark.

"Don't think **I'd** any help from Mr. Carnforth
here. He's a Member of Parliament in London,
and is far too much of a gentleman to concern himself with your fourpenny-ha'penny matters here. He
warned me before I began that being king of the
whole of your rotten island wasn't worth a dish of
beans; but I wouldn't believe him till I'd seen how
it was **for** myself.

"I'm here now through my **own** fault; I ought
to have remembered that niggers, and yellow-bellies,
and white men who have forgotten their colour,
could have no spark **of** gratitude. I'll not deny,
too, that I got to thinking about those fireflies, and
so wasn't keeping a proper watch; but here I am,
lashed up snug, and I guess you're going to make

the most of your chance.   By James, **though,** if you
weren't a pack of cowards, you'd cast me adrift, and
give **me my** gun again ! "

"Speaking as **a man** of peace," said the **ex-priest,**
" I fancy you are safest as you are, *amigo.*"

"**I'd** be king **of this** crowd again inside **three**
minutes if I was **loose,**" retorted Kettle.

El Cuchillo snapped his yellow fingers impatiently.
"**We are** wasting time," he **said.**   "Captain Kettle
seems still to dispute my supreme authority.   He
shall taste of it within the next dozen minutes; and
if he can see his way to resisting it, and asserting
his own kingship, he has my full permission to do so.
Here, you : go into the *ingenio,* and bring out that
machine."

A dozen ragged fellows detached themselves from
the onlookers, and went through a low stone doorway into the ruined sugar house.   In a couple of
minutes they reappeared, dragging with noisy
laughter a dusty, cumbersome erection, which they
set down in the open space before the piazza.

It was made up of a wooden platform on which
was fastened a chair and an upright.   On the upright
was a hinged iron ring immediately above the chair.
A screw passed through the upright into the ring,
with a long lever at its outside end, on either extremity of which was a heavy sphere of iron.   If
once that lever was set on the twirl, it would drive
the screw's point into whatever the iron ring con-
tained with a force that was irresistible.

The mulatto introduced the machine with a wave
of his yellow fingers.   "*El garotte,*" he said.   "A
mediæval survival which I did not dream of finding

here. Of its previous history I can form no idea.
Of its future use I can give a simple account. It will
serve to ease us of the society of this objectionable
Captain Kettle."

"Great **heavens,** man," Carnforth broke out, "this
is murder."

"**Ah,**" said el Cuchillo, "I will attend to your
case at the same time. You shall have the honour
of turning the screw which gives your friend his exit.
In that way we shall secure your silence afterwards
as to what has occurred."

"You foul brute," **said** Carnforth, **with a** shout,
"do you think I am an assassin like yourself?"

The mulatto took a long draught at his cigarette.
"What a horrible country England must be to live
in, if all the people there have tongues as long **as**
you two. Señor, if you do not choose to accept my
suggestion for pinning you to silence, I can offer you
another. **Refuse** to take your place at the screw,
and I promise **that** you shall be stood up against
the wall **of** this *ingenio* and **be shot** inside the
minute. The choice stands open before you."

"Mr. Carnforth," said Captain Kettle, "you
mustn't be foolish. You must officiate over me
exactly as you are asked, or otherwise you'll get
shot uselessly. Gingerbread and his friends mean
business. And if you still think you're taking a
liberty in handling the screw (in spite of what I say)
you may fine yourself **a** matter of ten shillings
weekly, and hand **it across** to Mrs. Kettle. I make
no doubt she would find that sum very useful."

"This is horrible," said Carnforth.

"It will be horrible for Mrs. Kettle and my young-

sters, sir, if you don't act sensibly and man the lever
as Gingerbread asks. If you get planted here alongside of me, I don't know any one at all likely to
give them a pension. It would afford me a great
deal of pleasure just now, Mr. Carnforth, if I knew
my family could still keep to windward of parish
relief."

"Of course," said Carnforth, with a white face,
"I will see your wife and children are all right if I
get clear; but it is too ghastly to think of purchas-
ing even my life on these terms."

"You seem slow to make up your mind, Señor,"
broke in the mulatto. "Allow me to hasten your
decision." He gave some directions, and the men
who had brought out the garotte took Captain
Kettle and sat him on the chair. They opened the
iron ring, which screeched noisily with its rusted
hinge, and they clasped it, collar-fashion, about his
neck. Then they led Carnforth up to the back
of the upright, and cast off the lashing from his
wrists.

"Now, Señor Carnforth," said the yellow man.
"I want that person garotted. If you do it for me,
I will give you a safe-conduct down to any seaport
in Cuba which you may choose. If I have to set on
one of my own men to do the work, you will not
have sight to witness it. I will stick you up against
that white wall, yonder, and have you shot, out of
hand. Now, Señor, I have the honour to ask for
your decision."

"Come, sir, don't hesitate," said Captain Kettle.
"If you don't handle the screw, remember some one
else will."

"That will be a flimsy excuse to remember afterwards."

"You will be paying a weekly fine, and can recollect that carries a full pardon with it."

"Pah," said Carnforth, "what is ten shillings a week?"

"Exactly," said Kettle. "Make it twelve, sir, and that will hold you clear of everything."

"What feeble, dilatory people you English are," said el Cuchillo. "I must trouble you to make up your mind at once, Señor Carnforth."

"He has made it up," said Kettle, "and I shall go smiling, because I shall get my clearance at the hands of a decent man. I'd have taken it as a disgrace to be shoved out of this world by a yellow beast like you, you shame of your mother."

The mulatto blazed out with fury. "By heaven," he cried, "I've a mind to take you out of that garotte even now and have you burnt."

"And we should lose a pleasant little comedy," said the ex-priest. "No, *amigo;* let us see the pair of them perform together."

"Go on," said the mulatto to Carnforth.

"Yes," said Kettle in a lower voice. "For God's sake go on and get it over. It isn't very pleasant work for me, this waiting. And you will make it twelve shillings a week, sir?"

"I will give your wife a thousand a year, my poor fellow. I will give her five thousand. No, I am murdering her husband, and I will give her all I have, and go away to start life afresh elsewhere. I shall never dare to show my face again in England or carry my own name." He gripped one of the iron spheres and threw his weight upon the lever. The bar buckled and sprang under his effort, but the screw did not budge.

"Quick, man, quick," said Kettle in a low, fierce voice. "This is cruel. If you don't get me finished directly, I shall go white or something, and those brutes will think I'm afraid."

Carnforth wrenched at the lever with a tremendous effort. One arm of the bar bent slowly into a semicircle, but the lethal screw remained fast in its socket. It was glued there with the rust of years.

Carnforth flung away from the machine. "I have done my best," he said sullenly to the men on the piazza, "and I can do no more. You have the satisfaction of knowing that you have made me a murderer in intent, if not in actual fact; and now, if you choose, you can stick me up against that wall and have me shot. I'm sure I don't care. I'm sick of it all here."

"You shall have fair treatment," said el Cuchillo, "and neither more or less. You have tried to obey my orders, and Captain Kettle is at present alive because of the garotte's deficiency, and not by your intention." He gave a command, and the men released the iron collar from Kettle's neck. "I will have the machine repaired by my armourer," he said, "and in the meanwhile you may await my pleasure out of the sunshine."

He gave another order, and the men laid hands upon their shoulders and led them away, and thrust them into a small arched room of whitened stone, under the boiler-house of the *ingenio*. The window

was a mere arrow-slit; the door was a ponderous
thing of Spanish oak, barred with iron bolts which
ran into the stonework; the place was absolutely
unbreakable.

The silence had lasted a dozen hours, although it
was plain that each of the prisoners was busily thinking. At last Kettle spoke.

"If I could only get a rhyme to 'brow,'" he
said, "I believe I could manage the rest."

"What?" asked Carnforth.

"I want a word to rhyme with 'brow,' sir, if you
can help me."

"What in the world are you up to now?"

"I've been filling up time, sir, whilst we've been
here by hammering out a bit of poetry about those
fireflies. I got the idea of it last night, when we
saw them flashing in and out against the black of
the forest."

"You don't owe them much gratitude that I can
see, Skipper. According to what you said, if you
hadn't been looking at them, you'd have been more
on the watch, and wouldn't have got caught."

"Perfectly right, sir. And so this poem should be
all the more valuable when it's put together. I'm
running it to the tune of 'Greenland's icy mountains,'
my favourite air, Mr. Carnforth. I'm trying to work
a parallel between those fireflies switching their
lights in and out, and a soul, sir. Do you catch the
idea?"

"I can't say I do quite."

Captain Kettle rubbed thoughtfully at his beard.
"Well, I'm a trifle misty about it myself," he ad-

mitted; "but it will make none the worse poetry for being a bit that way, if I can get the rhymes all right."

"'Plough' might **suit you**," Carnforth suggested.

"That's just the **word** I want, sir. 'The fields of heaven to plough.' That would be the very occupation the soul of the man I'm thinking about would delight in; something restful and in the agricultural line. I wanted to give him a good time up there. He was due for it," he added thoughtfully, and then he closed his eyes and fell to making further poetry.

Martin Carnforth knew the little ruffian's taste for this form of exercise, but it seemed to him jarringly out of place just then. "I am in no mood for verse now," he commented with a **frown.**

"I am," said Kettle, and tapped out the metre of a new line with a finger-tip upon his knee. "It always takes a set-to with the hands, or a gale of wind, or a tight corner of some kind, to work me up to poetry at all. And the worse the fix has been, the better I can rhyme. I find it very restful and pleasant, sir, to send my thoughts over a bit of a sonnet after times like these."

"Then you ought to turn out a masterpiece now," said Carnforth, "and enjoy the making of it."

Kettle took him seriously. "I quite agree with you there, sir," he said, and puckered his forehead and went on with his work.

Carnforth did not say any more, but turned again to brooding. Every time he looked at the matter, the more he cursed himself for leaving his snug pinnacle in England. The utmost boon he could have gained in Captain Kettle's society was not to be caught. Dangers, hardships, and exposures he was discovering are much pleasanter to hear of from a distance, or to read **about** in a well-stuffed chair by a warm fireside. The actual items themselves had turned out terribly squalid when viewed at first hand.

At last he broke out again. " Look here, Skipper," he said, " I'm fond enough of life, **but I** don't think I want to earn it by playing executioner. I'd prefer to let this rebel fellow parade me and bring out his platoon."

Kettle woke up from his work. " **I'm** not sweet on wearing the iron **collar** again, **and** that's a fact. It's horrible work waiting to have your backbone snapped without being able to raise **a** finger **to inter-**fere. I'm not a coward, Mr. Carnforth, but I **tell** you it took all the nerve I'd got to sit quiet in that chair without squirming whilst you were getting ready the ceremonial.

" It's no **new** thing for me **to** expect being killed before the hour was through. I've had trouble of all kinds with all sorts of crews, **but I've** always had my hands free and been able to use them, and I will **say** I've 'most always had a gun of some sort to help me. I might even go so far as to tell you, sir (and **you may** kick me for saying it if you like), I've felt **a** kind **of** joy regularly glow inside me during some of those kind of scuffles. Yes, sir, that's the kind of animal I am in hot blood I think no more of being killed than a terrier dog does."

" If there was only **a** chance of being knocked on the head in hot blood," said Carnforth, " I'd fight like a cornered thief till I got my quietus."

"And Mrs. Kettle would lose her twelve shillings a week if—— By James, sir, here they come for us."

He leapt up from the bench on which he had sat, and whirled it above his head. With a crash he brought it down against the whitened wall of the cell, and the bench split down its length into two staves. He gave one to Carnforth, and hefted the other himself like a connoisseur.

"Now, sir, you on one side of the door, and me on the other. They can't reach us from the outside there. And if they want us out of here, we've got to be fetched."

Carnforth took up his stand, and shifted his fingers knowingly along his weapon. He was a big man and a powerful one, and the hunger for fighting lit in his eye.

"Horatius Cockles and the other Johnnie holding the bridge," quoth he. "We can bag the first two, and the others will fall over them if they try a rush. What fools they were to untie our wrists and shins! But our fun won't last long. As soon as they find we are awkward, they will go around to the window-slit, and shoot us down from there."

"We aren't shot yet," said Kettle grimly, "and I'm wanting to do a lot of damage before they get me. Look out!"

The bolts grated back in the rusty staples, and the heavy door screamed outwards on its hinges. A negro came in, whistling merrily. The two halves of the bench flew down upon his head from either side with a simultaneous crash.

A white man's skull would have cruncbed like an

eggshell under that impact, but the African cranium is stout. The fellow toppled to the ground under the sheer tonnage of the blows, and he lay there with the whistle half-frozen on his lips, and such a ludicrous look of surprise growing over his features that **Carnforth** burst into an involuntary laugh. **Kettle,** however, was more business-like. The negro had a machete dangling from his hip, and the little sailor **darted** out and snatched it from its sheath. He jumped back again to cover with slim activity, and a couple of pistol bullets which followed him made harmless grey splashes on the opposite wall. **Then** there was a pause in the proceedings, and Carnforth felt his heart thumping **noisily against** his watch as he waited.

Presently a brisk footstep made itself heard on the flagging outside, and the voice of **the** mulatto leader spoke through **the** doorway.

" If you come out now, one of you shall be garot**ted, and** the other shall go free. If I have more trouble to fetch you, you shall both be roasted to death over slow fires."

" If—if—if !" retorted Kettle. " If your mother had stuck to her laundry work and married a nigger, she'd have kept a very great rascal out of the world. If I'd the sense of a sheep I'd come to you at once, and my poor wife would have twelve bob a week for life. If you want to talk, you frightened lump of gingerbread, come in here and do it, and don't squall out there like a cat on a garden wall."

The suave voice of **the** ex-priest made a comment. " Saints deliver us from these Englishmen's tongues. Truly they are not **fit to live ;** but why should we send our terriers into the rat pit? A little careful shooting through the window yonder will soon limit their capers, and if the shooting is carefully done, neither will be any the worse as a roast."

El Cuchillo answered him savagely. "Then do you see to it. The big man you may shoot as you please, but if you kill the sailor, look to yourself. That man is in my debt, and I want him in my hands alive, so that I may pay it."

"*Amigo*," said the unfrocked priest, "you may trust to my shooting. I will pink him most scientifically in one leg and the right arm, and I will guarantee that you shall get him in perfect condition to have your satisfaction on."

"Do so," said the mulatto, and the other marched briskly away on his rope-soled sandals. But in the meantime Kettle's active brain had formed a plan, and in dumb show he had telegraphed it across to Carnforth at the opposite flank of the doorway.

Of a sudden the pair of them rushed out simultaneously. Kettle handed the machete to his companion, and sprang upon the yellow man with greedy fingers. His feet he kicked away from beneath him, and at the same instant grappled him by the throat. It was a trick he had many a time before played upon mutinous seamen, and he had dragged the mulatto back into the cell almost before the man had time to struggle. Carnforth followed closely upon their heels, leaving signatures behind him written redly with the machete.

Captain Kettle bumped the mulatto's head against the wall as a way of quietening him, and keeping his fingers away from dangerous weapons, and then threw him on to the floor. He extracted a revolver and a knife from the man's belt, **and,** looked up to see the **face** of the ex-priest staring at him from the window. Then he sat **himself on** the chest of his prisoner, and prepared to treat for terms.

A shot rang out across the bivouac outside, and then another. The man at the window-slit turned **away his** face. There was a minute's pause, and then a dropping fire began, the sound of it coming **from two** distinct quarters.

The ex-priest's head went out of **sight.** It was the last they ever saw of him. Some one outside **the** doorway shouted " *Los Españoles !* " and **there** was the scuffle of bare feet running away **and fad-** ing into the distance. And, meanwhile, outside the windows the crackle of rifles grew more noisy, and **cries rose up** of men in pain. The light in the vaulted room grew faintly blue, and the air **was** soured with powder smoke.

" By James," said Kettle, " the Spanish regular troops have raided the camp, and the whole lot of them are fighting like a parcel of cats. Hark to the racket. Here's a **slice of** luck."

" I don't see it," said Carnforth. " If we're out of the fire, we're into the frying-pan. Sinking that Spanish warship was an act of piracy, and we shall be strung up if the Dons catch us, without the pre- lude of a trial. Listen ! There's a Maxim come into action. Listen ! I wonder which way the fight's going. They're making row enough over it. I'm going to get to the window and have a look."

4

"It's tempting," said the little sailor wistfully, "but I think, sir, you'd better not. If you're seen we shall be *gastados*, as they say, anyway. Whereas, if the rebels are licked, the Dons may march off again without knowing we are here. It's a chance. By James, though, I'd like to have a look. Hark to that. They're at hand-grips now. Hear 'em swear. And hear 'em scream.

"Some of them are beginning to run. Hark to that crashing as they're making their way through the cane."

"And hark to those shouts. It's like a lot of cockneys at a foxhunt."

"These Dagos always yell blue murder when they're in a fight," said Kettle contemptuously.

"The Maxim's stopped," said Carnforth, with a frown.

They listened on for awhile with straining ears, and then: "Perhaps that means the rebels have rushed it."

"They may have run. But the Dons ought to be browning the cover if they've cleared the camp. The fools! A Maxim would shoot through half a mile of that cane-jungle."

"Short of ammunition," said Kettle, " or perhaps it's jammed." A bugle shrilled out through the hot air, and its noise came to them there in the hot, dark room. "That means cease fire, and the Spaniards have won. Our mongrels had no bugles. Well, it's been a quick thing. I wonder what next!"

There was a dull murmur of many voices. Then orders were shouted, and noise came as of moving men, and a few more scattered shots rang **out,** most of them answered by cries or groans.

"Hullo?" said Kettle.

A weak voice from beneath him made explanation. "They are shooting their prisoners, Señores— the men who were my comrades. **It** is the custom— the custom of Cuba."

"So you have concluded to come to life again, have you?" asked the little sailor. "**I** thought I'd **bumped** you harder. What do you expect to be done with, **eh**?"

"I am in your hands," said the **mulatto** sullenly.

"That's no lie," said Kettle, "and I've a perfect right to kill you if I wish. But I don't choose to dirty my hands further. You've only acted according to your nature. And—when it came to me being able to move, I've beaten you every time. But now we'll have silence, please, for all hands. If those Spaniards are going to search this old sugar house, they'll do it, and up on a string we go the three of us; but there's no need to entice them here by chattering."

Their voices stopped, and the noises from without buzzed on. Of all the trials he had gone through, Carnforth felt that waiting to be the most intolerable of all. The Spanish soldiery were looking to their wounds and hunting through the bivouac. Some (to judge from their talk) had gathered round the rusted garotte and were examining it with interest. And a few strolled up to the ruined *ingenio,* and smoked their cigarettes under its piazza. Any moment the room beneath the boiler house might be peeped upon.

The sun beat down upon the stonework and the heat grew. The voices gradually drew away, till only the hum of the insects remained. And so an hour passed.

Another hour came and went without disturbance, and still another; and then there came the sound of a quavering tenor voice singing a scrap from the "Swanee River" from close outside the walls:

> "Oh, take me to my kind ole mudder!
> Dere let me live and die."

"That Yankee nigger," said Kettle, in a whisper. "He was wounded and delirious before we came, and he's been hidden amongst the cane. They can't have seen him before; but, poor devil, they'll shoot him now."

But no quietening rifle-shot rang out, and wonder grew on the faces of all three. They waited on with straining ears, and Carnforth raised his eyebrows in an unspoken question. Kettle nodded, and the big man rose gingerly to his feet, and peeped from the corner of the window-slit. He turned round with rather a harsh laugh. "The place is empty," he said. "I believe they've been gone these three hours."

Captain Kettle leapt to his feet and made for the door. "Quick," he cried, "or we shall have the rebels back again, and I'll own that I don't want to fight the whole lot of them again just now. We'll leave Gingerbread in here till his friends come to fetch him; and you and I, sir, will slip down to the beach, and get off in one of the old *Sultan's* quarter-boats."

They passed outside the door, and closed and bolted it after them.

"By the way," said Captain Kettle, " you couldn't happen to think of a rhyme to 'gleam,' could you?"

"No," said Carnforth.

"Well, I'll hammer it out on the road down, and then I'll have finished that sonnet, sir. But never mind poetry just now. I'll say the piece to you when we've got to sea. For the present, Mr. Carnforth, we must just pick up our feet and run."

And so they went off to the quarter-boat, and ten minutes later they were running her down the beach and into the sea.

CHAPTER III.

THE WAR-STEAMER, OF DONNA CLOTILDE.

I THINK it may be taken as one of the most remark-
able attributes of Captain Owen Kettle that, whatever circumstances might betide, he was always neat
and trim in his personal appearance. Even in most
affluent hours he had never been able to afford an
expensive tailor; indeed, it is much to be doubted if,
during all his life, he ever bought a scrap of raiment
any where except at a ready-made establishment ;
but, in spite of this, his clothes were always conspicu-
ously well-fitting, carried the creases in exactly the
right place, and seemed to the critical onlooker to be
capable of improvement in no one point whatso-
ever. He looked spruce even in oilskins and thigh
boots.

Of course, being a sailor, he was handy with his
needle. I have seen him take a white drill jacket,
torn to ribands in a rough and tumble with mutinous
members of his crew, and fine-draw the rents so wonderfully that all traces of the disaster were completely
lost. I believe, too, he was capable of taking a roll
of material and cutting it out with his knife upon
the deck planks, and fabricating garments *ab initio ;*
and though I never actually saw him do this with my
own eyes, I did hear that the clothes he appeared in

at Valparaiso were so made, and I marvelled at their neatness.

It was just after his disastrous adventure in Cuba; he trod the streets in a state of utter pecuniary destitution; his cheeks were sunk and his eyes were haggard; but the red torpedo beard was as trim as ever; his cap was spic and span; the white drill clothes with their brass buttons were the usual miracle of perfection; and even his tiny canvas shoes had not as much as a smudge upon their pipe-clay. Indeed, in the first instance I think it must have been this spruceness, and nothing else, which made him find favour in the eyes of so fastidious a person as Clotilde La Touche.

But be this as it may, it is a fact that Donna Clotilde just saw the man from her carriage as he walked along the Paseo de Colon, promptly asked his name, and, getting no immediate reply, despatched one of her admirers there and then to make his acquaintance, The envoy was instructed to find out who he was, and contrive that Donna Clotilde should meet the little sailor at dinner in the Café of the Lion d'Or that very evening.

The dinner was given in the *patio* of the café where palm-fronds filtered the moonbeams, and fire-flies competed with the electric lights; and at a moderate computation the cost of the viands would have kept Captain Kettle supplied with his average rations for ten months or a year. He was quite aware of this and appreciated the entertainment none the worse in consequence. Even the champagne, highly sweetened to suit the South American palate, came most pleasantly to him. He liked champagne according to its lack of dryness, and this was the sweetest wine that had ever passed his lips.

The conversation during that curious meal ran in phases. With the *hors d'œuvres* came a course of ordinary civilities; then for a space there rolled out an autobiographical account of some of Kettle's exploits, skilfully and painlessly extracted by Donna Clotilde's naïve questions; and then, with the cognac and cigarettes, a spasm of politics shook the diners like an ague.

Of a sudden one of the men recollected himself, looked to this side and that with a scared face, and rapped the table with his knuckles.

"Ladies," he said imploringly, "and Señores, the heat is great. It may be dangerous."

"Pah!" said Donna Clotilde, "we are talking in English."

"Which other people besides ourselves understand, even in Valparaiso."

"Let them listen," said Captain Kettle. "I hold the same opinions on politics as Miss La Touche here, since she has explained to me how things really are, and I don't care who knows that I think the present Government, and the whole system, rotten. I am not in the habit of putting my opinions in words, Mr. Silva, and being frightened of people hearing them."

"You," said the cautious man drily, "have little to lose here, Captain. Donna Clotilde has much. I should be very sorry to read in my morning paper that she had died from apoplexy—the arsenical variety—during the course of the preceding night."

"Pooh," said Kettle, "they could never do that."

"As a resident in Chili," returned Silva, "let me venture to disagree with you, Captain. It is a disease to which the opponents of President Quijarra are singularly addicted whenever they show any marked political activity. The palm trees in this *patio* have a reputation, too, for being phenomenally long-eared. So, if it pleases you all, suppose we go out on the roof? The moon will afford us a fine prospect—and—the air up there is reputed healthy."

He picked up Donna Clotilde's fan and mantilla. The other two ladies rose to their feet; Donna Clotilde, with a slight frown of reluctance, did the same; and they all moved off towards the stairway, Silva laid detaining fingers upon Captain Kettle's arm.

"Captain," he said, "if I may give you a friendly hint, slip away now and go to your quarters."

"I fancy, sir," said Captain Kettle, "that Miss La Touche has employment to offer me."

"If she has," retorted Silva, "which I doubt, it will not be employment you will care about."

"I am what they call here ' on the beach,'" said Kettle, "and I cannot afford to miss chances. I am a married man, Mr. Silva, with children to think about."

"Ah!" the Chillian murmured thoughtfully. "I wonder if she knows he's married? Well, Captain, if you will go up, come along, and I'm sure I wish you luck."

The flat roof of the Café of the Lion d'Or is set out as a garden, with orange trees growing against the parapets, and elephants' ears and other tropical foliage plants stood here and there in round green

tubs.   Around it are the other roofs of **the city,** which, with the streets between, look like **some** white rocky plain cut up by steep cañons. A glow comes from these depths below, and **with** it the blurred hum of people. But nothing articulate gets up to the Lion **d'Or, and** in the very mistiness **of** th**e noise** there is something indescribably fascinating.

Moreover, it is a place where the fireflies of Valparaiso most do congregate. Saving for the lamps of heaven, they have no other lighting on that roof. The owners (who are Israelites) pride themselves on this: it gives the garden an air of mystery; it has made it the natural birthplace of plots above numbering; and it has brought them **profits** almost beyond belief. Your true plotter, when his ecstasy comes upon him, is not the man to be niggardly with the purse. He is alive and glowing then; he may very possibly be dead to-morrow; and in the meanwhile money is useless, and the things money can buy—and the very best of their sort—are most desirable.

One more whispered **hint did** Mr. Silva give to Captain Kettle as they made their way together up the white **stone steps.**

"Do you know who and what our hostess is?" he asked.

"A **very** nice young lady," replied the mariner promptly, "with a fine taste in suppers."

"She is all that," said Silva; "but she also happens to be the richest woman in Chili. Her father owned mines innumerable, and when he came by his end in our last revolution, he left every dollar he had at Donna Clotilde's entire disposal. By some unfortunate oversight, personal fear has been left out of her composition, and she seems anxious to add it to the list of her acquirements."

Captain Kettle puckered his brows. "I don't seem to understand you," he said.

"I say this," Silva murmured, "because there seems no other way to explain the keenness with which she hunts after personal danger. At present she is intriguing against President Quijarra's Government. Well, we all know that Quijarra is a brigand, just as his predecessor was before him. The man who succeeds him in the Presidency of Chili will be a brigand also. It is the custom of my country. But interfering with brigandage is a ticklish operation, and Quijarra is always scrupulous to wring the necks of anyone whom he thinks at all likely to interfere with his peculiar methods."

"I should say that from his point of view," said Kettle, "he was acting quite rightly, sir."

"I thought you'd look at it sensibly," said Silva. "Well, Captain, here we are at the top of the stair. Don't you think you had better change your mind, and slip away now, and go back to your quarters?"

"Why, no, sir," said Captain Kettle. "From what you tell me, it seems possible that Miss La Touche may shortly be seeing trouble, and it would give me pleasure to be near and ready to bear a hand. She is a lady for whom I have got considerable regard. That supper, sir, which we have just eaten, and the wine, are things which will live in my memory."

He stepped out on to the roof, and Donna Clotilde

came to meet him. She linked her fingers upon his arm, and led him apart from the rest. At the further angle of the gardens they leaned their elbows upon the parapet, and talked, whilst the glow from the street below faintly lit their faces, and the fire-flies winked behind their backs.

"I thank you, Captain, for your offer," she said at length, "and I accept it as freely as it was given. I have had proposals of similar service before, but they came from the wrong sort. I wanted a man, and I found out that you were that before you had been at the dinner table five minutes."

Captain Kettle bowed to the compliment. "But," said he, "if I am that, I have all a man's failings."

"I like them better," said the lady, "than a half-man's virtues. And as a proof I offer you command of my navy."

"Your navy, Miss?"

"It has yet to be formed," said Donna Clotilde, "and you must form it. But, once we make the nucleus, other ships of the existing force will desert to us, and with those we must fight and beat the rest. Once we have the navy, we can bombard the ports into submission till the country thrusts out President Quijarra of its own accord, and sets me up in his place."

"Oh," said Kettle, "I didn't understand. Then you want to be Queen of Chili?"

"President."

"But a president is a man, isn't he?"

"Why? Answer me that."

"Because—well, because they always have been, Miss."

"Because men up to now have always taken the best things to themselves. Well, Captain, all that is changing; the world is moving on ; and women are forcing their way in, and taking their proper place. You say that no state has had a woman-president. You are quite right. I shall be the first."

Captain Kettle frowned a little, and looked thoughtfully down into the lighted street beneath. But presently he made up his mind, and spoke again.

"I'll accept your offer, Miss, to command the navy, and I'll do the work well. You may rely on that. Although I say it myself, you'd find it hard to get a better man. I know the kind of brutes one has to ship as seamen along this South American coast, and I'm the sort of brute to handle them. By James, yes, and you shall see me make them do most things, short of miracles.

"But there's one other thing, Miss, I ought to say, and I must apologise for mentioning it, seeing that you're not a business person. I must have my twelve pound a month, and all found. I know it's a lot, and I know you'll tell me wages are down just now. But I couldn't do it for less, Miss. Commanding a navy's a strong order, and, besides, there's considerable risk to be counted in as well."

Donna Clotilde took his hand in both hers.

"I thank you, Captain," she said, "for your offer, and I begin to see success ahead from this moment. You need have no fear on the question of remuneration."

"I hope you didn't mind my mentioning it," said

Kettle nervously. "I know it's not a thing gener-ally spoken of to ladies. But you see, Miss, I'm a poor man, and feel the need of money sometimes. Of course, twelve pound a month is high, but——"

"My dear Captain," the lady broke in, "what you ask is moderation itself; and, believe me, I respect you for it, and will not forget. Knowing who I am, no other man in Chili would have hesitated to ask "—she had on her tongue to say "a hundred times as much," but suppressed that and said—"more. But in the meantime," said she, "will you accept this hundred-pound note for any current expenses which may occur to you?"

A little old green-painted barque lay hove-to under sail, disseminating the scent of guano through the sweet tropical day. Under her square counter the name *El Almirante Cochrane* appeared in clean white lettering. The long South Pacific swells lifted her lazily from hill to valley of the blue water, to the accompaniment of squealing gear and a certain groaning of fabric. The Chilian coast lay afar off, as a white feathery line against one fragment of the sea-rim.

The green-painted barque was old. For many a weary year had she carried guano from rainless Chilian islands to the ports of Europe; and though none of that unsavoury cargo at present festered beneath her hatches, though, indeed, she was in shingle ballast and had her holds scrubbed down and fitted with bunks for men, the aroma of it had entered into the very soul of her fabric, and not all the washings of the sea could remove it.

A white whaleboat lay astern, riding to a grass-rope painter, and Señor Carlos Silva, whom the whaleboat had brought off from the Chilian beach, sat in the barque's deck-house talking to Captain Kettle.

"The Señorita will be very disappointed," said Silva.

"I can imagine her disappointment," returned the sailor. "I can measure it by my own. I can tell you, sir, when I saw this filthy, stinking, old wind-jammer waiting for me in Callao, I could have sat down right where I was and cried. I'd got my men together, and I guess I'd talked big about *El Almirante Cochrane*, the fine new armoured cruiser we were to do wonders in. The only thing I knew about her was her name, but Miss La Touche had promised me the finest ship that could be got, and I only described what I thought a really fine ship would be. And, then, when the agent stuck out his finger and pointed out this foul old violet-bed, I tell you it was a bit of a let down."

"There's been some desperate robbery some-where," said Silva.

"It didn't take me long to guess that," said Kettle, "and I concluded the agent was the thief, and started in to take it out of him without further talk. He hadn't a pistol, so I only used my hands to him, but I guess I fingered him enough in three minutes to stop his dancing for another month. He swore by all the saints he was innocent, and that he was only the tool of other men; and perhaps that was so. But he deserved what he got for being in such shady employment."

" Still, that didn't procure you another ship ?"

" Hammering the agent couldn't make him do an impossibility, sir. There wasn't such a vessel as I wanted in all the ports of Peru. So I just took this nosegay that was offered, lured my crew aboard, and put out past San Lorenzo island, and got to sea. It's a bit of a come down, sir, for a steamer-sailor like me," the little man added with a sigh, "to put an old wind-jammer through her gymnastics again. I thought I'd done with ' mainsail haul' and rawhide chafing gear, and all the white wings nonsense, for good and always."

" But, Captain, what did you come out for? What earthly good can you do with an old wreck like this ? "

" Why, sir, I shall carry out what was arranged with Miss La Touche. I shall come up with one of President Quijarra's Government vessels, capture her and then start in to collar the rest. There's no alteration in the programme. It's only made more difficult, that's all."   .

" I rowed out here to the rendezvous to tell you the *Cancelario* is at moorings in Tampique Bay, and that the Señorita would like to see you make your beginning upon her. But what's the good of that news, now? The *Cancelario* is a fine new war-ship of 3000 tons. She's fitted with everything modern in guns and machinery, she's three hundred men of a crew, and she lays always with steam up and an armed watch set. To go near her in this clumsy little barque would be to make yourself a laughing-stock. Why, your English Cochrane wouldn't have done it."

"I know nothing about Lord Cochrane, Mr. Silva. He was dead before my time. But whatever people may have done to him, I can tell anyone who cares to hear, that the man who's talking to you now is a bit of an awkward handful to laugh at. No, sir, I expect there'll be trouble over it, but you may tell Miss La Touche we shall have the *Cancelario*, if she'll stay in Tampique Bay till I can drive this old lavender-box up to her."

For a minute Silva stared in silent wonder.

"Then, Captain," said he, "all I can think is, that you must have enormous trust in your crew."

Captain Kettle bit the end from a fresh cigar. "You should go and look at them for yourself," said he, "and hear their talk, and then you'd know. The beasts are fit to eat me already."

"How did you get them on board?"

"Well, you see, sir, I collected them by promises —fine pay, fine ship, fine cruise, fine chances, and so on; and, when I'd only this smelling bottle here to show them, they hung back a bit. If there'd been only twenty of them, I don't say but what I could have hustled them on board with a gun and some ugly words. But sixty were too many to tackle; so I just said to them that *El Almirante Cochrane* was only a ferry to take us across to a fine war steamer that was lying out of sight elsewhere; and they swallowed the yarn, and stepped in over the side.

"I can't say they've behaved like lambs since. The grub's not been to their fancy, and I must say the biscuit was crawling; and it seems that as a bedroom the hold hurt their delicate noses; and, between one thing and another, I've had to shoot six of them before they understood I was skipper here. You see, sir, they were most of them living in Callao before they shipped, because there's no extradition there; and so they're rather a toughish crowd to handle."

"What a horrible time you must have had!"

"There has been no kid-glove work for me, sir, since I got to sea with this rose garden; and I must say it would have knocked the poetry right out of most men. But, personally, I can't say it has done that to me. You'd hardly believe it, sir, but once or twice, when the whole lot of the brutes have been raging against me, I've been very nearly happy. And afterwards, when I've got a spell of rest, I've picked up pen and paper and knocked off one or two of the prettiest sonnets a man could wish to see in print. If you like, sir, I'll read you a couple before you go back to your whaleboat."

"I thank you, Skipper, but not now. Time is on the move, and Donna Clotilde is waiting for me. What am I to tell her?"

"Say, of course, that her orders are being carried out, and her pay being earned."

"My poor fellow," said Silva, with a sudden gush of remorse, "you are only sacrificing yourself uselessly. What can you, in a small sailing vessel like this, do with your rifles against a splendidly armed vessel like the *Cancelario*?"

"Not much in the shooting line, that's certain," said Kettle cheerfully. "That beautiful agent sold us even over the ammunition. There were kegs put on board marked 'cartridges,' but when I came to break one or two so as to serve out a little ammunition, for practice, be hanged if the kegs weren't full of powder. And it wasn't the stuff for guns even ; it was blasting powder, same as they use in the mines. Oh, sir, that agent was the holiest kind of fraud."

Silva wrung his hands. "Captain," he cried, "you must not go on with this mad cruise. It would be sheer suicide for you to find the *Cancelario*."

"You shall give me news of it again after I've met her," said Captain Kettle. "For the present, sir, I follow out Miss La Touche's orders, and earn my £12 a month. But if you're my friend, Mr. Silva, and want to do me a good turn, you might hint that if things go well, I could do with a rise to £14 a month when I'm sailing the *Cancelario* for her."

The outline of Tampique Bay stood out clearly in bright moonshine, and the sea down the path of the moon's rays showed a canal of silver, cut through rolling fields of purple. The green-painted barque was heading into the bay on the port tack; and at moorings, before the town, in the curve of the shore, the grotesque spars of a modern warship showed in black silhouette against the moonbeams. A slate-coloured naphtha-launch was sliding out over the swells towards the barque.

Captain Kettle came up from below, and watched the naphtha-launch with throbbing interest. He had hatched a scheme for capturing the *Cancelario*, and had made his preparations; and here was an interruption coming which might very well upset everything most ruinously. Nor was he alone in his regard. The barque's topgallant rail was lined with faces; all her complement were wondering who these folk might be who were so confidently coming out to meet them.

A Jacob's ladder was thrown over the side; the slate-coloured launch swept up, and emitted—a woman. Captain Kettle started, and went down into the waist to meet her. A minute later he was wondering whether he dreamed, or whether he was really walking his quarterdeck in company with Donna Clotilde La Touche. But meanwhile the barque held steadily along her course.

The talk between them was not for long.

"I must beseech you, Miss, to go back from where you came," said Kettle. "You must trust me to carry out this business without your supervision."

"Is your method very dangerous?" she asked.

"I couldn't recommend it to an Insurance Company," said Kettle thoughtfully.

"Tell me your scheme."

Kettle did so in some forty words. He was pithy, and Donna Clotilde was cool. She heard him without change of colour.

"Ah," she said, "I think you will do it."

"You will know one way or another within an hour from now, Miss. But I must ask you to take your launch to a distance. As I tell you, I have made all my own boats so that they won't swim; but, if your little craft was handy, my crew would jump overboard and risk the sharks, and try to reach her in spite of all I could do to stop them. They won't be anxious to fight that *Cancelario* when the time comes, if there's any way of wriggling out of it."

"You are quite right, Captain; the launch must go; only I do not. I must be your guest here till you can put me on the *Cancelario*."

Captain Kettle frowned. "What's coming is no job for a woman to be in at, Miss."

"You must leave me to my own opinion about that. You see, we differ upon what a woman should do, Captain. You say a woman should not be president of a republic; you think a woman should not be sharer in a fight: I am going to show you how a woman can be both." She leant her shoulders over the rail, and hailed the naptha-launch with a sharp command. A man in the bows cast off the line with which it towed; the man aft put over his tiller, and set the engines a-going; and, like a slim, grey ghost, the launch slid quietly away into the gloom. "You see," she said, "I'm bound to stay with you now." And she looked upon him with a burning glance.

But Kettle replied coldly. "You are my owner, Miss," he said, "and can do as you wish. It is not for me now to say that you are foolish. Do I understand you still wish me to carry out my original plan?"

"Yes," she said curtly.

"Very well, Miss, then we shall be aboard of that war-steamer in less than fifteen minutes." He bade his second mate call aft the crew; but instead of remaining to meet them, he took a keen glance at the barque's canvas, another at her wake, another at the moored cruiser ahead, and then, after peering thoughtfully at the clouds which sailed in the sky, he went to the companion-way and dived below.

The crew trooped aft and stood at the break of the quarterdeck waiting for him. And in the meanwhile they feasted their eyes with many different thoughts on Donna Clotilde La Touche.

Presently Captain Kettle returned to deck, aggressive and cheerful, and faced the men with hands in his jacket pockets. Each pocket bulged with something heavy, and the men, who by this time had come to understand Captain Kettle's ways, began to grow quiet and nervous. He came to the point without any showy oratory.

"Now, my lads," said he, "I told you when you shipped aboard this lavender-box in Callao, that she was merely a ferry to carry you to a fine war-steamer which was lying elsewhere. Well, there's the steamer, just off the starboard bow yonder. Her name's the *Cancelario*, and at present she seems to belong to President Quijarra's Government. But Miss La Touche here (who is employing both me and you, just for the present) intends to set up a Government of her own; and, as a preliminary, she wants that ship. We've to grab it for her."

Captain Kettle broke off, and for a full minute there was silence. Then some one amongst the men laughed, and a dozen others joined in.

"That's right," said Kettle. "Cackle away, you scum. You'd be singing a different tune if you knew what was beneath you."

A voice from the gloom—an educated voice—answered him: "Don't be foolish, Skipper. We're not going to ram our heads against a brick wall like that. We set some value on our lives."

"Do you?" said Kettle. "Then pray that this

breeze doesn't drop (as it seems likely to do), or you'll lose them. Shall I tell you what I was up to below just now? You remember those kegs of blasting powder? Well, they're in the lazaret, where some of you stowed them; but they're all of them unheaded, and one of them carries the end of a fuse. That fuse is cut to burn just twenty minutes, and the end's lighted.

"Wait a bit. It's no use going to try and douse it. There's a pistol fixed to the lazaret hatch, and if you try to lift it that pistol will shoot into the powder, we'll all go up together without further palaver. Steady now there, and hear me out. You can't lower away boats, and get clear that way. The boat's bottoms will tumble away so soon as you try to hoist them off the skids. I saw to that last night. And you can't require any telling to know there are far too many sharks about, to make a swim healthy exercise."

The men began to rustle and talk.

"Now, don't spoil your only chance," said Kettle, "by singing out. If on the cruiser yonder they think there's anything wrong, they'll run out a gun or two, and blow us out of the water before we can come near them. I've got no arms to give you; but you have your knives, and I guess you shouldn't want more. Get in the shadow of the rail there, and keep hid till you hear her bump. Then jump on board, knock everybody you see over the side, and keep the rest below."

"They'll see us coming," whimpered a voice. "They'll never let us board."

"They'll hear us," the Captain retorted, "if you

gallows-ornaments bellow like that, and then all we'll have to do will be to sit tight where we are till that powder blows us like a thin kind of spray up against the stars. Now, get to cover with you, all hands, and not another sound. It's your only chance."

The men crept away, shaking, and Captain Kettle himself took the wheel, and appeared to drowse over it. He gave her half a spoke at a time, and by invisible degrees the barque fell off till she headed dead on for the cruiser. Save for the faint creaking of her gear, no sound came from her, and she slunk on through the night like some patched and tattered phantom. Far down in her lazaret the glowing end of the fuse crept nearer to the powder barrels, and in imagination every mind on board was following its race.

Nearer and nearer she drew to the *Cancelario*, and ever nearer. The waiting men felt as though the hearts of them would leap from their breasts. Two of them fainted. Then came a hail from the cruiser: " Barque, ahoy, are you all asleep there?"

Captain Kettle drowsed on over the wheel. Donna Clotilde, from the shadow of the house, could see him nodding like a man in deep sleep.

"Carrajo! you barque, there! Put down your helm. You'll be aboard of us in a minute."

Kettle made no reply : his hands sawed automatically at the spokes, and the glow from the pinnacle fell upon close-shut eyes. It was a fine bit of acting.

The Chilians shouted, but they could not prevent the collision, and when it came there broke out a yell as though the gates of the pit had been suddenly unlocked.

The barque's crew of human refuse, mad with terror, rose up in a flock from behind the bulwarks. As one man they clambered over the cruiser's side and spread about her decks.

Ill provided with weapons though they might be, the Chilians were scarcely better armed. A sentry squibbed off his rifle, but that was the only shot fired. Knives did the greater part of the work,—knives and belaying pins, and whatever else came to hand. Those of the watch on deck who did not run below were cleared into the sea; the berth deck was stormed; and the waking men surrendered to the pistol nose.

A couple of desperate fellows went below, and cowed the firemen and engineer on watch. The mooring was slipped, steam was given to the engines, and whilst her former crew were being drafted down into an empty hold, the *Cancelario* was standing out at a sixteen-knot speed towards the open sea under full command of the raiders. Then from behind them came the roar of an explosion and a spurt of dazzling light, and the men shuddered to think of what they had so narrowly missed. And as it was some smelling fragments of the old guano barque lit upon the afterdeck, as they fell headlong from the dark sky above.

Donna Clotilde went on to the upper bridge, and took Captain Kettle by the hand.

"My friend," she said, "I shall never forget this." And she looked at him with eyes that spoke of more than admiration for his success.

" I am earning my pay," said Kettle.

" Pah !" she said, " don't let money come between us. I cannot **bear to** think of you in connection with sordid things like that. I put you on a higher plane. Captain," **she** said, and turned her head away, " I shall choose a man like you for husband."

" Heaven mend your taste, Miss," said Kettle ; " but—there may be others like me."

" There are not."

" Then you must be content with the nearest you can **get.**"

Donna Clotilde stamped her foot upon the planking of the bridge.

" **You** are dull," **she cried.**

" **No,**" he said, " **I have got** **clear** sight, Miss. Won't you go below now and get **a spell of** sleep ? Or will you **give me** your orders first **?** "

" No," she answered, " I will not. We must settle this matter first. You have a wife in England, I know, but that is nothing. Divorce is simple here. I have influence with the Church ; you could be set **free** in a day. Am I not the woman you would choose **?** "

" **Miss La** Touche, you are my employer."

" **Answer** my question."

" Then, Miss, if you will have it, you are not."

" **But** why ? Why ? Give me your reasons? You are brave. Surely I have shown courage too ? Surely you must admire that ? "

" I like men for men's work, Miss."

" But that is an exploded notion. Women have got to take their place. They must show themselves the **equals** of men in everything."

" But you see, Miss," said Kettle, " I prefer to be linked to a lady who is my superior—as I am linked at present. If it pleases you, we had better end this talk."

" No," said Donna Clotilde, " it has got to be settled one way or the other. You know what I want. Marry me as soon as you are set free, and there shall be no end of your power. I will make you rich ; I will make you famous. Chili shall be at our feet ; the world shall bow to us."

" It could be done," said Kettle with a sigh.

" Then marry me."

" With due respect, I will not," said the little man.

" You know you are speaking to a woman who is not accustomed to be thwarted?"

Captain Kettle bowed.

" Then you will either do as I wish, or leave this ship. I give you an hour to consider it in."

" You will find my second mate the best navigating officer left," said Kettle, and Donna Clotilde, without further words, left the bridge.

The little shipmaster waited for a decent interval, and then sighed, and gave orders. The men on deck obeyed him with quickness. A pair of boat davits were swung out-board, and the boat plentifully victualled and its water-breakers filled. The *Cancelario's* engines were stopped, and the tackles screamed as the boat was lowered to the water, and rode there at the end of its painter. Captain Kettle left the bridge in charge of his first officer, and went below. He found the lady sitting in the commander's cabin, with head pillowed upon her arms.

" You still wish me to go, Miss ?" he said.

" If you will not accept what is offered."

" I am sorry," said the little sailor, "very sorry. If I'd met you, Miss, before I saw Mrs. Kettle, and if you'd been a bit different, I believe I could have liked you.   But as it is——"

She leaped to her feet, with eyes that blazed.

" Go ! " she cried.   " Go, or I will call upon some of those fellows to shoot you."

" They will do it cheerfully, if you ask them," said Kettle, and did not budge.

She sank down on the sofa again with a wail.

"Oh, go," she cried.   " If you are a man go, and never let me see you again."

Captain Kettle bowed, and went on deck.

A little later he was alone in the quarter-boat. The *Cancelario* was drawing fast away from him into the night, and the boat danced in the cream of her wake.

" Ah, well," he said to himself, "there's another good chance gone for good and always. What a cantankerous beggar I am."   And then for a moment his thoughts went elsewhere, and he got out paper and a stump of pencil, and busily scribbled an elegy to some poppies in a cornfield.   The lines had just flitted gracefully across his mind, and they seemed far too comely to be allowed a chance of escape.   It was a movement characteristic of his queerly ordered brain.   After the more ugly moments of his life, Captain Owen Kettle always turned to the making of verse as an instinctive relief.

CHAPTER IV.

EVEN before he left Jeddah, Captain Kettle was quite aware that by shipping pilgrims **on** the iron deck of the *Saigon* for transit across the Red Sea, he was trangressing the laws of several nations, especially those of Great Britain and her Dependencies. But what else could the **poor man do?** Situated as he was, with such a tempting opportunity ready to his hand, he would have been less than human if **he** had neglected to take the bargain which was offered. And though the list of things that has been **said** against Captain Owen Kettle is both black and long, I am not aware that anyone has yet alleged that the little sailor was anything more or less than human in all his many frailties.

Cortolvin came to the chart-house and put this matter of illegality to him in plain words when the engines chose to break down two days out of Jeddah, **and** the *Saigon* lolled helpless in the blazing Red **Sea heat.**

Cortolvin up to that time had not made himself remarked. He had **marched** on board from the new Jeddah quay where the railway is, and posed as an Arab of **the Sahara who was** glorying in the newly-acquired green turban of a Hadji; he was nicked on the mate's tally **as a** " nigger," along with some three hundred and **forty** dark-skinned followers of the Prophet ; **and he** had **spent** those two **days** upon an orthodox **square of** ragged carpet, spread on the rusted iron plating **of the** lower fore deck.

When the pilgrims had mustered **for victualling,** he had filed in with the rest, and held out a **brass** *lotah* **for his** ration of water, and a tattered square of canvas **for** his dole of steamed rice. You could **count his** ribs twenty yards away ; but he'd the look **of a** healthy man ; and when on mornings he helped **to** throw overboard those of his fellow-pilgrims who had died during the night, it was plain to see that **he** was **a fellow of more** than **ordinary** muscular strength.

He came to Captain Kettle in the chart-house to report that the pilgrims contemplated seizing the *Saigon* so soon as ever the engines were once more put in running order. " They've declared a *jehad* against you, if you know what that is," said Cortolvin.

" A holy war, or some such skittles, isn't it ? " said Kettle.

" That's about the size of it," said the Hadji ; "you'll have to look out if you intend to remain master of this steamboat."

" I don't require any teaching of my business from passengers," said Captain Kettle stiffly.

"All right," said Cortolvin, "have it your own way. But I think **you** might be decently grateful. I've risked my **life by** coming to give you news of what was in the **wind.** And you can't pretend that the information is **not** useful. You've a coolie crew who will be absolutely foolish **if** trouble comes—

these Lascars always are that way. You've just your two white engineers and two white mates to back you up, and the five of you wouldn't have a show. You've three hundred and forty fanatics to deal with, who are all fighting bred, and fighting fit. They're all well armed, and they wouldn't a bit object to die scrimmaging in such a cause.

"You know it's part of their creed that if they peg-out whilst fighting *giaours*, they go slick to paradise by lightning express. That wily old camel-driver of Mecca painted his heaven as just the sort of dandy place to suit this kind of cattle, and as most of them have a beast of a time on this earth, they're anxious to move along upstairs whenever a decent opportunity offers to get there."

"They'll be an ugly crowd to tackle: I grant that."

"They are so, and don't you forget it. I might point out, Captain, that, personally speaking, I'd been a lot safer if I'd stayed down on the lower fore deck yonder, and held my tongue. They'd have got you to an absolute certainty if they'd ambushed you as was intended, and I could have kept out of the actual throat-cutting and preserved a sound skin. They've all got profound respect for me: I'm a very holy man."

"And as it is?"

Hadji Cortolvin shrugged his shoulders. "Oh, I chip in with you."

"Will you tell me why?"

"Cousinship of the skin I suppose. You're white by birth, and I believe I should turn out to be white also if I kept out of the sun for awhile, and had several Turkish baths. Of course I've a snuff-coloured hide on me now, and during this last two years I've been living with men of colour, and following their ways, and thinking their thoughts. Funny isn't it? I come across you; I don't know you from Adam; I can't say I particularly like what I've seen of you; and yet here am I, rounding on my former mates, and chipping in with you on the clear knowledge that I shall probably get killed during the next few hours for my pains."

"May I ask your name?" said Kettle. "I believe, sir," he added with a bow, "that you are a gentleman."

The Hadji laughed. "So far as I recollect, I was that once, Captain. Sorry I haven't a card on me, but my name's W. H. Cortolvin, and I lived near Richmond, in Yorkshire, before I was idiot enough to go wandering off the Cook's tourist routes into the middle of Arabia."

"I'm Welsh myself," said Kettle, "but I've known men from Yorkshire. Shake hands, sir, please. Will you have a whisky-peg?"

"Pour it out, Captain. I haven't tasted a Christian drink for thirty weary months. And you've got a *chattie* hung up in the draught of a port! Cool water, ye gods! *Bismillah!* But it is good to be alive sometimes."

Captain Kettle looked with distaste at the Hadji's attire.

"Won't you sling that filthy night-gown thing of yours overboard," he asked, "and have a wash? I can rig you out with some pyjamas from the slop chest."

But Cortolvin would not change his dirt and

squalor just then.   He had worn it too long to be affected by it ; " and," said he, " I don't want to advertise the fact that I'm an Englishman just at present.
If my dear friends down yonder on the lower deck
knew it, they'd not wait for the engines to be repaired.
They'd fizzle up just like gunpowder there and then,
and the whole lot of us white men would be pulled
into tassels before we'd time to think."

" I don't know about that," said Kettle. " I've
faced some of the ugliest crowds that have floated
on the seas before this, and they thought they were
going to have it all their own way, but they found
that when it came to shooting that I could keep my
end up very handily."

He waved his guest to a deck chair, placed a box
of cheroots hospitably open on the chart-table, and
then he went outside the chart-house, and leant over
the bridge deck rail. The awning above him threw
a clean-cut shade which swung to and fro as the
Saigon rolled over the faint oily swell ; and outside
its shelter the sun's rays fell like molten brass, and
the metal-work was hot enough to raise a blister.
The air was motionless and stagnant, and greasy
with the smell of humanity. The whole fabric of the
steamer shimmered in the dancing heat.

For the dense mass of pilgrims below the situation approached the intolerable. Left to itself, the
rusted iron deck beneath their bare skins would
have grown hot enough to char them. Nothing but
a constant sluicing with water made it in any way to
be endured. And as the water from alongside came
up to them as warm as tea, it did but little to refresh.

The African can withstand most temperatures

which are thrown from above on to the face of this planet, but even the African can at times die from heat as glibly as his betters. Even as Kettle watched, one of the pilgrims, a grizzle-headed Haûsa from the Western Soudan, was contorted with heat apoplexy; breathed stertorously for a minute or so; and then lay still, and immediately became a prey to flies innumerable. Two of his nearest comrades bestirred themselves to look at him, pronounced that life was extinct, stood up, and with an effort carried the body out of the press, and heaved it over the hot iron bulwark into the oily sea beneath. It is not good that the dead should remain with the quick even for minutes in circumstances such as those.

And whilst the bearers carried him away, an old white-haired negro from Sokoto stood upon his feet swaying to the roll of the ship, and faced the heat-blurred East with bowed head. Aloud he bore witness that God was great; and that Mahomet was the Prophet of God; and that of mortals, each man's fate was writ big upon his forehead. And then the rest of the pilgrims bent their foreheads to the torturing deck plates, and made profession of the faith, following his words.

Captain Kettle from his stand against the rail of the bridge deck pitied the heathen, and thought with a complacent sigh of a certain obscure chapel in South Shields; but at the same time he could not avoid being impressed by the heathen's constancy. They might die, but they forebore to curse God in doing it, and the omission gave him an insight into the workings of fatalism which made him think more of what Cortolvin had said.

Every man amongst the pilgrims had sword, or spear, or mace, or rifle within grip of his fist; and as a fighting force—with fatalism to back them—he began to realise that they could make a very ugly company to manœuvre against. A regulation of the pilgrim trade requires that all weapons shall be taken from this class of passengers during the voyage, but Kettle had omitted to disarm them through sheer contempt for what they could do. If they chose to fight amongst themselves, that was their own concern; it never even occurred to him as they came off Jeddah quay, noisy and odorous, that they would dare to contend against his imperial will; but now he sincerely wished that the means of serious offence were not so handy to their fingers.

I do not say that he was afraid, for, knowing him well, I honestly believe that the little ruffian has never yet feared man that was born of woman; but the safety of the *Saigon* was a matter just then very near to his heart, and he had forebodings as to what might happen to her.

He went back again inside the chart-house, sat himself upon the sofa, and ran a finger round inside the collar of his white drill coat.

"Do you like the cheroots, sir?" he said to his tattered guest.

"Nice cheroots," said Cortolvin: "wonder how many I'll smoke. Those True Believers are a pretty tough crowd, aren't they? There's one Soudanese fellow in a Darfur suit of mail. Did you notice him? He's been a big war sheik in his day. He helped to smash up Hicks Pasha's army, and com- manded a thousand men at the storming of Khartoum ; but he got sick of Mahdiism about a year back, and set out to perform the Hadj. When it comes to fighting, you'll see that man will shine."

"He shall have my first shot," said Kettle.

"It surprises me," said Cortolvin, "that you ever went in for this pilgrim-carrying business at all. You must have been pretty hard pushed, Captain."

"Hard wasn't the word for it," said the ship-master with a sigh. "I met misfortune, sir, in Chili. I disagreed with my employer, who was a lady, and went off cruising in a boat by myself. A tea steamer picked me up and put me in Colombo. I got from there to Bombay as second mate of a tramp, but I couldn't stand the old man's tongue, and went ashore without my wages. I guess, sir, I'm no good except in command ; I can't take an order civilly.

"Well, in Bombay I'd a regular nip-gut time of it. I bummed round the agents' offices till I almost blushed to look at their punkah-coolies ; but I'd no papers to show that would do me any good ; and none of them would give me a ship the size of a rice mat.

"At last, when I was getting desperate, and pretty near put to going to sea before the mast, a Cardiff man I once knew came to the lodgings, and gave me a tip. He'd been master of a country steamer ; he'd been sacked (he didn't deny it) for drunkenness ; he'd not drawn a sober breath for months, and didn't see any prospect of changing his habits ; and there was the berth vacant, and I might have it for the asking.

"The pay wasn't much ; only 100 rupees a month

and percentage on profits; and the owner was a Parsee. I'd never been low enough down to sign on under a black man before, but I guess I was past being very nice in my tastes just then. The owner was fat and oldish, and wore a thing on his head like a top hat turned upside down, and I will say I did not give him much politeness. But he knew his place; he *sahib'd* me quite respectfully; and he said he'd be honoured if I'd take his steamer under my charge. 'She was all he'd got,' he said; 'he loved her like his life, and he'd not trust her to any-one except a *pukka sahib.*'

"Of course he lied a good deal—all natives do that—and he fixed up our bargain so that I'd little to win and he'd a good deal, which is those Parsees' way. But I will say he was always most respectful, and in the matter of victualling he really surprised me. Why, he actually put Bass's ale on board at four annas the bottle!

"We cleared from Bombay in corn, and cottons, and earthenware, consigned to Jeddah, and the owner told me I'd have no trouble in getting a cargo of dates and coffee to bring back. But the Jeddah merchants seemed to think different. I cut down freights to near vanishing point, but they wouldn't look at them anyhow. I couldn't get a ton of cargo on board for any spot in the known globe, no, not if I'd offered to carry it for nothing. The *Saigon* might have swung there at moorings till the bottom rotted out of her; and expenses were running up all the time.

"The climate was sickly too; I lost my *serang* before I'd been there a week, and two more of the coolies died in the next ten days. So when this cargo of pilgrims offered, I tell you I just jumped at it. Of course this old wreck was not fitted for the trade. She's small, she's iron decks, she's only two boats, and she's not near enough water tanks. There'd be big penalties if she was caught. But I shipped a second rice steamer, and signed that charter-party smiling.

"It wasn't as if I'd got to go through the Ditch to one of the Morocco ports ; the pilgrims had only to be taken across to Kosseir ; and squaring an Egyptian custom officer is only a case of how much *backshish*."

"You do know your trade," said Cortolvin.

"The under side of it," said Kettle, with a sigh. "A man with luck like mine has to. He never gets on with the decent steamboat lines, where every-thing is square and above board. He can only get the little hole-and-corner owners, who you've got to make dividends for somehow and no questions asked or else just up and take the dirty sack.

"I'm a man," he added with a frown, "that can do the job well, and they know it, and keep me to it. But I despise myself all the time. It isn't in my nature, Mr. Cortolvin. Put me ashore, give me a farm, and let me bend yellow gaiters and a large-pattern coat, and there wouldn't be a straighter, sweeter-natured man between here and heaven."

The Hadji swept the perspiration from his fore-head with the back of a grimy knuckle.

"There's no accounting for taste, Captain. I'm the owner of acres near Richmond, and if I chose I could ride about my park, and see the farms, and live the life of a country gentleman just in the way you think you'd like. But I tired of it."

"Perhaps you have no wife, sir," suggested the sailor.

His guest gave a short laugh.

"Oh, Lord, yes," he said, "I've a wife."

He paused a minute and then threw his half-smoked cheroot savagely out into the sunshine.

"You can take it from me that I have a wife, Captain. But—well, you see, I've always been an Arabic scholar, and I thought I'd come out to the Hedjaz to study dialects for a year or so. It would be a pleasant change after the milk and honey of a country life. I don't seem to have got killed, and I think I've liked it on the whole. It's been exciting, and I know more about bastard Arabic than any European living now that poor Palmer's dead, if that's any satisfaction. If I chose to go home now, I could pose as no end of a big boss in that line. The only thing is, I can't quite make my mind up whether to risk it. By God, yes," he added, with a stare out into the baking sunshine beyond the doorway, "oh, yes, I've a wife."

Captain Kettle did not quite follow all this, so he said politely and vaguely: "Well, of course, you know your own affairs best, sir." Then he took a long and steady look at his guest. "You'll excuse me, sir, but your name seems familiar. I wonder if you'd got that beard and some of your hair off whether I should recognise you."

"I fancy not."

"Cortolvin," the little man mused. "I'm sure I've seen that name before somewhere."

The Hadji laughed. "I'm afraid that neither I nor any of my people have been celebrated enough to have come into public notice, Skipper; but we had a namesake some years back who was famous. A horse named Cortolvin won the Grand National in '67. That's what you'll have got in your mind."

Captain Kettle stiffened. "I beg your pardon, sir," he said with acid politeness, "but I don't see you've earned a right to insult me. When I am at sea I am what circumstances make me. When I am ashore in England, I would have you know I am a different person. I am a regular attender at chapel, and a man who (outside business matters) tries to keep entirely straight. In England, sir, I take an interest in neither pocket-picking, horse-racing, nor sacrilege ; and I have it on the word of a minister I sit under, that there is very little to choose between the three."

Cortolvin faced the situation with ready tact. That this truculent little ruffian who could flirt with homicide without a second thought should so strongly resent the imputation of being interested in a horse race did not surprise him much. He had met others of the breed before. And he smoothed down Captain Kettle's ruffled feelings with the easy glibness of a man of the world. But the needs of the moment were again recurring to him with violence, and he broke off artistically to refer to them.

"Don't you think," he said, "my fellow pilgrims will bear a little attention now, Skipper?"

"I will be off and make up a bit of a surprise packet for them," said Kettle. "Excuse me, sir, for two minutes, whilst I go and give instructions to my chief." And he swung on his pith helmet and left the chart-house.

The sun climbed higher into the fleckless sky, and lolled above the *Saigon* in insolent cruelty. The Red Sea heat grew, if anything, yet more dreadful. The men's veins stood out in ropes upon their streaming bodies, and it scorched them to draw in a breath. Drink, too, was scarce. The Hedaz is a region almost waterless; the desert at the back drains up all the moisture, and the *Saigon* had left Jeddah with her tanks only half filled. She had to depend upon her condenser, and this was small. And in the tropics, condenser-water must be dealt out in a sparing ration, or a dozen hours may easily see a whole ship's company down with raging dysentery.

The *Saigon* carried a spar-deck amidships, and the pilgrims were grouped in two bodies forward and aft of this on the iron plating of the fore and main decks. The spar-deck was officially reached from these lower levels by a couple of slender iron ladders, but it was not unscaleable to a fairly active climber. There was an alley-way passing beneath the spar-deck, but this could easily be closed by the iron doors in the two bulk-heads, which fastened inside with heavy, clamping screws.

The chief engineer came into the chart-house, and hitched up his grimy pyjamas, and mopped his face with a wad of cotton waste. He looked meaningly at the whisky-bottle, but Kettle ignored his glance.

"Well, Mr. McTodd?" said he.

"I'm a' ready for the pagans, sir, when ye're willing to gi' the worrd."

" What are your engines like now ? "

" A wee bittee less fit for the scrap-heap than they were a dozen hours back, but no' very much to boast of." Mr. McTodd spat out into the sunshine. "They're the rottenist engines ever I fingered," said he, "and that's what I think of them. A man ought to have double my pay to be near them. They're just heart-breaking."

" You knew she wasn't the P. and O. when you signed on."

" We're neither of us here, Captain Kettle, because we were offered fatter berths."

Kettle frowned. " I'll trouble you, Mr. McTodd, to attend to the matter in hand. You have those steam pipes ranged ? "

"Both forrard and aft."

" Commanding both ladders ? "

" Just like that."

" And you've plenty of steam ? "

"Ye can hear it burring through the escape this minute if ye'll use your ears. It's been vara exhausting work toiling down yonder in that a'ful heat."

"Well, Mr. Cortolvin here assures me that the niggers will begin to play up the minute we get under weigh, so you see we know where we are, and must be ready for them. I shall want you and the second engineer on deck of course, so you must arrange for one of your crew to run the engines till we've got the business settled."

" I've a greaser down yonder who can open the throttle," said McTodd gloomily, "but he's got no notion of nursing sick engines like these, and as like

as not he'll drive them off their bedplates in a score
of revolutions. Ye'd better let me keep the engine-
room myself, Captain. I'm a sick man, and I'm no'
fit for fighting with my throat as dry as it is now."

Captain Kettle poured out a liberal two fingers
of whisky and handed it across. "Now, Mac," said
he, "wet your neck, and let's have no more of this
nonsense. You'll have to fight for your life inside
ten minutes, and you'll do it better sober."

The engineer eyed the whisky and poured it
slowly down its appointed path.

"Mon," he said, "ye've an a'ful poor opinion o'
my capaacity. I'll just be off and give yon coolie
greaser some instructions, and get my side-arms, and
be with you again in forty clock-ticks."

"I pity the nigger that comes to hand grips with
McTodd," said Kettle, when the grimy man in the
grey pyjamas had left the chart-house, "He's an
ugly beggar to handle when he's sober as he is now.
We'll get ready now, sir, if you please. You go to
the after end of the bridge deck with McTodd and
the second mate, and I'll look after the forrard end
with the old mate and the second engineer. When
they try to rush the ladder, McTodd will give them
the steam, and they'll never be able to face it. All
you and the second mate have to do is to see they
don't climb up over the rail."

"I wish it could be avoided,' said Cortolvin sadly.
"That high-pressure steam will scald some of them
horribly."

"It will do more than that," said Kettle. "It
will strip the meat clean off their bones."

"I have lived amongst those men or their sort for

two solid years, and many of them have shown me kindnesses."

"You should have thought of that, sir, before you came to me here in the chart-house."

"I did think of it; but I couldn't be a renegade to my colour; and so I came. But, Captain, will you let me speak to them? Will you let me tell them that their scheme is known and prepared for? Will you let me explain to them what they will have to face if they start an outbreak?"

Captain Kettle frowned. "You will understand that I am not frightened of the beasts?" he said.

"I quite know that," said Cortolvin, "and I am sorry to spoil a fight. But it is their lives I am begging for."

"Very well," said Kettle, "you can fire away. I don't speak their *bat*, and it's as well they should know from someone what they have to look forward to. Here's a life-preserver which you may find useful. It's the only weapon I have to offer you. My own pistol is the only gun we have in the ship."

The pair of them went outside the chart-house and walked to the head of the forward ladder. A newly-fitted steam pipe, with the joints all greasy with white lead, lay on the deck planks, and the second engineer stood beside it with thumbs in his waist-strap. On the deck below, the pilgrims no longer squatted on their carpets, but stood together in knots, and talked excitedly. Cortolvin clapped his hands, and the sea of savage faces turned towards him.

There were representatives in that mob from half the Mahommedan peoples of Northern Africa.

There were lean Arab camel-breeders of the desert, jet-black farmers from the Great Lakes and the upper Nile, Haûsas from the Western Soudan, limp Fellaheen from Lower Egypt, an Egba who had served in the British Police Force at Lagos, merchants from the back of the Barbary States, workers in metal from Sokoto, and weavers from Timbukhtu.

They were not all holders of the title of Hadji; for though by the Mahommedan law every male must make the Mecca pilgrimage at least once in a lifetime, unless debarred by poverty or lameness, the journey may be done by deputy. And these deputies, fierce, truculent ruffians, who had lived their lives amongst incessant wars and travel, were perhaps the most dangerous of all the lot.

The black men listened to their late associate with a momentary hush of surprise. He spoke to them in fluent Arabic. He did not appeal to their better feelings: he knew his audience. He said it was written that if they tried this thing, if they attempted to capture the steamer, they should surely fail; that all things were prepared to give them battle; and that a horrible death awaited those who persisted in their design.

And then he tried to point out the nature of the *Saigon's* defences, but there he failed. It is ill work to explain the properties of high-pressure steam to savages. A murmur rose amongst them which grew. They let out their voices, and roared defiance. And then the great black mass of them rushed for the iron ladder.

Captain Kettle clapped a whistle to his lips and blew it shrilly.

"Now then, Mr. Cortolvin," he cried, "away with you aft to help McTodd. These cattle here want something more than talk, and I'm going to give it them."

In answer to his whistle, steam had been turned on from below. The second engineer unhitched his thumbs from his waistbelt, took a lump of waste in each grimy hand, and lifted the iron pipe. It was well-jointed, and moved easily, and he turned the nozzle of it to sweep the ladder. In that baking air, the steam did not condense readily ; it travelled three yards from the nozzle of the pipe before it became even thinly visible ; and it impinged upon the black naked bodies, and burned horribly without being seen.

At first they did not flinch. With a dreadful valour they faced the torment, and fought with each other to be first upon the rungs, and then when those in front would have held back, the mob behind pressed them irresistibly onwards. In a moment or so the first rank began to go down before that withering blast, and then others trod on them and fell also, till the hill of writhing black humanity grew to half the height of the iron ladder.

And in the meantime others of the pilgrims were trying to storm the bridge deck at other points; but on the port side, the grey-headed old man fighting *baresark* with an axe, and to starboard, Captain Kettle, with pistol and knuckleduster, battled like wild-cats to keep the sacred planking inviolate.

What was going on at the after end of the *Saigon* they could not tell. From behind them came the roar of the fighting Haûsa, and the savage war-cries of the desert, just as they rose up from before their faces. But in its first flush the fight was too close for any man's thoughts to wander from his own immediate adversaries.

It seemed, however, that the battle was over first in the after part of the steamer, and whether this was because the attack there was less heartful, or because Mr. McTodd's artillery was more terrible, cannot now be known. The question was debated much afterwards without coming to a decision. But, anyway, by the time Captain Kettle's adversaries had ceased to rage against him, Cortolvin was free to come and stand by his side as interpreter.

The wounded lay sprawling and writhing about the iron decks; below them the survivors—and scarcely one of these was without his scald—huddled against the doors of the forecastle; and the grimy second engineer held the belching steam pipe upwards, so that a grey pall hung between the *Saigon* and the sun.

" Now, sir," said Kettle, " kindly translate for me. Tell those animals to chuck all their hardware over the side, or I'll cook the whole lot of them like so many sausages."

Cortolvin lifted up his voice in sonorous Arabic.

" It was written," he cried, " that the *giaour* should prevail. It is written also that those amongst you having wit shall cast your weapons into the sea. It is written, moreover, that those others of you who do not on this instant disarm shall taste again of the scorching breath of Eblis."

A stream of weapons leapt up through the air and fell into the swells alongside with tinkling splashes.

" It would be a weariness to guard you," Cortolvin went on. "Swear by the beard of the Prophet to make no further attempt against this ship, or we shall gaol you fast in death."

A forest of trembling black hands shot up before him.

"We swear!" they cried.

"Then it is written that you keep your vow," said Cortolvin. "God is great! See now to your sick." He turned to Kettle and touched his ragged turban, after the manner of an officer reporting. " The mutiny is ended, sir," he said.

Captain Kettle swung himself lightly on to the upper bridge and telegraphed "Full speed ahead " to the engine-room ; the propeller splashed in the oily swells, and the *Saigon* gathered way. Sullen and trembling, the pilgrims began to tend their hurts, and presently McTodd with a large copper kettle in his hand descended amongst them, and distributed oil and surgical advice.

" There were none actually killed at my end," said Cortolvin.

" I dropped four," said Kettle. " I had to. It was either me or them. And my old mate axed half-a-dozen before they let him be. We'd a tight time here whilst it lasted."

" It will require a good lunp of *backshish* to explain it all satisfactorily at Kosseir."

"Oh, I can't go near there now after this. No custom house for me, sir. I shall just run in-shore a dozen miles short of it, and put the beggars on the beach in my boats, and let them get into Kosseir as best they can. I suppose you'll come back with me ?"

" I suppose so.   Anyway, I can't go on with them. It is the first time **any of** them have discovered I was not a genuine Arab."

" I can imagine," said Kettle drily, "they'd **give** you a lively **time, if they** had you **to** themselves for five minutes.   The Sons of the Prophet don't admire having Europeans messing about the Kaaba But I owe you something, sir, and I shall be happy to go out of my way to serve you.   I will drop you at Suakim, **or** at Aden, or at Perim, **where I** am going **to coal,** whichever you please."

" But **what** about yourself ? "

" Oh, I shall be all right.   I am seldom in need of a nursery-maid, sir."

" But if this affair **gets** into the newspapers, in- quiries will be made, **and** you'll very possibly find yourself in an ugly hole."

"It won't get in the newspapers," said **Kettle** thoughtfully. " The pilgrims can't tell, my officers daren't for their own **sakes, and you** leave me to see my coolies don't. Newspapers," he repeated dreamily ; " queer the hint should have come like that."

" What hint ?   What are you talking about ? "

" I remembered then where I'd seen your name, sir. It was in the *Times of India's* general news column."

" What was said ? "

" Well, **sir,** I suppose **you'd** better be told.   But you must hold up for a hardish knock.   Will you come into the chart-house for a minute, and have a peg ? "

" No, get along, man, get along."

7

" I think it was about your wife, sir. Does she hunt ? "

" All the season."

" Then it will be her. I remember now it said Richmond in Yorkshire, and the name was Mrs. W. H. Cortolvin. She's broken her neck, sir."

Cortolvin clutched at the white rail of the bridge. " My God ! " he cried, " dead ! Julia dead ! Is that all, Captain ? "

" It was only a two-line paragraph. You'll please understand how sorry I am to carry such sad news, Mr. Cortolvin."

" Thanks, Skipper, thanks."   He turned away and walked to the end of the bridge and stayed there for a while, leaning against an awning stanchion, and staring at the baking levels of the Red Sea which were slipping past the *Saigon's* rusty flanks. And then he came back again and stood at Kettle's side, looking down at the pilgrims anointing their scalds below.

" I have learned to be something of a fatalist, Captain," he said, " when I was amongst these people. This is how I sum the situation. It was written that my wife should die whilst I was away. It was written also that I should live. God ordered it all. God is great."

Captain Kettle gripped his hand in sympathy. " I'm sorry for you, sir ; believe me, I am truly sorry. If you think a bit of poetry about the occasion would help you at all, just you say, and I'll do it. I'm in the mood for poetry now. All things put together, we've been through a pretty heavy time during these last few hours."

"Thanks, Skipper, thanks," said Cortolvin. "I know you mean well. And now if you don't mind I'll leave you. I think I'd like to be alone for a bit."

"You do, sir. Go and lie down on my bunk. I'll have you a beautiful elegy written by the time you're back on deck again. It will comfort you."

CHAPTER V.

CORTOLVIN came out under the bridge deck awning up through the baking heat of the companionway, and dropped listlessly into a deck chair. He was dressed in slop-chest pyjamas of a vivid pattern, and had a newly-shaven chin, which stood out refreshingly white against the rest of his sun-darkened countenance.

"Well," said Captain Kettle, as he shoved across the box of cheroots, "are we any nearer getting under way?"

"I looked in at the engine-room as I came past," said the tall man with a laugh, "and the Chief had a good deal to say. I gathered it was his idea that the fellow who last had charge of those engines ought to die a cruel and lingering death."

"It's a sore point with McTodd when she breaks down. But did he say how long it would be before he could give her steam again? I'm a bit anxious. The glass is tumbling, hand over fist ; and what with that, and this heat, there's small doubt but what we'll have a tornado clattering about our ears directly. There's the shore close aboard, as you can see for yourself, and if the wind comes away anywhere from the east'ard, it'll blow this old steamboat half way into the middle of Africa before we can look round us. It's a bad season just now for tornadoes."

The clattering of iron boot-plates made itself heard on the brass-bound steps of the companion-way. "That'll be the Chief coming to answer for himself," said Cortolvin.

Mr. Neil Angus McTodd always advertised his calling in the attire of the outward man, and the eye of an expert could tell with sureness at any given moment whether Mr. McTodd was in employment or not, and, if so, what type of steamboat he was on, what was his official position, what was his pay, and what was the last bit of work on which he had been employed.

The present was the fourth occasion on which the *Saigon's* machinery had chosen to break down during Captain Kettle's two months of command, and after his herculean efforts in making repairs with insufficient staff and materials, Mr. McTodd was unpleasant both to look upon and associate with. He was attired in moist black boots, grey flannel pyjama trousers stuffed into his socks, a weird garment of flannel upon his upper man, a clout round his neck, and a peaked cap upon his grizzled red hair, anointed with years of spraying oil. His elbows and his forehead shone like dull mirrors of steel, and he carried one of his thumbs wrapped up in a grimy, crimson rag. His conversation was full of unnecessary adjectives, and he was inclined to take a cantankerous view of the universe.

"They'd disgrace the scrap-heap of any decent yard, would the things they miscall engines on this rotten tub," said he, by way of preface.

"They are holy engines, and that's a fact," said Kettle. "How long can you guarantee them for this time?"

The engineer mopped his neck with a wad of cotton waste. "Ten revolutions, if you wish me to be certain. It's a verra dry ship, this."

"And how many more? We shall want them. There's a tornado coming on."

"I'm no' anxious to perjure mysel', Captain, but they might run on for a full minute, or they might run on for a day. There's a capreciousness about the rattle-traps that might amuse some people, but it does not appeal to me. I'm in fear of my life every minute I stand on the foot-plates."

"I'd not have taken you for a frightened man."

"I'm no' that as a usual thing, but the temperature of yon engine-room varies between a hundred and twenty and hundred and thirty of the Fahrenheit scale, and it's destroying to the nerves. All the aqueous vapour leaves the system, and I'm verra badly in need of a tonic. Is yon whusky in the black bottle, Captain?"

"Take a peg, Mac."

"I'll just have a sma' three fingers, now ye mention it." He laid the thickest part of his knotty knuckles against the side of the tumbler, and poured out some half a gill of spirit. "Weel," said he, "may we get as good whusky where we are going to," and enveloped the dose with a dextrous turn of the wrist. After which ambiguous toast, he wiped his lips with the cotton waste, and took himself off again to the baking regions below; and presently a dull rumbling, and a tremor of her fabric, announced that the *Saigon* was once more **under way.**

The little steamer had coaled at Perim Island, in the southern mouth of the Red Sea, had come out into the Indian Ocean through the straits of Bab-el-Mandeb, had rounded Cape Guardafui, and was on her way down to Zanzibar in response to the cabled orders of her Parsee owner in Bombay. Cortolvin was still on board as passenger. His excuse was that he wanted to inspect the Island and City of Zanzibar before returning to England and respectability ; his real reason was that he had taken a fancy to the little ruffian of a skipper, and wished to see more of him.

"Cheerful toast, that of McTodd's," said Cortolvin.

"Those engines are enough to discourage any man," said Kettle, "and the heat down there would sour the temper of an archangel."

Cortolvin loosened a couple more buttons of his pyjamas and bared his chest. "It's hard to breathe even here, and I thought I'd learnt what heat was out in those Arabian deserts. There's a tornado coming on, that's certain."

"It will clear the air," said Kettle. "But it will be a sneezer when we get it. Mr. Murgatroyd!" he called.

The old, grizzle-headed mate thrust down a purple face from the head of the upper bridge ladder— "Aye, aye?"

"Get all the awnings off her," the shipmaster ordered; "put extra grips on the boats, and see everything lashed fast that a steam crane could move. We're in for a bad breeze directly."

"Aye, aye," rumbled the mate, and clapped a leaden whistle to his mouth, and blew it shrilly. A minute later he reported: "A big steamer lying-to just a point or two off the starboard bow, Captain. I haven't seen her before because of the haze." He examined her carefully through the bridge binoculars, and gave his observations with heavy deliberation. "She's square-rigged forrard, and has a black funnel with a red band—no, two red bands. Seems to me like one of the German mail-boats, and I should say she was broke down."

Captain Kettle rose springily from his deck chair, and swung himself onto the upper deck bridge. Cortolvin followed.

A mist of heat shut the sea in a narrow ring. Overhead was a heavy, purply darkness, impenetrable as a ceiling of brick. The only light that crept in came from the mysterious unseen plain of the horizon. From every point of the compass uneasy thunder gave forth now and then a stifled bellow, and, though the lightning splashes never showed, sudden thinnings of the gloom would hint at their nearness. The air shimmered and danced with the baking heat, and though lurid greys and pinks predominated, the glow which filled it was constantly changing in hue.

The scene was terrifying, but Kettle regarded it with a satisfied smile. The one commercial prayer of the shipmaster is to meet with a passenger steamer at sea, broken down, and requiring a tow; and here was one of the plums of the ocean ready to his hand and anxious to be plucked. The worse the weather, the greater would be the salvage, and Captain Kettle could have hugged himself with joy when he thought of the tropical hurricane's nearness.

He had changed the *Saigon's* course the instant he came on the bridge, and had pulled the syren string and hooted cheerfully into the throbbing air to announce his coming. The spectral steamer grew every moment more clear, and presently a string of barbaric colours jerked up to the wire span between her masts. There was no breath of wind to make the flags blow out; they hung in dejected cowls; but to Kettle they read like the page of an open book.

"Urgent signal H. B.!" he cried, and clapped the binocular back in the box, and snapped down the lid. "H. B., Mr. Cortolvin, and don't you forget having seen it. '*Want immediate assistance*,' that means."

"You seem to know it by heart," said Cortolvin.

"There's not a steamboat officer on all the seas that doesn't. When things are down with us, we take out the signal book, and hunt up H. B. amongst the urgent signals, and tell ourselves that some day we may come across a Cunarder with a broken tail-shaft, and be able to give up the sea and be living politely on £200 a year well invested, within the fortnight. It's the steamboat officer's dream, sir, but there's few of us it ever comes true for."

"Skipper," said Cortolvin, "I needn't tell you how pleased I'll be if you come into a competence over this business. In the meanwhile, if there's anything I can do, from coal-trimming upwards, I'm your most obedient servant."

" I thank you, sir," said Kettle. "And if you'd go and carry the news to the chief, I'll be obliged. I · know he'll say his engines can't hold out. Tell him they must. Tell him to use up anything he has sooner than get another breakdown. Tell him to rip up his soul for struts and backstays if he thinks it'll keep them running. It's the one chance of my life, Mr. Cortolvin, and the one chance of his, and he's got to know it, and see we aren't robbed of what is put before us. Show him where the siller comes in, sir, and then stand by and you'll see Mr. McTodd work miracles."

Cortolvin went below, and Kettle turned to the old mate. "Mr. Murgatroyd," said he, " get a dozen hands to rouse up that new manilla out of the store. I take you from the foredeck, and give you the afterdeck to yourself. I'll have to bargain with that fellow over there before we do anything, and there'll be little enough time left after we've fixed upon prices. So have everything ready to begin to tow. We'll use their wire."

" Aye, aye," said the mate. "But it won't do to tow with wire, Captain, through what's coming. There's no give in wire. A wire hawser would jerk the guts out of her in fifteen minutes."

Kettle tightened his lips. " Mr. Murgatroyd," said he, " I am not a blame' fool. Neither do I want dictation from my officers. I told you to rouse up the manilla. You will back the wire with a double bridle of that."

" Aye, aye," grunted the mate ; " but what am I to

make fast to ?   Them bollards aft might be stepped in putty for all the use they are. They'd not tow a row-boat through what's coming. I believe they'd draw if they'd a fishing line made fast to them."

" I should have thought you'd been long enough at sea to have known your business by this time," said Kettle unpleasantly. " D'ye think that every steamboat that trades is a bran new ' Harland and Wolff ' ? "

" Well," said the mate sullenly, " I'm waiting to be taught."

" Pass the manilla round the coaming of the after-hatch, and you won't come and tell me that's drawn while this steamboat stays on the water-top."

" Aye, aye," said the mate, and stepped into his slippers and shuffled away. Captain Kettle walked briskly to the centre of the upper bridge and laid a hand on the telegraph. He gave crisp orders to the Lascar at the wheel, and the *Saigon* moved in perfect obedience to his will.

Ahead of him the great slate-coloured liner lay motionless on the oily sea. Her rail was peopled with the anxious faces of passengers. Busy deck-hands were stripping away the awnings. On the high upper bridge were three officers in peaked caps and trim uniforms of white drill, talking together anxiously.

The little *Saigon* curved up from astern, stopped her engines, and then, with reversed propeller, brought up dead, so that the bridges of the two steamers were level, and not more than twenty yards apart. It was smartly done, and (as Kettle had intended) the Germans noticed it, and commented. Then began the barter of words.

"Howdy, Captain," said Kettle, "I hope it's not a funeral you've brought up for? This heat's been very great. Has it knocked over one of your passengers?"

A large-bearded man made reply : "We haf seen a slight mishap mit der machinery, Captain. My ingeneers will mend."

"Oh, that's all right. Thought it might be worse. Well, I wish you luck, Captain. But I'd hurry and get steam on her again, if I were you. The breeze may come away any minute now, and you've the shore close aboard, and you'll be on it if you don't get your steamboat under command again by then, and have a big loss of life. If you get on the beach, it'll surprise me if you don't drown all hands."

Captain Kettle put a hand on the telegraph, as though to ring on his engines again, but the bearded German, after a preliminary stamp of passion, held up his hand for further parley. But for the moment the opportunity of speech was taken from him. The passengers were either English, or for the most part understood that tongue when spoken ; and they had drunk in every word that was said, as Kettle had intended; and now they surged in a writhing, yelling mob at the foot of the two bridge ladders, and demanded that assistance should be hired, let that cost what it might.

There was no making a hail carry above that frightened uproar, and the German shipmaster raved, and explained, and reasoned for full a dozen moments before he quelled it. Then, panting, he came once more to the end of his bridge, and addressed the other steamer.

"Dose bassengers vas nervous," said he, "because dey thought dere might come some leetle rain squall; so I ask you how mooch vould you take my rope and tow me to Aden or Perim?"

"Phew!" said Kettle. "Aden! That's wrong way for me, Captain. Red Sea's where I've come from, and my owner cabled me to hurry and get to Zanzibar."

"Vell, how mooch?"

"We'll say £100,000, as your passengers seem so anxious."

"Hondred tousand teufels! Herr Gott, I haf not Rhodes on der sheep!"

"Well, Captain, take the offer or leave it. I'm not a tow-boat, and I'm in a hurry to make my passage. If you keep me waiting here five minutes longer, it'll cost you £120,000 to be plucked in anywhere."

The shipmaster on the other bridge went into a frenzy of expostulation; he appealed to all Captain Kettle's better feelings; he dared him to do his worst, he prayed him to do his best. But Kettle gazed upon the man's gesticulating arms, and listened to his frantic oratory unmoved. He lit a cheroot, and leant his elbows on the white railing of the bridge, and did not reply by so much as a single word.

When the other halted through breathlessness, even then he did not speak. He waved his hand towards the fearsome heavens with their lurid lights, and pointed to the bumping thunder, which made both steamers vaguely tremble, and he let those argue for him. The clamour of the passengers rose again in the breathless, baking air, and the Captain of the liner had to yield. He threw up his arms in token of surrender, and a hush fell upon the scene like the silence of death.

"My gompany shall pay you hondred tousand pound, Captain, und—you haf der satisfaction dot you make me ruined man."

"I have been ruined myself," said Kettle, "heaps of times, and my turn for the other thing seems to be come now. I'll run down closer to you, Captain, or do you bid your hands heave me a line from the fo'c's'le head as I come past. You've cut it pretty fine. You've no time left to get a boat in the water. The wind may come away any moment now.

Captain Kettle was changing into another man. All the *insouciance* had gone from him. He gave his orders with crispness and decision, and the mates and the Lascars jumped to obey them. The horrible danger that was to come lay as an open advertisement, and they knew that their only way to pass safely through it—and even then the chances were slim—was to obey the man who commanded them to the uttermost tittle.

The connection between the steamers had been made, the snaky steel-wire hawser had been hauled in through a stern fair-lead by the *Saigon's* winch, and the old mate stood ready with the shackle which would link it on to the manilla.

The heavens yielded up an overture like the echo of a Titan's groan. "Hurry there, you slow-footed dogs!" came Kettle's voice from the bridge.

The Lascars brought up the eye of the hawser, and Murgatroyd threaded it on the pin of the shackle. Then he cried, "All fast," and picked up a spike, and screwed home the pin in its socket. Already the engines were on the move again, and the *Saigon* was steaming ahead on the tow-line. It was a time for hurry.

The air thickened and grew for the moment if anything more hot, and the tornado raced down upon them as a black wall stretching far across the sea, with white water gleaming and churning at its foot. It hit the steamers like a solid avalanche, and the spin'drift in it cut the faces of the men who tried to withstand it, as though whips had lashed them.

The coolie quarter-master clung on to the *Saigon's* wheel-spokes, a mere wisp of limp humanity, incapable of steering or of doing anything else that required a modicum of rational thought. The little steamer fell away before the blast like a shaving in a dry street; the tonnage of the tornado heeled her till her lee-scuppers spouted green water in-board; and she might well have been overturned at the very outset. But Kettle beat the helpless Lascar from his hold, and spoked the wheel hard down; and the engines, working strongly, brought her round again in a wallowing circle to face the torrent of hurricane.

She took five minutes to make that recovery, and when she was steaming on again, head to the thunderous gusts, the tale of what she had endured was written in easy lettering. On both fore and main decks the bulwarks were gone level with the covering boards: the raffle of crates, harness casks, gang planks, and so on, that a small trader carries in view to the sky, had departed beyond the ken of man; and, indeed, those lower decks were scoured clean to the naked rusted iron. The port life-boat hung stove from bent davits, and three of the coolie crew had been swept from life into the grip of the eternal sea.

Cortolvin fought his way up on to the upper bridge step by step against the frantic beating of the wind, and, without being bidden, relieved at the lee spokes of the wheel. Captain Kettle nodded his thanks. The *Saigon* had no steam steering gear, and in some of the heavier squalls the wheel threatened to take charge, and pitch the little shipmaster clean over the spokes.

Amid the bellowing roar of the tornado, speech, of course, was impossible, and vision, too, was limited. No human eye could look into the wind, and even to let it strike the face was a torture. The sea did not get up. The crest of any wave which tried to rise was cut off remorselessly by the knives of the hurricane, and spread as a stinging mist throughout the wind. It was hard indeed to tell where ocean ceased and air began. The whole sea was spread in a blurr of white and green.

The big helpless liner astern plucked savagely at the *Saigon's* tail, and the pair of them were moving coast-wards with speed. Left to herself, and steaming full-speed into the gale, the little *Saigon* would have been able to maintain her position, neither losing ground nor gaining any. With the heavy tow in charge, she was being driven towards the roaring surf of the African beach with perilous speed.

It was possible to see dimly down the wind, and

when Cortolvin turned his face away from the stinging blast of the tornado, he could understand with
clearness their exact position. Close astern was the
plunging German liner, with her decks stripped and
deserted, and only the bridge officers exposed. Beyond was cotton-white sea ; and beyond again were
great leaping fountains of whiteness where the tor-
tured ocean roared against the yellow beach.

Thirty minutes passed, each second of them
brimmed with frenzied struggle for both man and
machinery. The tornado raged, and boomed, and
roared, and the backward drift was a thing which
could be measured with the eye.

Then the old mate heaved himself up the bridge
ladder by laborious inches. His clothes were whipping from him in tattered ribbons ; his hat was gone ;
and the grizzled hair stood out from the back of his
head like the bristles of a broom. He clawed his
way along the rail, and put his great red face close
to Kettle's ear.

"We can't hold her," he roared. "She's taking
us ashore. We shall be there in a dozen minutes,
and then it will be ' Jones ' for the lot of us."

Captain Kettle glared, but made no articulate
reply. If he could have spared a hand from the
wheelspokes, it is probable that Mr. Murgatroyd
would have felt the weight of it.

The old fellow bawled at him again. "The hands
know it as well as me, and they say they're not going
to be drowned for anybody. They say they're going
to cast off the hawser."

This time Captain Kettle yelled back a reply.
"You thing!" he cried. "You putty man, get back

to your post ! **If you** want to live, keep those niggers' fingers off **the** shackle. By James, if that tow is cast off, I'll turn the *Saigon* for the beach, and drown the **whole** crew of **you inside** three minutes. By James ! yes, and you know me, and you know I'll do it too. You ham-faced jelly-fish, away aft with you, and save your blooming life !"

The man winced under the little captain's **tongue,** and went away, and Captain Kettle looked **across** the wheel at his assistant.

Cortolvin shrugged his shoulders, and glanced backward at the beach, and nodded. Kettle leant across and shouted :

"I know it, sir, as **well** as you **do.** I know it as well **as they do.** But I've got a fortune in tow yonder, and I'd rather **die** than set it adrift. It isn't one fortune, **either; it's a** dozen fortunes, and I have just got **to grab one of** them. I'm a married man, sir, with a family, and I've known what it was to watch and see 'em hungry. You'll stand by me, Mr. Cortolvin ?"

"It seems I promised. . You know I've been long enough with Mohammedans, Skipper, **to be** somewhat a fatalist. So I say : 'God is **great !** and our fates are written on **our** foreheads, **and** no man can change by an inch the path which **it is** foreordained he **should** tread.' But they are **queer** fates, some of them. I went away from England because of my wife ; I step out of the middle of Arabia, and stumble across you, and **hear that** she is dead ; I look forward to going **home and living** a peaceful country life ; and now it appears I'm to be drowned obscurely, out of the touch of newspapers. However, I'll be consistent, I won't grumble, and you may hear me **say it aloud**: ' *La Allah illah Allah!* ' "

Captain Kettle **made no** reply. Through the infernal **uproar of the** tornado he did not hear much **of what** was said, and part of what did reach his ears was beyond his comprehension. Besides, his mind was, not unnaturally, occupied with more selfish considerations.

Astern of him, in the German liner, were some thousand passengers, **who** were all assets for salvage. **The** detail of human life did not enter much **into** his calculations. He had been brought up in a **school** where life **is cheap,** and not **so pleasant and** savory a thing that it is set much store on. The passengers were part of the ship, just **as much as** were **her** engines, and the bullion which **he hoped she carried.**

The company which owned her was responsible for **all; their credit** would be damaged if all or a part of **her was lost;** and **he,** Owen Kettle, would reap a proportionate reward if he could drag her into any civilized port. **And when** he thought of the roaring beach so terribly close astern, he bit **his** beard in an agony **of** apprehension lest the fates should steal this fortune from **him.**

And, meanwhile, the line of surf was growing ever nearer. So close, indeed, were they to the hateful **shore that,** when for a moment the fountains of white water subsided where **the** breakers raged upon the beach, **they** could see dimly beyond through the sea smoke, palm trees, and ceibas and great silk cotton-woods, whipping and crashing before the insane blast of the tornado.

All hands on the *Saigon's* deck had many minutes before given themselves up for as good as dead. Their only chance of salvation lay in casting off the tow-rope, and no one dared touch the linking shackle. They quite knew that their savage little skipper would fulfil his threat if they disobeyed his orders. Indeed, old purple-faced Murgatroyd himself sat on the hatch-coaming with an opened clasp knife, and vowed death on any one who tampered with either shackle or manilla. The clumsy mate had swallowed rough words once, but he preferred drowning to living on and hearing Captain Kettle address him as coward.

The shore lay steep-to, but the back-wash creamed far out into the sea. Already the stern of the German liner was plunging in the whitened water, and destruction seemed a question of seconds.

Then a strange thing happend. It seemed as though the Finger of God had touched the wind; it abated by visible graduations, and the drift of the steamer grew more slow ; it eased to a mere gale, and they held their place on the lip of the boiling surf ; and then with a gasp it sank into quietude, and a great oily swell rose up as if by magic from the bowels of the deep, and the little *Saigon* forged ahead and drew the helpless passenger liner away from the perilous beach. Those tropical hurricanes of the Eastern Seas progress in circles, and this one had spurned them from its clutch, and let them float on a charmed ring of calm.

Cortolvin bowed over the wheel in silent thankfulness, but the shipmaster rejoiced aloud.

"How's that, umpire?" said he. " By James, wasn't

it worth hanging on for? I've got a wife, sir, and kids, and I'm remembering this moment that they'll always have full bellies from now onwards, and good clothes and **no more cheap** lodgings, but **a** decent house semi-detached, and money to plank down in the plate when they go to chapel on Sundays. **The** skipper **of that** Dutchman will **be ruined** over this last half-hour's job, but **I can't** help that. It's myself I have to think of first; one **has to in** this world, or no one else will; and, Mr. Cortolvin, I'm **a made man.** Thanks to McTodd——"

From below there came a sudden *whirr* of machin-**ery, as** though the engines had **momentarily** gone mad, and then a bumping and a banging which jarred every plate of the *Saigon's* fabric, and then a silence, broken only by the thin distant scream of **a hurt man.** Presently the boom of steam **broke** out from the escape-pipe beside the funnel, and a minute later the chief engineer made his way leisurely up on to the bridge.

He was bleeding from a cut on **the** forehead and another gash showed red amongst **the** grime on his stubby cheek. He was shredding tobacco with a clasp-knife as he walked, and seemed from his man-ner to be a man quite divorced **from all** responsible occupations. He halted **a** minute **at** the head of the bridge ladder, replaced the tobacco cake in the pocket **of** his pyjama coat, and rolled up the shred-dings in the palms of his crackled hands. Then he filled **a short** briar pipe, lit it, and surveyed the avail-able universe.

"Yon'll be the tornado, 'way ahead there, I'm thinking?" said he.

"Are those blame' engines broke down again?" asked Kettle sharply.

"Aye, ye may put it they're broke down."

"Then away with you below again, Mr. McTodd, and get them running again. You may smoke when we bring up in Aden."

McTodd puffed twice more at his pipe, and spat on the wheel grating.

"By James!" said Kettle, "do you hear me?"

"My lugs are a bit muzzy, but I can hear ye for a' that, captain. Only thing is, I can't do as you'd like."

Captain Kettle stiffened ominously. "Mr. McTodd," he said, "if you force me to take you in hand, and show you how to set about your work, you'll regret it."

"Man," said the engineer, "I can do some kind of impossibeelities. Ye've seen me do them. Ye've seen me keep them palsied rattle-traps running all through that blow. But if ye ask me to make a new propeller out of rod iron and packing cases, I'll have to tell you that yon kind of meeracle's beyond me."

"My great James!" said Kettle, "you don't mean to tell me the propeller's gone?"

"Either that, or else all the blades have stripped off the boss. If ye'd been below on my foot-plates, ye'd have kenned it fine. When it went, those puir engines raced like an auld cab-horse tryin' to gallop, and they just got tied in knots, and tumbled down, and sprawled fifteen ways at once. I was on the platform, oiling, when they jumped, and that nigger second of mine tried to get at the throttle to close her down."

" Well, get on man, get."

" Weel, he didn't, that's all ; he's lying in the low pressure crank pit this minute, and the top of his skull'll be to seek somewhere by the ash lift. Mon, I tell ye, yon second o' mine's an uncanny sight. So I had to do his work for him, and then I blew off my boilers, and came up here.

" It would have been verra comforting to my professional conscience if I could have steamed her into Aden. But I'm no' as sorry as I might be for what's happened. I have it in mind that yon Parsee owner of ours in Bombay'll lose siller over this breakdown, and I want that beggar punishing for all the work he's given me to do on a small wage. Mr. Cortolvin, ha' ye a match?"

A hail came from the liner astern.

" *Saigon* ahoy ! Keep our hawser taut."

" You're all right for the present," Kettle shouted back.

" Der vind might return onless you get in the middle of him."

" Then if it does," retorted Kettle, " you'd better tell your passengers to say their prayers. You'll get no further help from me. I'm broken down myself. Lost my propeller, if you want to know."

" *Herr lieber Gott !* "

" I shouldn't swear if I were you," said Kettle. " If the breeze comes this way again, you'll be toeing the mark in the other place inside five minutes." He turned and gave an order : " After deck, there. Mr. Murgatroyd, you may cast off their rope ; we've done towing."

Now after this, a variety of things might have happened. Amongst them it was quite possible that both steamers, and all in them, might have been spewed up as battered refuse high upon the African beach. But as Providence ordered it, the tornado circled down on them no more; a light air came off the shore which filled their scanty canvas, and gave them just steerage way; and they rode over the swells in company, as dry as a pair of bridge-pontoons, and about as helpless. All immediate danger was swept away; nothing but another steamer could relieve them; and in the meantime it was a time for philosophy.

Captain Kettle did not grumble; his fortune was once more adrift and beyond his grasp; the Parsee in Bombay would for a certainty dismiss him from employment; and Mrs. Kettle and her family must continue to drag along on such scanty doles as he could contrive to send them. All these were distressing thoughts, but they were things not to be remedied; and he took down the accordion and made sweet music, which spread far over the moving plains of ocean.

But Mr. McTodd had visions of more immediate profit. He washed with soap until his face was brilliant, put on a full suit of slop-chest serge, took boat, and rowed over to the rolling German liner. It was midnight when he returned, affluent in pocket and rather deep in liquor. He went into the chart-house, without invitation, smiled benignly, and took a camp-stool.

"They thought they would get me down into the mess-room over yonder," said he, "and I'll no' deny it was a temptation. I could ha' telled those Dutch engineers a thing or two. But I'm a' for business first when there is siller ahead. So I went aft to the saloon. They were at dinner, and there were puir appetites among them. But someone spied me standing by the door and lugged me into a seat, and gave me meat and drink—champagne, no less! —and set me on to talk. Lord! once I got my tongue wagging, you should have seen them. There was no more eating done. They wanted to know how near death they'd been, and I telled 'em; and there was the Old Man and all the brass-edged officers at the ends of the tables fit to eat me for giving the yarn away. But a (*hic*) fat lot I cared. I set on the music, and they sent round the hat. Losh! There was twenty-four pound English when they handed it over to me. Skipper, ye should go and try it for yourself."

" Mr. McTodd," said the little sailor, " I am not a dashed mendicant!"

The engineer stared with a boiled eye, and swayed on his camp-stool. He had not quite grasped the remark.

" I'm Scotch mysel'!" exclaimed he, at length.

" Same thing," said Kettle; " I'm neither. I'm a common, low-down Englishman, with the pride of the Prince of Wales, and a darned ugly tongue; and don't you forget it either."

McTodd pulled a charred cigar stump from his waistcoat pocket and lit it with care. He nodded to the accordion.

" Go on with your noise," said he.

Captain Kettle's fingers began to twitch suggestively; and Cortolvin, in order to keep the peace, offered to escort McTodd to his room.

"I thank ye," said the engineer: "it's the climate. I have maleria in the system, and it stays there in spite of all that drugs can do, and affects the perambulatory muscles of the lower extremities. Speakin' of which, ye'll na doot have seen for yoursel'——"

"Oh, you'd better come along to bed," said Cortolvin.

"Bide a wee, sonny," said the man in the blue serge, solemnly. "There's a thought come to me that I've a message to give. Do ye ken anybody called Calvert?"

"Archie Calvert, by any chance?"

"'Erchie' was the name he gave. He said he kenned ye weel."

"We were at Cambridge together."

"Cambridge, were ye? Weel, I should have been a D.D. of A-berdeen mysel' if I'd done as my father wished. He was Free Kirk meenister of Ballindrochater——"

"Yes, but about Calvert?"

"Ou ay, Calvert! Erchie Calvert, as ye say. Weel, I said we'd you aboard, and this Calvert— Erchie Calvert—said he'd news for you about your wife."

"All right, never mind that now. She's dead, I know, poor woman. Let me help you down to your bunk."

"Dinna be so offensive, man, and bide a wee to hear ma news. Ye're no a widow after all—widow-man that is. Your guid wife didna dee as ye think.

She'd a fall from a horse, which'll probably teach her to leave horse-riding alone to men in the future; and it got in the papers she was killed; but it seems a shaking was all she earned. And, talking of horses now, when I was a bairn in Ballindrochater——"

Cortolvin shook him savagely by the arm.

"My God!" he cried; "do you mean to say she's not dead?"

"Aren't I telling you?"

Cortolvin passed a hand wearily over his eyes. "And a minute ago," he whispered, "I thought I was going home." His hand dropped limply to his side, and his head slid to the chart-house deck in a dead faint.

McTodd swayed on the camp-stool and regarded him with a puzzled eye. "Losh!" he said, "here's him drunk as well as me. Two of us, and I never kenned it. It's a sad, immoral world, skipper. Verra sad, skipper, I say. Here's Mr. Cortolvin been—Oh Lord, and he isn't listening either."

Captain Kettle had gone out of the chart-house. The thud of a propeller had fallen upon his ear, and he leant over the *Saigon's* rail and sadly watched a triangle of lights draw up through the cool, purple night. A cargo steamer freighted with rails for the Beira railway was coming gleefully towards them from out of the north, to pick up the rich gleanings which the ocean offered.

CHAPTER VI.

THE ESCAPE.

"You've struck the wrong man," said Captain Kettle. "I'm most kinds of idiot, but I'm not the sort to go ramming my head against the French Government for the mere sport of the thing."

"I was told," said Carnegie wearily, "that you were a man that feared nothing on this earth, or I would not have asked you to call upon me."

"You were told right," said Kettle. "But those that spoke about me should have added that I'm not a man who'll take a ticket to land myself in an ugly mess unless some one pays my train fare and gives me something to spend at the other end. I'm a sailor, sir, by trade or profession, whichever you like to name it, and on a steamboat, when a row has been started, I'll not say but what I've seen it through more than once out of sheer delight in wrestling with an ugly scrape. Yes, sir, that's the kind of brute I am at sea.

"But what you propose is different; it's out of my line; it's gaol-breaking, no less; with a spell of seven years in the jug if I don't succeed, and no kind of credit to wear, or dollars to jingle, if I do carry it through as you wish. And may I ask, sir, why I should interest myself in this Mr. Clare? I never heard of him till I came in this room half-an-hour ago in answer to your advertisement."

" He is unjustly condemned," Carnegie repeated, as though he were quoting from a lesson. " He is suffering imprisonment in this pestilential place—er —Cayenne for a fault which some one else has committed ; and unless he is rescued he will die there horribly. I am appealing to your humanity, Captain. Would you see a fellow-countryman wronged ? "

" I have only to look in the glass for that," retorted Kettle. " Most people's kicks come to me when I am anywhere within hail. And you'll kindly observe, sir, that I've nothing but your bare word to go on for Mr. Clare's innocence. The French Courts and the French people, by your own admitting, took a very different view of the matter. They said with clearness that he did sell those plans of fortresses to the Germans, and, knowing their way of looking at such a matter, it only surprises me he wasn't guillotined out of hand."

" It is my daughter who is sure of his guiltlessness in the matter," said Carnegie with a flush. " And," he added, " I may say that she is the chief person who wishes for his escape."

Captain Kettle bowed, and fingered the tarnished badge on his cap. He had a chivalrous respect for the other sex.

" And it was she who made me advertise vaguely for a seafaring man who had got daring and the skill to carry out so delicate a matter. We had two hundred answers in four posts : can you credit such a thing ? "

" Easily," said Kettle. " I am not the only poor devil of a skipper who's out of a job. But a hundred pounds is not enough, and that's the beginning and the end of it. There's two ways of doing this business, I guess, and one of them's fighting, and the other's bribery. Well, sir, a man can't collect much of an army for twenty five-pun' notes; and as for bribery, why it's hardly enough to buy up a deputy Customs inspector in the ordinary way of business, let alone a whole squad of Cayenne warders with a big idea of their own value and importance.

" Then there's getting out to French Guiana, and geting back, and steamer fare for the pair of us would come to more than a couple of postage stamps. And then where do I come in? You say I can pocket the balance. But I'm hanged if I see where the balance is going to be squeezed from. No, sir; a hundred pounds is mere foolishness, and the kindest thing I can do is to go away without further talk. By James, sir, I can say that if you'd given me this precious scheme as your own, there's a man in this room who would have had a smashed face for his impudence; but, as you tell me there's a lady in the case, I'll say no more."

Captain Kettle stood up, thrust out his chin aggressively, and swung on his cap. Then he took it off again, and coughed with politeness. The door opened, and the girl they had been speaking about came into the room. She stepped quickly across and took his hand.

"Captain Kettle," she said, " I could not leave you alone with my father any longer. I just had to come in and thank you for myself. I knew you would be the man to help us in our trouble. I knew it from your letter."

The little sailor coughed again, and reddened slightly under the tan. " I'm afraid, miss," he said, " I am useless. As I was explaining to your—to Mr. Carnegie, before you came in, the job is a bit outside my weight. You see, when I answered that advertisement, I thought it was something with a steamboat that was wanted, and for that sort of thing, with any kind of crew that signs on, I am fitted, and no man better. But this——"

" Oh, do not say it is beyond you. Other prisoners have escaped from the French penal settlements. It only requires a strong, determined man to arrange matters from the outside, and the thing is done."

Kettle fidgeted with the badge on his cap. " With respect, miss," said he, " what any other man could do, I would not shy at ; but the thing you've got here's impossible ; and the gentleman will just have to stay where he is and serve out the time he's earned."

" But, sir," the girl broke out passionately, " he has not earned it. He was accused unjustly. He was condemned as a scapegoat to shield others. They were powerful—he was without interest ; and all France was shrieking for a victim. Mr. Clare was a subordinate in a Government office through which these plans of fortresses had passed. He was by birth half an Englishman, and so it was easy to raise suspicion against him. They forged great sheaves of evidence ; they drew off attention from the real thieves ; they shamed him horribly ; and then they sent him off to those awful Isles de Salut for life. Yes, for life—till age or the diseases of the place should free him by death. Can you think of anything more frightful?"

"Mr. Clare is fortunate in having such a friend."

"A friend!" she repeated. "Has not my father told you? I am his promised wife. Fancy the irony of it! We were to have been married the very day he was condemned. It was my money and my father's which defended him at the trial, and it nearly beggared us. And now I will spend the last penny I can touch to get him free again."

Captain Kettle coughed once more. "It was upon a question of money that Mr. Carnegie and I split, miss. I said to him a hundred pounds would not work it, and there's the naked truth."

"But it must," she cried, "it must! You think us mean—niggardly. But it is not that; we can raise no more. We are at the end of our funds. Look around at this room; does this look like riches?"

It did not. They were in a grimy Newcastle lodging, *au troisième*, and at one side of the room the flank of a bedstead showed itself in outline against a curtain. The paper was torn and the carpet was absent, and from the shaft of the stairway came that mingled scent of clothes and fried onion which is native to this type of dwelling.

Carnegie himself was a faded man of fifty. His daughter carried the recent traces of beauty, but anxiety had lined her face, and the pinch of *res angustæ* had frayed her gown. All went to advertise the truth of what the girl had been saying, and Kettle's heart warmed towards her. He knew right well the nip of poverty himself. But still, he did not see his way to perform impossibilities, and he lifted up his voice and said so with glum frankness.

"I am not remembering for a minute, miss," he explained, "that I am a fellow with a wife and children dependent on my earnings. I am looking at the matter as though I might be Mr. Ciare's relative, and I have got nothing new to tell you. A hundred pounds will not do it, and that is the end of the matter."

The girl wrung her hands and looked pitifully across at her father.

"Well," said Carnegie with a heavy sigh, "I will scrape up a hundred and twenty, though that will force us to go hungry. And that is final, Captain. If my own neck depended upon it, I could not lay hands on more."

Captain Owen Kettle's face wore a look of pain. He was a man of chivalrous instincts; it irked him to disoblige a lady; but the means they offered him were so terribly insufficient. He did not repeat his refusal aloud, but his face spoke with eloquent sympathy.

The girl sank into one of the shabby chairs despairingly. "If you fail me, sir," she said, "then I have no hope."

Kettle turned away, still fingering the tarnished badge on his cap, and stared drearily through the grimy window-panes. A silence filled the room. Carnegie broke it.

"Other men answered the advertisement," he suggested.

"I know they did," his daughter said; "and I

9

read their letters, and I read Captain Kettle's and if there is one man who could help **us out** of all those that answered, he is here now in this room. My heart went out to him at once when I saw his **ap-plication.** I had never heard of him before, but, when I read the few pages he sent, it came to me that I knew him intimately from then onwards, and **that** he and no other in all the world could do the service which we want. **Sir," she** said, addressing the little **sailor** directly, " I **learnt** from that letter that you **made** poetry, and **I** felt that the romance of this **matter** would carry **you on** where any other man **with merely** commercial instincts would fail."

" Then **you** like poetry, miss ? "

" I write it," she said, " for the magazines, and sometimes **it** gets **into** print."

" Would **you mind** shaking hands with me ? " asked Captain Kettle.

" I want to **do so,"** she answered, " if you will let that mean the signing of our contract."

Captain **Kettle** held out his fist. " Put it there, miss," said he. " The French Government is a lump-ing **big** concern, **but** I've bucked against a Govern-ment before and come out top side, **and,** by James, I'll do **it** again. You stay at home, miss, and write poetry, and get **the** magazines to **print** it, instead of those rotten adventure yarns they're so fond of, and you'll be doing Great Britain a large service. What the people **in** this country need is nice rural poetry to tell **them** what sunsets are like, and how corn grows, and all that, and not cut-throat stories they might **fill** out for themselves from the morning news-papers if they only knew the men and the ground.

"If I can only know you're at home here, miss, doing that, I can set about this other matter with a cheerful heart. I don't think the money will be of much good; but you may trust me to get out to French Guiana somehow, even if I have to work my way there before the mast; and I'll collar hold of Mr. Clare for you and deliver him on board a British ship in the best repair which circumstances will permit. You mustn't expect me to do impossibilities, miss; but I'm working now for a lady who writes poetry for the magazines, and you'll see me go that near to them you'll probably be astonished."

Turn now to another scene. There is a certain turtle-backed isle in the Caribbean Sea sufficiently small and naked to be nameless on the charts. The Admiralty hydrographers mark it merely by a tiny black dot; the American chartmaker has gone further and branded it as "shoal," which seems to hint (and quite incorrectly) that there is water over it at least during spring tides.

The patch of land, which is egg-shaped, measures some 180 yards across its longer diameter, and, although no green seas can roll across its face, it is sufficiently low in the water for the spindrift to whip every inch of its surface during even the mildest of gales. On these occasions the wind lifts great layers of sand from off the roof of the isle, but ever the sea spews up more sand against the beaches; and so the bulk of the place remains a constant quantity, although the material whereof it is built is no two months the same.

As a residence the place is singularly undesirable,

and it is probable that, until Captain Owen Kettle scraped for himself a shelter-trench in the middle of the turtle back of sand, the isle had been left severely alone by man throughout all the centuries.

Still human breath was hourly drawn in the immediate neighborhood, and when the airs blew towards the isle, or the breezes lay stagnant, sharp, human cries fell dimly on Kettle's ear to tell him that men near at hand were alive, and awake, and plying their appointed occupations. The larger wooded island, which lay a long rifle shot away, was part of the French penal settlement of Cayenne; and the cries were the higher notes of its tragic opera. But they affected Captain Kettle not at all. He was there on business; he had been at much pains to arrive at his present situation, and had earned a bullet scar across the temple during the process; and, as some time was to elapse before his next move became due, he was filling up the intervening hours by the absorbing pursuit of literature.

He squatted on the floor of his sandpit, with his teeth set in the butt of a cold cigar, and rapped out the lines of sonnets, and transferred them to a sheet of sea-stained paper. He used the stubby bullet of a revolver cartridge from lack of a more refined pencil, and his muse worked with lusty pace—as, indeed, it was always wont to do when the world went more than usually awry with him.

To even catalogue the little scamp's adventures since his parting with Miss Carnegie in that Tyneside lodging, would be to write a lengthy book; and they are omitted here *in toto*, because to detail them would of necessity compromise worthy men, both French and English, who do not wish their traffic with Kettle to be publicly advertised.

Suffice it to say, then, that he made his way out to French Guiana by ways best known to himself; pervaded Cayenne under an alias, which the local gendarmerie laid bare; exchanged pistol shots with those in authority to avoid arrest; and, in fact, put the entire penal colony, from the governor down to the meanest convict, into a fever of unrest entirely on his especial behalf.

He was put to making temporary headquarters in a mangrove swamp, and completing his preparations from there, and, to say the least of it, matters went hardly with him. But at last he got his preliminaries settled, and left his bivouac among the maddening mosquitos, and the slime, and the snaky tree roots, and took to the seas again in a lugsail boat, which he annexed by force of arms from its four original owners.

A cold-minded person might say that the taking of that boat was an act of glaring piracy; but Kettle told himself that, so far as the French of Cayenne were concerned, he was a " recognised belligerent," and so all the manœuvres of war were candidly open to him. He had no more qualms in capturing that lugsail boat from a superior force than Nelson once had about taking large ships from the French in the Bay of Aboukir.

He had a depôt of tinned meats *cachéd* by one of his agents up a mangrove creek, and under cover of night he sailed up and got these on board, and built them in tightly under the thwarts of his boat so that they would not shift in the seaway. And finally, again cloaked by friendly darkness, he ran on to the beach of the turtle-backed isle, hid his boat in a gully of the sand, scooped out a personal residence where he would be visible only to God and the sea-fowl, and sat himself down to wait for an appointed hour.

By day the sun grilled him, by night the sea-mists drenched him to the skin, and at times gales lifted the surface from the Caribbean and sent it whistling across the roof of the isle in volleys of stinging spindrift. Moreover, he was constantly pestered by that local ailment, chills-and-fever, partly as a result of two or three trifling wounds bestowed by the gendarmerie, and partly as payment for residence in the miasmatic mangrove swamps ; so that, on the whole, life was not very tolerable to him, and he might have been pardoned had he cursed Miss Carnegie for sending him on so troublesome an errand. But he did not do this. He remembered that she was occupying herself at home in New-castle with the creation of poetry for the British magazines according to their agreement, and he for-got his discomforts in the glow of a Mæcenas. It was the first time he had been a *bona fide* patron of letters, and the pleasure of it intoxicated him.

A fortnight passed by—he had given Clare a fort-night in the message he smuggled into the convict station for him to make certain preparations—and at the end of that space of time Captain Kettle rolled his MSS. inside an oilskin cover, and addressed it to Miss Carnegie—in case of accidents. He put beckets on the top of his cap, slipped his revolver into these, and put the cap on his head ; and then.

stripping to the buff, he left his form and got up on to the sand, and walked down its milk-warm surface to the water's edge.

The ripples **rang like a** million of the tiniest bells upon the fine shingle, and **the stars in** the **velvet** night above were reflected in the water. It was far too still a night for his purpose—far too dangerously clear. He would have preferred rain, or even half a gale of wind. But he had fixed his appointment, **and he** was not the man **to let any detail of** added **danger** make him break a tryst. So he waded down into the lonely **sea,** and struck **out at** a steady breast stroke for the **Isle** de Salut, which loomed in low black outline across the waters before him.

A more hazardous business than this part of **the** man's expedition **it** would be hard **to** conceive. There were no prisoners in the world more jealously guarded than those **in** the pestilential settlement ahead of him. They were forgers, murderers, or, what the French hate still more, traitors and foreign spies; and once they stepped ashore upon **the** beach they were there for always. **They were all** life-sentence men. Until ferocious labor or the batterings **of** the climate sent them to rest below the soil, they **were** doomed to pain with **every** breath they **drew.**

Desperate gaoling like this makes desperate men, **and did any** of the prisoners—even the most cowardly of them—see the glimmer of a chance to escape, he would leap **to** take it, even though he knew that a certain hailstorm of lead would pelt along his trail. And as a consequence the rim of **the** isle **bristled** with armed warders, all of them marksmen, who shot **at** anything that moved, and who had as little compunction in dropping a prisoner as any other sportsman would have in knocking over a partridge.

To add to Captain Kettle's tally of dangers, the phosphorescence that night was peculiarly **vivid**; the sea glowed where he breasted it; his wake was lit with streams of silver fire; his whole body stood out like a smoulder of flame on a cloth of black velvet. His presence moved upon the face of the waters as an open advertisement. He was an illuminated target for every rifle that chose to sight him, and, far worse, he **was a** fiery bait bright enough to draw every shark **in the** Caribbean. And sharks swarmed **there**. His limbs crept as he swam with them.

To move fast was to increase the phosphorescence; to move slow was to linger in that horrible suspense; and I think it is one of the highest testimonials to Kettle's indomitable courage when I can say that **not** once during that ghastly voyage did he either hurry, or scurry, or splash. He was a prey to the most abominable dread; he expended an hour and a half over an hour's swim, and it seemed to him a space **of** years; and when he grounded on the beach of **the** Isle de Salut he was almost **fainting** from the strain of his emotions, and for awhile lay on the sand sobbing like a hysterical schoolgirl.

But a sound revived him and sent full energy into his limbs again without a prelude. From the distance there came to him the noise of shod feet crunching with regulation tread along the shingle. He was lying in the track of a sentry's beat.

By instinct his hand dragged the revolver from its beckets on his cap, and then he rose to his feet and darted away like some slim pink ghost across the beach into the shelter of the thickets. He lay there holding his breath, and watched the sentry pace upon his patrol. It was evident that the man had not seen him; the fellow neither glanced towards the cover nor searched the beach for foot-tracks; and yet he carried his rifle in the crook of his arm ready for a snap shot, and flickered his eyes to this side and to that like a man habitually trained to sudden alarms and a quick trigger finger. His every movement was eloquent of the care with which the Isle de Salut was warded.

Kettle waited till the man had gone off into the dark again and the soundless distance, and then stepped out from his ambush, and ran at speed along the dim, starlit beach. The sand-pats sprang backwards from his flying toes, and the birds in the forest rim moved uneasily as he passed. The little man was sea-bred first and last; he had no knowledge of woodcraft; a silent stalk was a flight far beyond him; and he raced along his way, revolver in hand, confident that he could shoot any intruding sentry before a rifle could be brought to bear.

Of course, the discharge of weapons would have waked the isle, and brought the whole wasps' nest about his ears. But this was a state of things he could have faced out brazenly. Throughout all his stormy life he had never yet shirked a *mêlée*, and perhaps immunity from serious harm had given him an over-estimate of the percentage of bullets which go astray. At any rate, the thrill of brisk fighting was a pleasure **he well** knew, and **he** never went far **out of** his way to avoid it.

But, as it was, he **sped** along his path unnoticed. The blunders of chance threaded him through the shadows and the chain of sentries so that no **living** soul picked up the alarm, till at last he pulled up panting at the edge of the open space which edged in the grim convict barrack itself.

And now began a hateful tedium of waiting. The day he had fixed with Clare was the right one; the hour of the rendezvous was vague. He had said **" as near** midnight as may be " in his message; but he was only able to guess at the time himself, and he expected that Clare was in a similar plight. Anyway, the man was not there, and Kettle gnawed his fingers with impatience as he awaited **him.**

The night under the winking stars was full **of** noise. In the forest trees the jarflies and the tree-crickets and the katydids kept up their maddening chorus. The drumming mosquitoes scented **the** naked man from afar and put every inch of his body **to** the torment. **The** moist, damp heat of the place made him pant to get his breath. The prison itself was full of the uneasy rustling of men sleeping in discomfort, and at regular intervals some crazy wretch within the walls cried **out** "*Dieu, Dieu, Dieu!*" **as** though **he** were a human cuckoo clock condemned **to** chime after stated lapses of minutes.

An hour passed, and still the uneasy night dozed on without notice **that** a prisoner was trying to escape. Another hour went **by,** and Captain Kettle began to contemplate the possibilities of attacking the grim building with his own itching fingers, and dragging Clare forth in the teeth of whatever opposition might befall. "*Dieu, Dieu, Dieu!*" rang out the tormented man within the walls, and then from round the further angle of the place a figure came running, who stared wildly about him as though in search of some one.

Kettle stepped out from his nook of concealment, a clear, pale mark in the starlight. The runner swerved, stopped, and hesitated. Kettle beckoned him, and the man threw away his doubt and raced up. The little sailor thrust out a moist hand. "You'll be Mr. Clare, sir, I presume?"

"Yes."

"I'm very pleased to have the honor of meeting you. I'm Captain Kettle, that was asked as a favor by Miss Carnegie——"

"Let us get away, quick. They will be after me directly, and if they catch me I shall be shot. Mr. Kettle, quick, where is your boat?"

But the little naked man did not budge. "I am accustomed, sir," he said stiffly, "to having my title."

"I don't understand. Oh, afterwards; but let us get away now at once."

"*Captain* Kettle, sir."

"Captain Kettle, certainly. But this waiting may cost us our lives."

"I am not anxious to take root here, sir, but, as for the boat, you've a good swim ahead of you before we reach that." And he told of the way he had come. "There was no other plan for it, Mr. Clare. It would have been sheer foolishness to have brought my boat to this island with all these busy people

with guns prowling about. I had just got to leave
her at my headquarters, and you must make up
your mind to swim and risk the sharks if you wish
to join her."

"I am open to risking anything," said Clare.
"It's neck or nothing with me after what I did five
minutes back in that hell over yonder. One of the
warders——" he broke off and dragged a hand across
his eyes. "Look here, Captain, we are bound to
be seen if we go back round by the beach. Come
with me and I'll show you a track through the
woods."

He started off into the cover without waiting for
a reply, and Kettle with a frown turned and followed at his heels. Captain Kettle preferred to do
the ordering himself, and this young man seemed
apt to assert command. However, the moment
was one for hurry. The night was beginning to
thin. So he got up speed again, and the trees and
the undergrowth closed behind him.

"*Dieu, Dieu, Dieu !*" cried out the tormented prisoner within the walls as a parting benediction.

Some men, like the historical Dr. Fell, have the
knack, unknown to themselves, of inspiring dislike
in others, and Clare had this effect upon Captain
Owen Kettle. The little sailor's dislike was born
at the first moment of their meeting. It grew as
he ran through the forest of the Isle de Salut ; and
even when Clare fell upon a sentry and beat the
sense out of him as neatly as he could have done it
himself, Kettle failed to admire or sympathise with
him.

On the return swim to the turtle-backed island he came very near to wishing that a shark would get the man, although such a calamity would have meant his own almost certain destruction ; and when they lay together, packed like a pair of sardines, in the shelter pit, under the intolerable sunshine of the succeeding day, it was with difficulty he could keep his hands off this fellow whom he had gone through so much to help.

Clare put in what of talking was done ; the sailor preserved a sour, glum silence. He felt that if he gave his vinegary tongue the freedom it wished for, nothing could prevent a collison.

He argued out with himself the cause for this dislike during the succeeding night. They had got the boat in the water, had mastheaded the lug, and were running northwest before a snoring breeze towards the British West Indian Islands. He himself, with main-sheet in one hand and tiller in the other, was in solitary command. Clare was occupied in baiing back the seas to their appointed place.

For a long time the utmost he could discover against the man was that on occasions he "was too bossy," and with bitter satire he ridiculed himself for a childish weakness. But then another thought drifted into his mind, and he picked it up, and weighed it, and balanced it, and valued it, till under the fostering care it grew, and the little sailor felt with a glow and a tightening of the lips that he had now indeed a real and legitimate cause for hate.

What mention had this fellow Clare made of Miss Carnegie ? Practically none. He, Kettle, had stated by whom he was sent to the rescue, and Clare had received the news with a casual " Oh ! " and a yawn. He had offered further information (when the first scurry of the escape was over, and they were *cachéd* in the sandpit) upon Miss Carnegie's movements and her condition as last viewed in New-castle, and Clare had pleaded tiredness and suggested another hour for the recital. Was this the proper attitude for a lover? It was not. Was this meet behaviour for the future husband of such a woman as Miss Carnegie, who was not only herself, but who also wrote poetry for the magazines? Ten thousand times over, it was not.

He sheeted home the lug a couple of inches in response to a shift of the breeze, and opened his lips in speech.

" Miss Carnegie, sir," he began, " is a lady I esteem very highly."

" She is a nice girl," assented the man with the baler.

" She is willing to beggar herself to do you service, sir."

" Yes, I know she is very fond of me."

" And I should like to know if you are equally fond of her ? "

" Steady, Captain, steady. I don't quite see what you have got to do with it." He paused and looked at the sailor curiously. " Look here, I say, you seem to talk a deuce of a deal about Miss Carnegie. Are you sweet on her yourself? "

Captain Kettle glared, and it is probable that, if such an action would not have swamped the boat, he would have dropped the tiller and left the marks of his displeasure upon Clare's person without further barter of words. But, as it was, he deigned to speak.

"You dog," he said, "if you make a suggestion like that again, I'll kill you. You've no right to say such a thing. I just honor Miss Carnegie as though she were the Queen, or even more, because she writes verse for the magazines, and the Queen only writes diaries. And, besides, there could be nothing more between us; I'm a married man, sir, with a family. But about this other matter. It seems to me I'm the party that kind of holds your fate just at present, young man. If I shove this tiller across, the boat'll broach to and swamp, and, whatever happens to me —and I don't vastly care—it's a sure thing you will go to the place where there's weeping and gnashing of teeth. How'd you like that?"

"Not a bit. I want to live. I've gone through the worst time a human being can endure on that ghastly island astern there, and I'm due for a great lot of the sweets of life to make up for it. And if it interests you to know it, Captain—I do owe you something personally, I suppose, and you have some right to be in my confidence—if it interests you to hear such a thing, I may tell you I shall probably marry Miss Carnegie as soon as I get back to her."

"Then you do love her?"

"I don't quite know what love is. But I like her well enough, if that will do for you. Hadn't we better take down a reef in the lug? I can hardly keep the water under."

"By James, you leave me to sail this boat," said Kettle, "and attend to your blessed baling, or I'll knock you out of her."

The conversation languished for some hours after this, and Kettle, with every nerve on the strain, humored the boat as she raced before the heavy following seas, whilst the ex-convict scooped back the water which eternally slopped in green streams over her gunwale. It was Clare who set up the talk again.

"Did she know anything about those plans of the French fortresses?"

"Miss Carnegie had the most definite ideas on the subject."

"I suppose she'd found out by that time that I really did get hold of them out of the office myself, and sell them to the Germans?"

For one of the few times in his life Captain Kettle lied. "She knew the whole yarn from start to finish."

"Well, I was a fool to muddle it. With any decent luck I ought to have brought off the *coup* without anybody being the wiser. I could have laid quiet a year or two till the fuss blew over, and then had a tidy fortune to go upon, and been able to marry whom I pleased, or not marry at all. Eh— well, skipper, that bubble's cracked, and I suppose the best thing I can do now is to marry old Carnegie's girl after all."

"Then you've quite made up your mind to marry this lady?"

"Quite."

"That's what you say," retorted Kettle. "Now you hear me. Miss Carnegie thinks you are in love with her, and you are not that by many a long fathom ; so there goes item the first. In the second

place, she thought you were sent to Cayenne unjustly, whereas by **your** own showing, **you're a dirty
thief,** and deserved all you got. And, thirdly, I
don't approve of squeezing fathers-in-law **as an in-**
dustry for young men newly out of **gaol."**

"You truculent **little** ruffian, **do** you dare **to**
threaten me?"

"I'd threaten the Emperor of Germany if I was
close **to him** and **didn't** like what he was doing.
Here, you! Don't you lift that báler **at** me, or I'll
slip some lead through your mangy **hide** before you
can wink. Now you'll just understand, for the rest
of this cruise, till we make our port, **you** stay forrard,
and I'm on the quarter-deck. If **you move aft** I'll
shoot you dead, and thank you for giving me **the**
chance. But if you **get** ashore all in one piece, **I'll**
spike your guns in another way."

"How?" asked **the** man sullenly.

"**You'll find** out when you get there," said **Kettle**
grimly. "**And now don't you** speak to **me** again.
You aren't wholesome. **Get** on with your baling.
D'ye hear me, there? Get on **with** that baling; I
don't want my boat to be swamped through your
cursed laziness."

Now, to which port **it** was **of** the British West
India Islands that the lugsail boat and its occupants
arrived, **I** never quite made out, and indeed the
method **in** which Captain Kettle " spiked " Mr.
Clare's " guns " was hidden from **me** till quite recently. A week ago, however, a letter of his drifted
into my hands, and, as **it** seems to explain all that
10

is necessary, I give it here exactly as it left his pen.

WEST INDIA ISLANDS.

To MISS CARNEGIE,
       JESMOND STREET,
            NEWCASTLE, ENGLAND.

HONOURED MADAM,

Am please to report have carried out part of y^r esteemed commands. Went to Cayenne, as per instruction, and took Mr. Clare away from French Government, they not consenting. Landed him in good condition at this place. Having learnt that he did steal those plans, and, moreover, he saying he did not care for you the way he ought, have taken liberty to guard lest he should trouble you in future. To do this, found old coloured washerwoman here (widow) who was proud to have white husband. Him objecting, I swore to tell French Consul if he did not marry, and get him sent back to Cayenne. So he married. She weighs 250 lbs. I enclose copy of their marriage lines, so you can see all is correct.

Trust you will excuse liberty. He has made one escape ; you have made another.

The weather is very sultry here, but they say there is fine scenery up-country.

Shall get English magazines some day, when things blow over a bit, and I can come that way again, to look for your poetry.

Hoping this finds you in good health as it leaves me at present.

Y^rs obedient,

O. KETTLE (Master).

1 Inclosure.

CHAPTER VII.

" No, **Mr.** Carnforth," said Kettle; "it would be lying if I was to say I knew anything **about** pearl-fishing. I've heard of it **of** course; **who hasn't?** And, for the matter of that, **I've had** on **a** diving-suit myself, and gone down and examined **a ship's** bottom to see if the divers that **had** been **sent** down to look at some started plates **had** brought **up a** true report. But I've never done more than pass through those North Australian seas. They tell me the pearl-fishing's done from small luggers of some ten or fourteen tons, sailing out of Thursday Island."

" It **is,**" said the big man. " And——"

" Well, sir, you'd better get another captain. I'm a steamer sailor by bringing up, **and on a** steamer I know my business, and can do it with any other man alive. But you'd not find me much **good on** a little wind-jammer like **a** Thursday Island pearler. I'm a hard-up man, Mr. Carnforth, and desperately in want **of a** berth; I hope, too, you'll not think it undue **familiarity** when I say that I like you personally; **but,** honestly, I don't think you'd better engage me as your skipper for **this** trip. You could get a so much better man for your money."

Carnforth laughed. " My dear Kettle," he said, " I don't think I ever came across a fellow with less real notion of looking after his own interests. As you are aware, I know your peculiar qualifications pretty thoroughly ; I'm an eminently practical business man : I offer you a handsome salary with both eyes open ; and yet you refuse because you are afraid of robbing me of my money."

"Mr. Carnforth," said the little sailor stiffly, "I have my own ideas of what's right. You have seen me at sea using violence and ugly words. But you will kindly remember that I was in service of an employer then, and was earning his pay by driving his crew. It's another thing now ; we are ashore here, and I would have you know that ashore I am a strict chapel member, with a high-pressure conscience, and a soul that requires careful looking after. I could never forgive myself if I thought I was taking your pay without earning it thoroughly."

"If you'll let me get a word in edgeways," said the other irritably, "and not be so beastly cocksure that you can rob me—which you could no more do than fly—perhaps you'd understand what I'm offering, and not sneeze at a good chance. The lugger is your own invention, and so is the idea that I'm merely going pearl-fishing in the ordinary way. My notion is to go pearl-poaching, which is a very different matter ; to get rich quick, and take the risks, and climb over them and to go at the business in a steamer with a strong enough crew to—ar—do what's needful."

"And you're already a rich man," said Kettle, "with a fine position in the country, and a seat in Parliament. Some people never do know when they're well off."

"Some people don't," said Carnforth, "and you're another of them, skipper. For myself, I do a mad thing now and again because—oh, because I like the excitement and flurry of it. But you!—You go and refuse a profitable billet that would fit you down to the boots, merely for the sake of a whim. A quarter of an hour ago you told me you were practically destitute—*ar*—' on the streets' your own words were; and here you are chucking up a certain **twenty pounds** a month, and a possible ninety, when it's ready to your hand."

"I didn't know about the steamer," said Kettle, "and that's a fact."

"Well, I'm telling you now, Captain, and if you don't take charge of her upper bridge, it will be your own fault. Why, man, there isn't a job between here and New Jerusalem that would suit you better; and besides, I'm keen to go there myself, and you are the one man in the world I want to have as a shipmate, and I ask you to come as a personal favour.

"I'm sick of this smug, orderly, frock coated life here. Nature intended me for a pirate, and fate has made me a successful manufacturer. I've tasted the wild unregenerate life of the open air once under your auspices, and rubbed against men who were men, and I want to be there again. I'm tired of fiddling amongst men and women who are merely dollar-millers and dress-pegs. I'm sick of what they call success. I'm sick of the whole blessed business."

Captain Kettle thought of Mrs. Kettle and her children in the squalid house in South Shields, with the slender income and **the** slim prospects, and he sighed drearily. But he did not utter those thoughts aloud. He said, instead, that he was very grateful to Mr. Carnforth for his magnificent offer, and **would** do his best to earn thoroughly the lavish income which was held out to him.

Carnforth reached out and gripped his hand.

"Thanky, Kettle," he said ; " and mind, I'm going **to try and** lug you into a competency over this. You might just as well have given way before. I **always get my own** way over this sort of thing. And **now** probably you'd like to **hear a bit** more about **the poaching ground ?**"

"**If you** please, sir."

"Well, I can't quote you latitude and longitude off-hand, but I'll show you the whereabouts of the place marked on the chart afterwards. It's Japan way, and the Japs have chosen to claim all the bits of reefs thereabouts, and to proclaim a sort of close season against all foreign pearlers. Now the place **I've got news of is in** their area, but so far it has **never** been fished. It's enormously rich, **and it's** absolutely virgin. Why, man, if we can put in six months' work there undisturbed, we can easily carry off a million pounds' worth of shells and pearls."

"Six months!" said Kettle. "That's a big order. I've **no doubt** that with a decent steamer and a few rifles we could beat off one of their gunboats when we get there, and do, **say,** a week's fishing. But if that gunboat steams back to Nagasaki, or wherever her port is, and brings **out** a whole blessed navy at her heels, we may find the contract outside our size. **Of course, if you are** going to fit out a real big steamboat, with a gun or two, and a hundred men——"

Carnforth laughed. "Wait a bit," said he. "You're going ahead too fast. There's no question of fighting a whole navy. In fact we mustn't fight at all if there's any means of wriggling out of it. I believe fighting would amount to piracy, and piracy's too lively even for my tastes. Besides, if we got very noisy, we'd have some cruiser of the British China Squadron poking her ugly nose in, and that's a thing we couldn't afford to risk at any price."

"Then how are you going to manage it?"

"What we must hope for is to be left undisturbed. There's every chance of it. The reef is out of all the steam-lanes and circle tracks, and the Japs' gun-boat patrol is not very close. In fact the place has only been newly charted. It was found quite by accident by the skipper of a sea-sealing schooner, and he missed the plum because he happened to have been a brute to one of his hands."

"But I thought you said this reef was out of all ship tracks?"

"Don't hustle me. The schooner had been seal-ing off the Commander Islands. She was coming home, and got into heavy weather. She was blown away three days by a gale, and picked up the surf of this reef one morning at daybreak, ran down in-to the lee, and lay there till the breeze was over. The reef wasn't charted and the skipper, who was 'on the make,' wondered how he could gather dividends out of it. In the off-sealing season he was in the Thursday Island trade, and his thoughts naturally ran upon pearls and shell. He'd a diving suit on board, and he rowed into the lagoon, made one of his crew put on the suit, and sent him down.

"Now observe the result," said Carnforth with sly relish, "of being too severe on one's hands. This sailor, who was sent down in the diving-suit, had been having a dog's time of it on the sealing schooner, and when he got on the floor of the lagoon and saw the place round him literally packed with shell that had never been touched by human fingers, he made up his mind that the time had come to repay old scores. So when he came up out of the water again, he said, sulkily enough, that there was nothing below but seaweed and mud; and the boat rowed back out of the lagoon; and the schooner let draw her forestay-sail sheet and ran away on her course.

"The skipper reported the new reef, and in due course it got on the charts; and the sailor kept holding his tongue till he could find a market for his information.   He didn't find one at once; he had to wait two years, in fact; and then he found me. I guess that skipper would be easier on his hands in future if he only knew what he'd lost, eh, Kettle?"

The sailor frowned.

"A shipmaster, sir, has to get the full amount of work out of his hands, or he's neglecting his duty. I can picture that schooner, Mr. Carnforth, and I picture her Old Man hearing what he's missed, and still carrying on the driving game.   The things we have to ship as sailors are beasts, and you have to treat them as such; and if you can show me a master who's popular in the forecastle, I can show you a man who's letting his hands shirk work, and not earning his owner's pay."

"H'm!" said Carnforth. "I've seen you handle a crew, and I know your theories and little ways, and I know also that you're far too obstinate an animal to change your opinions in a hurry. I've a pretty strong will myself, and so I can sympathise with you. However, we'll let that matter of ethics slide for the present, and go into the question of ways and means"—and on the dry detail of this they talked till far into the night.

Here, however, the historian may for awhile withhold his pen, since those in the shipping interest can fill the gap for themselves, whilst to all others, these small questions of ways and means would be infinitely tedious.

The yacht's voyage out to Japanese waters may also be omitted. The English papers announced its commencement in one of the usual formal paragraphs: "*Mr. Martin Carnforth, M. P. for the Munro division of Yorkshire, has started in his fine steam yacht, the Vestris, for a lengthened tour in China seas to study Oriental questions on the spot, and will probably be absent some considerable time.*"

The official log kept on board was meagre and scanty, being confined to arid statements of distances run, and the ordinary meteorological happenings of the ocean; and towards the latter entries, even these were skilfully fictitious. Indeed, when the vessel neared the scene of action, her yellow funnel changed to black with a crimson band, a couple of squarish yards were crossed on her foremast, her dainty gaff-sails vanished and were replaced by serviceable trysails, and the midship house was soiled by the addition of a coat of crude white lead above the trimly polished teak, and straddled over by a clumsy iron bridge defended by ill fitting canvas dodgers and awnings.

There was no making the expert believe, of course, that she was a mere trader that had always been a trader. But to the nautical eye she was unsuspicious: she looked one of those ex-yachts that have been sold out of the petticoat-cruising service of Cowes, and been adapted to the more homely needs of the mercantile marine; and in the Mediterranean, the Australian seas, and China waters, there are many of this breed of craft making a humble living for their owners. A couple of weeks' neglect will make any brass-work look un-yachtlike, and a little withholding of the paint-brush soon makes all small traders wonderfully kin.

Re-christening of course is but a clumsy device, and one which is (the gentle novelist notwithstanding) most seldom used. A ship at her birth is given a name, and endowed with a passport in the shape of " papers." Without her papers she cannot enter a civilised port; she could not " clear " at any custom house; and to attempt doing so would be a blatant confession of " something wrong." So when the paint brushes went round, and the name *Vestris* on counter, boats, and lifebuoys was exchanged for *Governor L. C. Walthrop* (which seemed to carry a slight American flavor) a half sigh went up from some of the ship's company, and a queer little thrill passed through the rest, according to their temperaments. They were making themselves sea pariahs from that moment onwards, until they should deem fit to discard the alias.

Captain Kettle himself finished lettering the last of the lifebuoys and put down his brush, and shook his head.

Carnforth **was** watching him from a deck chair. "You don't like it?" he said.

"I never did such a thing before," said Kettle, "and I never heard of it being done and come to any good. We're nobodies now, and **it's** every one's business to meddle with a nobody. If you're a somebody, only the proper people can interfere."

"I can't help it," said Carnforth. "The *Vestris* is well-known at home, and I'm well-known **too**; and we've just got to see this business through one way or the other, under pursers' names. She's the *Governor L. C. Walthrop*, and I'm Mr. Martin, **and** you **can be what you** like."

"I'll **still** use my own name, sir. I've carried it a good many years **now**, through most kinds of weather; and it's had so **many** stones thrown at it that **a** few more won't hurt. If we get through with this little game, all right; if we get interrupted, I guess the only thing left will be to attend our own funerals. I'm not going to taste the inside of **a** Japanese gaol at any price."

"I **never** saw such **a** fellow as you for looking at the gloomy side of things," said Carnforth irritably.

"It's the gloomy side that's mostly come my way, sir."

"I wish to goodness I'd never been idiot enough to come out here on this harebrained scheme."

"Why!" said Kettle in surprise, "you've got the remedy to your hand. You give your orders, Mr. Carnforth, and I'll bout-ship this minute and take you home."

"And don't you want to go through with it, skipper?"

"I don't see my tastes need be mentioned," said the sailor stiffly. "You are my owner, sir. I'm here to do as I'm bid."

"Captain Owen Kettle," said the other, with a laugh that had got some sour earnest at the back of it, "you're a cantankerous little beggar. I sailed with you before, and found you the most delightful of shipmates. I sail with you now, and you keep me always at boat-hook's length away from you. Be hanged if I see what I've done to stiffen you."

"Sir," said Kettle, "on the *Sultan of Borneo* you were my guest; on this yacht you are my owner; there's all the difference in the world."

"You wish to point out, I suppose, that a ship-master looks upon an owner as his natural enemy, as he does the Board of Trade. Still, I don't think I personally have deserved that."

"I am as I have been made, sir, and I suppose I can't help it."

"You are a man with some wonderfully developed weaknesses. However, as to going back, I'm not going to stultify myself by doing that now. We'll see the thing through now, whatever happens."

Martin Carnforth nodded curtly, and got up and walked the deck. He was conscious of a fine sense of disappointment and disillusionment. He had started off on this expedition filled with a warm glow of romance. He had been grubbing along at distasteful business pursuits for the larger part of his life, and adventure, as looked at from the outside, had always lured him strongly. Once in Kettle's company he had tasted of the realities of adventure amongst Cuban revolutionists; had got back safely, and settled down to business again for a time; and then once more had grown restless. He had the virus of adventure in his blood, and he was beginning to learn that it was a cumulative poison.

So, once more he had started off, but this time he was being chilled from the outside. Properly treated, the prospects of the trip would have been rosy enough. Handled by Captain Owen Kettle, the whole affair was made to assume the aspect of a commercial speculation of more than doubtful sanity. And, as he walked, he cursed Kettle from his inmost heart for bringing him to earth and keeping him there amongst sordid considerations.

The little mariner himself was seated in a deck-chair under an awning, turning in the frayed sleeve of a white drill jacket. His sewing tackle stood in a pictured tin biscuit box on the deck beside him. He unripped the old stitches with a pocket-knife, and resewed the sleeve with exquisite accuracy and neatness. His fierce eyes were intent on the work. To look at his nimble fingers, one would think that they had never held anything more deadly than the ordinary utensils of tailoring. Carnforth broke off his walk, and stood for a moment beside him.

"Skipper," he said, "you're a queer mixture. You've lived one of the most exciting lives any man's ever gone through, and yet you seem to turn your more peaceful moments to tailoring **or** poetry indifferently, and enjoy them with gusto."

" Mr. Carnforth," said **the** little sailor, " I guess we're all discontented animals. We always like most what we get least of."

" Well, I suppose that's intended to sum up my character as well as your own," said Carnforth, and **sat** down and watched the sewing.

The mate on the yacht's upper bridge picked up the reef with his glasses that evening a couple of hours after sundown. The night was velvet-black, with only a few stars showing. A sullen ground-swell rolled the seas into oily hills and valleys, and the reefs ahead showed themselves in a blaze of phosphorescence where the swell broke into thunderous surf. It seemed as though the yacht was steaming towards the glow and din of some distant marine volcano. The watch below were all on deck, drawn there by curiosity, and along one bulwark the watch on duty were handling the deep-sea lead At intervals came the report, trolled in a minor key, of " No bottom."

The engines were running half speed ahead, and presently they stopped, and the order was given for the yacht to lay-to where she was till daybreak. A light breeze had sprung up, bringing with it a queer slender taint into the sweet sea air.

For a long time Carnforth had been snuffling diligently. " I'm sure I smell something," he said at last.

" It's there," said Kettle. " Have you ever been **in a** north country. Norwegian port, sir? "

"By Jove! yes, skipper. It's just the same. Decaying fish."

"There's **not another** stink like it **on this earth.** You know what it means here?"

"I suppose some other fellows are in the lagoon before us and they're rotting out shell."

"That's it,"said Kettle ; "and we're going to have our work **cut** out to get **a** cargo. But we'll do it, Mr. Carnforth, never you fear. I suppose there'll be trouble, but that'll have to be got over. We've **not** come all this way to go back with empty holds."

Carnforth looked at the little man slily. Here **was** a very different Captain Kettle from the fellow who had been mending the white drill coat half-a-dozen hours before. He was rubbing his hands, his eye was bright, his whole frame had stiffened. He was whistling a jaunty tune, and was staring keenly out at the phosphorescent blaze of the breakers, as though he could see what was behind them, and was planning to overcome all obstacles. An hour before Martin Carnforth had been cursing the tedium of **his** expedition. A little chill **went** through him **now.** Before many more hours were past he had a **strong** notion he would be scared at its liveliness. **He had** seen Captain Kettle's methods before when things **went** contrary to his plans and wishes.

Slowly **the** night dragged through, and by degrees the blackness thinned. The Eastern waters grew grey, **and the** sky above them changed to dull sulphur yellow. Then a coal of crimson fire burned out on the horizon, and grew quickly to a great half-dish of scarlet ; and then the rest of the sun was shot up, as an orange pip is slipped from the fingers; and it was brilliant, staring, tropical day.

For full an hour the yacht had been under weigh at half steam with lead going, circling round the noisy reefs. The place was alive with the shout of breakers and the scream of seafowl. Inside, beyond the hedge of spouting waters, were three small turtle-backs of yellow sand, and a lugger at anchor.

The water outside was clear as bottle-green glass, and of enormous depth. The only entrance to the lagoon was a narrow canal between the reefs, shown up vividly by the gap in the ring of creaming surf. It was not likely that any one from the lugger would lend a hand for pilotage—or be trusted if they offered. So Kettle steamed the yacht to some half-mile off the entrance, called away the whale-boat, and went off in her himself with a crew and a couple of leadsmen to survey the channel. He did it with all deliberation; returned; took his perch in the fore-crosstrees, where he could see the coral floor through the clear water beneath, and conned the yacht in himself. Carnforth leant over the bridge-end and watched.

The coral floor with its wondrous growths came up towards him out of the deep water. The yacht rolled into the pass on the backs of the great ocean swells, and the reef-ends on either side boomed like a salute of heavy guns. The white froth of the surges spewed up against her sides, and the spindrift pattered in showers upon her deck planks. The stink of the place grew stronger every minute.

Then she shot through into a mirror of still, smooth water, slowed to half-speed, and with hand lead going diligently, steamed up to an anchorage in sixteen fathoms off one of the sandy islets. A white whale-boat put off from the lugger, rowed by three Kanakas, and by the time the yacht's cable was bitted, a man from her had stepped up the accommodation ladder, and was looking about him on deck.

He was a biggish man in striped pyjamas, barefooted, roughly-bearded, and wearing a crumpled pith helmet well down on the back of his head. His face was burnt to a fine mahogany colour by the sun, and, dangling over his chest at the end of a piece of fine sinnet, was a gold-rimmed eyeglass which glittered like a diamond when it caught the sun. He touched his helmet to Kettle.

"You've brought a fine day with you, Captain," said he,

"Rather warm," said Kettle. "I haven't looked at the glass this morning. I hope it's going to keep steady."

The visitor glanced round and sized up the yacht and its resources. "Oh, I should say it's likely to for the present. You've a nice little boat here, and a likely looking lot of men. You'll be having ten of a crew all-told, Captain, eh?"

"Thirteen," said Kettle.

"Humph, it's an unlucky number. Well, Captain, if I were you I wouldn't stay here too long. The weather's a bit uncertain, you know, in these seas."

"We want some pearls and shell before we go."

"I might have guessed that. Well, it's a nuisance from our point of view, because we thought we'd the lagoon to ourselves, and intended to skim it

11

clear ourselves if the Japs didn't interrupt. But, take the tip, Captain, and don't **be too** greedy. If you stay too long, **the glass** may fall suddenly and——"

"Take care, my lad," snapped Kettle, "**I'm a man** that accepts threats from no man living."

"Oh, all right," said the stranger carelessly. "**But** who have we here?" And he stuck the glass into his eye and whistled.

Captain Kettle made a formal introduction. "My owner, sir, **Mr.** Martin, of New York."

"Humph," said the **visitor**: "you used to be Carnforth up at Cambridge, **didn't you?** M. Carnforth, I remember, **and** M. might possibly stand for Martin."

Captain **Kettle** smiled grimly, **and** Carnforth swore.

"Bit of a surprise **to find** you pearl-poaching, Carnforth. I **see your name** in the Australian **papers** now and again, and got a notion you were something big at home. Had a bust-up?"

"No," said Carnforth. "I'm all right there. **Come** below and **have a drink and a talk.** By the way, it's awfully **rude** of me; I haven't tumbled **yet to who** you are."

"Never mind my name," said **the** visitor coolly. "**I don't** suppose **you'd** remember me. I was a reading man up there, and you weren't. You did **your** best **to torment** my life **out.** I took **a** big degree and **made a** fizzle of after-life. You got ploughed and became a commercial success. So you see we've little enough in common; and, besides, I was here first, and I resent your coming."

"Oh, rubbish, man! Come below and have a cocktail."

"Thanks, no. I prefer not to be under the tie of bread and salt with—*er*—trade rivals." He dropped his eyeglass, and walked to the head of the accommodation ladder. "Look here, Master Carnforth," he said, "I'll give you a useful tip. Clear out!" Then he went down into his whale-boat, and the brown men pulled him back to the lugger.

"Curse that beggar's impudence," said Carnforth hotly. "I wonder who the deuce he is?"

"Maybe we'll find out," said Kettle. "I tried to catch your eye whilst he was speaking. If I had my way, he'd be on board now, kept snug till we were through with our business here. He'd have been a lot safer that way."

"Oh, no!" said Carnforth. "We couldn't have done the high-handed like that on the little he said. Wonder who he can be, though? Some poor beggar whose corns I trod on up at Cambridge. Well, anyway twenty years and that beard have completely changed him out of memory. However, if he chooses to come round and be civil, he can; and if he doesn't, I won't worry. And now, Captain, —pearls. The sooner we get to work, the more chance we have of getting a cargo under hatches and slipping away undisturbed."

"Right-o," said Captain Kettle. "They've got the other two sandbanks, and, by the stink, they're doing a roaring business. We'll bag this empty one near us, and set about fishing this very hour, and plant our shell to rot there. It'll smell a bit different to a rose-garden, Mr. Carnforth, but it'll be a sight more **valuable.**"

Then began a period of frantic **toil and** labour. Every man **on board was** "on shares," **for** it had pleased Carnforth's whim to use this old buccaneer's incentive. Half of **the** profits went to the ship, **and** the rest to the crew. Each man had so many shares, according to his rating. Carnforth himself, in addition to his earnings as owner, earned also as an **ordinary** seaman, and sweated, and strained like any of the hands. From an hour before daybreak to an hour after sunset he was away in the boats, under the dews **of morn** and eve, or the blazing torrent of midday sunshine. Every night he tumbled into his bed-place dog-tired, and exulting in his tiredness. Every morning he woke eager for the fierce toil. **He** was unshaven, **sun-burned**, blood-smeared from the scratches of the shell, filthy with rank sea mud. But withal he was entirely happy.

Kettle toiled with equal vigour, working violently himself, and violently exhorting the others. Neither his arms nor his tongue were ever tired. But he was **always** neat, and seldom unclean. Dirt seemed to **have** an antipathy for the man, and against his dishevelled owner, he looked like a park dandy beside a rag picker.

At the other **side of** the lagoon the white man from Cambridge, and a white friend, and their crew of ten Kanakas, worked with similar industry. The ring of the lagoon was some half mile in diameter, with lanes of deep water running through its floor where divers could not work. There was no clashing of the two parties. One of these water lanes seemed

to set out a natural boundary, and neither transgressed it. On each submarine territory there was
enough shell to work on for the present, and each
party toiled with the same frantic energy, and spread
out the shell on the sun-baked sandbanks, and
poisoned heaven with the scent of decay. But
there was no further intercourse between the two
bodies of men, nor indeed any attempt at it. How
the others were doing, the yacht's party neither knew
nor cared. Theirs was a race against time for wealth,
and not one striver amongst them all had leisure to
be curious about his neighbors.

In a nicer life, the smells of the place would have
offended them monstrously; here they were a matter
for congratulation. The more the putrefaction, the
more the profit. They ripped the shells from the
sea, and spread them upon the beaches. The
roasting sun beat upon the spread-out shell-fish,
and melted away their soft tissues in horrible decay.

The value was all a gamble. There might be
merely so much mother-o'-pearl for inlay work; or
seed pearls, such as the Chinese grind up for medicine; or larger pearls of any size and colour and shape,
from the humble opalescent sphere worth its meagre
half-a-crown, to the black pearl worth its score of
pounds, or the great pear-shaped pink pearl worth a
prince's ransom. It was all a gamble, but none the
less fascinating for that. Carnforth was mad over
the work; Kettle, with all his *nonchalance* gone, was
nearly as bad.

But the process of realising their wealth was none
too fast, and, in fact, seemed to them tedious beyond

words. Every filled shell, with its latent possibilities of treasure lying out there upon the sand, was so much capital left in a perilously insecure investment. They were so bitterly afraid of interruptions. The dark shadow of Japan was always before their eyes.

Still at last came the first moment of realisation. They had toiled a month, and they had collected that day the fruits of their first day's labour. The mother-o'-pearl shell was packed in the hold; the little crop of pearls stood in a basin on the cabin table, and they gloated over them as they supped.

Carnforth stirred them lovingly with the butt of his fork. "Pretty little peas, aren't they, skipper?"

"For those they amuse, though I like to see a bit more colour in a woman's ornaments myself."

"Matter of taste and matter of fasion. Pearls are all the rage just now. Diamonds are slightly commonplace; but women will spend their money on something, and so the price of pearls is up."

"So much the better for us, sir. It's a pity, though, that some of them seem a bit off colour, like that big grey chap for instance."

"Grey, man! Why, that's a black pearl, and probably worth any ten of the rest put together."

"Well," said Kettle, "I don't set up for being a pearl merchant. Poaching them's trouble enough for me."

"Pass the biscuit, will you?" said Carnforth, yawning. "I suppose that little lot—is worth— worth—anything over—a thousand pounds," and with that he dropped back dead asleep in his chair with a forkful of food in mid-air. Captain Kettle

finished his meal, but he, too, man of wire though
he was, suddenly tumbled forward and went to sleep
with his head on the table. It was no new thing for
them to do. They had dropped off like this into
unconsciousness more than once during that month
of savage toil.

The next day they had a smaller crop ready to
glean—a bare five hundred pounds' worth, in fact.
But they did not lament. There would be an enormous quantity ready for the morrow.

That further realisation of their wealth, however,
never came. During the night another lugger sailed
into the lagoon, and upset all their plans. She was
the consort of the lugger commanded by the Cambridge man, and she had taken away to a safe place
their first crop of pearls and shell. Further, she was
manned by fourteen whites, all armed, and all quite
ready to defend what they considered their poachers'
monopoly. As a consequence, they pulled across
to the yacht some two hours before daybreak, and
Carnforth and Captain Kettle found themselves
waked by three men who carried Marlin repeating
rifles, and were quite ready to use them if pressed.

But the little sailor was not easily cowed. "By
James!" he cried, "this is piracy!"

"It'll be a funeral," said the man with the eyeglass, "if you don't bring your hand out from under
that pillow, and bring it out empty. Now, don't
risk it, skipper. I'm a good snap shot myself, and
this is only a two-pound trigger."

Captain Kettle did not chuck his life away uselessly. He let go his revolver and drew out his hand.
"Well," he said, "what are you grimy pirates going

to do next?   By the look of you, you've come here
to steal our soap and hairbrushes."

"Carnforth," shouted the man with the eyeglass,
"come in here and be told what's going to happen.
I say, you fellows, bring Carnforth into the skipper's
room."

Martin Carnforth came into Kettle's room sullenly
enough, with his hands in his pockets.

"Now I'll give you the whole case packed small,"
said the spokesman. "A crowd of us found this
place, and discovered the pearls and the shell. We
were all badly in want of a pile, and we took the
risks, and started in to get it. Most of us went
away with the first cargo, and only two white men
were left with a few Kanakas. Then you came.
You were told you're not wanted, but you gently
hinted at *force majeure*, and were allowed to stay.
Finally the rest of our crowd comes back, and it's
force majeure on the other side, and now you've got
to go. If you've the sense of oysters, you'll go
peacefully. There isn't enough for all of us ; at any
rate we don't intend to share."

"Mr. Carnforth," said Kettle, "I told you we'd
better have bottled that dirty man with the window-
pane eye who's been talking."

"Look here," said Carnforth hotly. "This is all
nonsense. We've got as much right here as
you."

"Right !" said the pearler. "Right had better
not enter into the question. We're all a blooming
lot of poachers, if it comes to that. You know that,
Mr. Martin, or Carnforth, or whatever you choose
to call yourself for the time being. You come here

under a purser's name, your yacht is guyed out like
a Mediterranean tunny fisher; and I guess you look
upon the thing much as you did bagging knockers
and brass door-plates in the old days at Cambridge—
half the fun's in dodging the bobby."

"You're taking the wrong sort of tone," interrupted Carnfoth. "I'm not used to being hectored
at like this."

"I can believe it," said the pearler drily. "You
are a successful man."

"And let me tell you this. You've got the upper hand for the present, that I admit. You may
even force us out of the lagoon. But what then? I
guess the account would not be closed; and when
a man chooses to make me his enemy, I always see
that he gets payment in full sooner or later."

"All right," said the man with the eyeglass, "pay
away. Don't mind us."

"A hint at one of the Japanese ports as to what
was goin' on would soon upset your little game."

"Not being fools," said the pearler coolly, "of
course we've thought of that. We've——"

A hail came down the saloon skylight outside,
from the deck above. "Scoot, boys, scoot! The
Philistines be upon us."

"What's that?" shouted the man with the eyeglass.

"Well, it's one of those confounded Jap gunboats,
if you want to know. Hurry, and we shall just get
off. We'll leave these fools to pay the bill."

"Humph!" said the pearler, "that settles the
matter another way. I must go, and I suppose
you'll try to hook it too. Ta, ta, skipper; you're

a good sort—I like you. By-bye Carnforth, can't recommend the **Jap gaols.** Hope you get caught, and that'll square up for your giving me a bad time at Cambridge."

He followed the others out on deck, and a moment later their whale-boat was pulling hard for where the luggers rode lazily at their anchors. Carnforth and Kettle went after him, and the engineers and the yacht's crew, who had been held down in the forecastle at rifle's muzzle, came on deck also.

It did not require any pressing to get the engine room staff to their work. The boilers were cold; but never were fires lit quicker. Paraffin, wood, small coal, grease, anything that would burn, was coaxed into the furnace doors. The cold gauges began to quiver, but as every man on board well knew, no human means could get a working steam pressure under half-an-hour.

On deck the crew had run the boats up to davits, had hove short by hand, and then stood like men on the drop, waiting their fate. The luggers had mastheaded their yards, and were beating down the lagoon against a spanking breeze. One after the other they tumbled out through the passage, and swung on the outer swell; and then, with their lugs goose-winged, fled like some scared seafowl out over the blue sun-scorched waters.

But though the yacht had canvas, Kettle knew that she could not beat to windward, and so dare not break his anchor out of the ground till the engineers had given her steam. There was nothing for it but to wait with what patience they could.

The Japanese gunboat had been sighted far enough off, and, as she was coming up from the farther side of the ring of reefs, she had to circle round them before she could gain the only entrance. Moreover her utmost paper pace was eight knots, and she happened to be foul, and so her advance was slow. But still to the watching men it seemed that she raced up like a Western Ocean greyhound.

The sun rose higher. The stink of the rotting shell-fish came to them in poisonous whiffs. At another time it would have spoken of wealth in sweet abundance. But now they disregarded it. Prison and disgrace were the only things before them, and these filled the mind.

Then the chief engineer called up to the bridge through the voice-tube that he could give her enough steam for steerage way in another minute.

"Foredeck there!" cried Kettle. "Break out that anchor! By hand!" And the men laboured with the hand gear, so as to save the precious steam. Then a thought flashed across Captain Kettle's brain and he quickly gave it to Carnforth. "It's only a beggarly chance, sir, but we'd better try it, I suppose?"

"Yes," said Carnforth.

"If only we hadn't painted out those names, we might have done it more safely. As it is, we must risk it. Off with you below, sir, and get into some decent clothes. You'd give the whole show away if you stayed up on the bridge here in those filthy rags. You may be a yacht owner, sir, but, by James, you look far more like an out-of-work coal trimmer."

Carnforth ran down the ladder, and Kettle gave crisp orders to the hands on deck, who disappeared also, and presently came back dressed as spruce yachtsmen, in white trousers, white drill jumpers, and straw hats; and by that time the yacht was under way, and steaming slowly to the pass.

The gunboat was coming in with her crew at quarters, officers with swords on, and everything cleared for action. The Japanese flag ran up to her peak.

Promptly an English royal yacht club burgee broke out at the poacher's main truck, and a British blue ensign fluttered up to her poopstaff, and dipped three times in salute.

Carnforth came up on to the bridge. "Now, sir," said Kettle, "you must do the talking. I guess it's got to be lies, and lying's a thing I can't do."

"What shall I say?"

"Say what's needed," replied Kettle concisely; "and don't say it wrong. Remember, sir, you're lying for your liberty. It's neck or nothing. She's got two big guns trained on us, and a shot from either would send us to Jones before we could get in a smack in return."

"What ship's that?" came the hail in perfect English.

"Steam yacht *Vestris*. Lord Martin, owner," said Carnforth, who knew the value of titles on the foreigners. "I am Lord Martin."

"What are you doing in here?"

"Been watching those poachers."

"Heave to and explain."

"I shall do nothing of the sort, and if you dare

to fire on me I will bring the British fleet about your ears."

The Japanese spokesman gasped, and consulted with a superior, and the steamers drew abreast.

"But you must heave to."

"I shall do nothing of the kind."

"But you are in forbidden waters."

"Then you should put up a notice to say so. I shall report this to my Admiralty in London."

"Go it," said Kettle, *sotto voce*. "For blooming cheek, give me an M. P."

"But you must stop," said the Japanese, "or I shall be compelled to fire."

"You can do as you please," said Carnforth. "I shall report you to your commander-in-chief at Nagasaki. I never came across such insolence. You heard my name—Lord Martin. You'll hear more of it before long."

Steam was rising in the gauges, and the yacht was getting into her stride of twelve knots. She sped out through the passage, and rolled in the trough of the glistening swells beyond. The crew of the war-ship still stood to their guns, but the officers were in a dilemma. These pestilential Britishers always did make such a row if any of their vessels were fired on; and this, apparently, was a yacht, though grotesquely unkempt, and tricked out with a black and red funnel; and, moreover, she was owned by a peer of the realm.

A last despairing hail came over the waters: "Are you noble?"

"Yes, haven't I told you? Lord Martin. You'll know it better when you're next in port."

And that was the last word.   The gunboat turned and steamed out after them, but her turning circle was large, and her speed slow.   By midday she was hull down astern; by evening her mast trucks were under the water.

Carnforth strutted the deck complacently. "Rather a gorgeous bluff, eh, Skipper?" he said at last.

"You're the only man on this ship that could have done it," said Kettle admiringly.   "It takes a parliamentary education to lie like that."

Again the silence grew between them, and then Carnforth said, musingly: "I wonder who that Cambridge man was."

"He seemed to hate you pretty tenderly."

"He did that.   I suppose I must have played some practical joke on him.   Well, I know I used to be up to all sorts of larks in those days, Skipper, but that's long enough ago now, and all that sort of foolishness is past."

Captain Kettle laughed.   "Have you done with pearl-poaching, sir?   Or are you going to have another try at it?   But don't paint out the name of your ship next time.   If that Jap had had the eyes of a mole he'd have seen the change, and he'd have taken his chances and fired.   *Governor L. C. Walthrop* is no name for an English milord's yacht."

THE LINER AND THE ICEBERG.

CAPTAIN KETTLE had been thanking Carnfoth for getting him command of the Atlantic liner *Armenia*. "But," he went on, "qualifications, sir, are all my eye. Interest's the thing that shoves a ship-master along. Yes, Mr. Carnforth, interest and luck. I've got qualifications by the fathom, and you know pretty well what they've ever done for me. But you're a rich man and an M. P.; you've got interest; you come up and give me a good word with an owner, and look, the thing's done."

"Well, I sincerely wish you a long reign," said Carnforth. "The *Armenia's* the slowest and oldest ship on the line, but she was the best I could get the firm to give you. It's seldom they change their captains, and they promote from the bottom, upwards. You've got all the line before you, Kettle, and the rest must depend on yourself. I'd sincerely like to see you commodore of the firm's fleet, but you'll have to do the climbing to that berth by your own wit. I've done all I can."

"You've done more for me, sir, than any other creature living's done, and believe me, I'm a very grateful fellow. And you can bet I shall do my best to stick to a snug berth now I've got it. I'm a married man, Mr. Carnforth, with children; I've them always at the back of my memory; and I've known what it is to try all the wretched jobs that the knock-about ship-master's put to if he doesn't choose his belongings to starve. The only thing I've got to be frightened of now, is luck, and that's a thing which is outside my hands, and outside yours, and outside the hands of every one else on this earth. I guess that God above keeps the engineering of luck as His own private department; and He deals it out according to His good pleasure; and we get what's best for us."

Now the S.S. *Armenia*, or the old *Atrocity*, as she was more familiarly named, with other qualifying adjectives according to taste, was more known than respected in the Western Ocean passenger trade. In her day she had been a flier, and had cut a record; but her day was past. Ship-building and engine-building are for ever on the improve, and with competition, and the rush of trade, the older vessels are constantly getting outclassed in speed and economy. So heavy stoke-hold crews and extravagant coal consumption no longer made the *Armenia* tremble along at her topmost speed. The firm had built newer and faster boats to do the showy trips which got spoken about in the newspapers; and in these they carried the actresses, and the drummers, and the other people who run up heavy wine bills and insist on expensive state-rooms; and they had lengthened the *Armenia's* scheduled time of passage between ports to what was most economical for coal consumption, and made her other arrangements to match. They advertised first-class bookings from Liverpool to **New York** for £11 **and** upwards, and passengers who economised and bought £11 tickets, fondly imagining that they were going **to cross in** one of the show boats, were wont to find **themselves** consigned to berths in inside cabins on the *Armenia*.

The present writer (before Captain Kettle took over command) knew the *Armenia* well. A certain class of passengers had grown native to her. On **outward** trips she was a favourite boat **for** Mormon missionaries and their converts. **The** saints themselves voyaged first-class, and made a **very** nasty exhibition of manners ; **their** wives **were in the second** cabin ; and the ruck of the converts—Poles, Slavs, Armenians, and other noisome riff-raff—reposed in stuffy barracks far below the water-line, and got **the** best that could be given them for their contract transport price of three-pound-ten a head. **Besides** the Mormons (and shunning them as oil does **water**) there were civilized passengers who shipped by the *Armenia* either because the cheap tariff suited their purses, or because an extra couple of days at sea did not matter to them, and they preferred her quiet *régime* to the hurry, and noise, and dazzle, and vibration of the crowded and more popular greyhounds.

On to the head of this queer family party, then, Captain Owen Kettle was pitchforked by the Fates **and Mr.** Carnforth, and at first he found the position bewilderingly strange. He was thirty-seven years of age, and **it** was his *début* as an officer on a passenger boat. The whole routine was new to him. Even the deckhands were of a class strange to his experience, and did as they were bidden smartly and efficiently, and showed no disposition to simmer to a state of constant mutiny. But newest of all, he came for the first time in contact with an official called a Purser (in the person of one Mr. Reginald Horrocks) at whose powers and position he was inclined to look very much askance.

It was Mr. Horrocks who welcomed him on board, and the pair of them sized one another up with diligence. Kettle was suspicious, brusque, and inclined to assert his position. But the Purser was more a man of the world, and, besides, he was by profession urbane, and a cultivator of other people's likings. He made it his boast that he could in ten minutes get on terms of civility with the sourest passenger who was ever put into an undesirable room ; and he was resolved to get on a footing of geniality with the new skipper if his art could manage it. Mr. Horrocks had sailed on bad terms with a captain once in the days of his novitiate, and he did not wish to repeat the experience.

But Kettle was by nature an autocrat, and could not shake down into the new order of things all at once. The *Armenia* was in dock, noisy with stevedores working cargo, when the new captain paid his first preliminary visit of inspection. Horrocks was in attendance, voluble and friendly, and they went through every part of her, from the sodden shaft-tunnel, to the glory-hole where the stewards live. The Purser was all affability, but Kettle resented his tone, and at last, when they had ended their excursion, and walked together into the chart-house on the lower bridge, the little sailor turned round and faced the other, and put the case to him significantly.

" You will kindly remember that I am Captain of this ferry," he said.

"You're Captain all the way, sir," said Horrocks genially. " My department is the care of the passengers as your deputy, and the receiving in of stores from the superintendent purser ashore ; and I wish to handle them all according to your orders."

" Oh," said Kettle, " you'll have a pretty free hand here. I don't mind telling you I'm new to this hotel-keeping business. I've been in cargo boats up to now."

" Well, of course, Captain, a Purser's work is a profession to itself, and the details are not likely to have come in your way. I suppose I'd better run things on much as before to start with, and when you see a detail you want changed, you tell me, and I'll see it changed right away. That's where I come in ; I'm a very capable man at carrying out orders. And there's another thing, Captain ; I know my place : I'm just your assistant."

Captain Kettle pressed the bell. " Purser," said he, " I believe we shall get on well. I hope we shall ; it's most comfortable that way." A bareheaded man in a short jacket knocked, and came in through the chart-house door. " Steward, bring a bottle of whisky, and put my name on it, and keep it in the rack yonder ; and bring some fresh water and two glasses—Purser, you'll have a drink with me ? "

" Well, here's plenty of cargo," said Kettle, when the whisky came.

" Here's plenty of passengers and a popular ship," said the Purser.

But if Mr. Horrocks was civil and submissive in

words on the *Armenia*, it was because he had mastered the art of only saying those things which are profitable, and keeping his private thoughts for disclosure on more fitting occasions. When he sat at tea that night with his wife across in their little house in New Brighton, he mentioned that the new captain did not altogether meet with his august approval. " He's a queer savage they've got hold of, and no mistake this time," said he ; " a fellow that's lived on freighters all his life, and never seen a serviette, and doesn't know what to do with his entertainment money."

" Tell the firm," suggested Mrs. Horrocks.

" Not much. At least, not yet. He's new, and so naturally they think he's a jewel. I'm not going to make myself unpopular by complaining too soon. Give this new old man string enough, and he'll hang himself neatly without my help."

" Like the last ? "

" Oh, this one's worse than him. In fact I'm beginning to be sorry I ever did get our last old man the push. He was all right so long as I didn't make my perquisites too big. But as for this one, I don't suppose he'll understand I've a right to perquisites at all."

" But," said Mrs. Horrocks, " you're Purser. What does he suppose you live on ? He must know that the pay don't go far."

" Well, he didn't seem to know what a Purser was, and when I tried to hint it to him, he just snapped out that he was Captain of this blooming ship."

" And then ? "

Mr. Horrocks shrugged his shoulders. "Oh, I agreed right away. May as well tickle a fool as tease him, my dear. He thinks because he's a splendid seaman—and he may be that, I'll admit—he's fit to skipper a Western Ocean passenger boat. He's a lot to learn yet, and I'm the man that's going to educate him."

Now the exasperating part of it was, that not only did this process of "education" promptly begin, but Captain Kettle knew it. Never before had he had any one beneath him on board ship who had dared to dispute his imperial will, and done it successfully. There was no holding this affable purser, no pinning him down to a specific offence. If he mapped out a plan of action, and Captain Kettle objected to it, he was all civility, and would give it up without argument. "Certainly, sir," he would say. "You're captain on this boat, as you say, and I'm Purser, and I just know my place." And then afterwards would invariably come a back thrust which Captain Kettle could never parry.

There were three long tables in the saloon, headed by the Captain, the Purser, and the Doctor ; and when the passengers came on board at Liverpool or New York, it was Mr. Horrocks who arranged their meal places. He had a nice discrimination, this Purser, and from long habit could sum up a passenger's general conversational qualities at a glance. He knew also Captain Kettle's tastes and limitations, and when that redoubtable mariner had been making things unpleasant, he rewarded him with dinner companions for the next run who kept him in a state of subdued frenzy. It was quite an easy thing

to do, and managed craftily, it was a species of torture impossible to resent.

In fact it may be owned at once that as a conversational head to a liner's table, Captain Kettle
did not shine. The situation was new and strange
to him. Up till then he had fought his way about
the seas in cargo tramps, with only here and there
a stray passenger ; and, at table, professional topics
had made up the talk, or, what was more common,
glum, scowling silence had prevailed.

Here, on this steam hotel, he suddenly found
himself looked up to as a head of society. His own
real reminiscences of the sea he kept back ; he felt
them to be vastly impolite ; he never dreamed that
they might be interesting.

His power of extracting sweet music from the accordion he kept rigidly in the background. Accor-
dions seemed out of place somehow with these finick-
ing passengers. He felt that his one genteel taste
was for poetry, but only once did he let it slip out.
It was half-way across the Atlantic on a homeward
trip, and conversation had lagged. The Purser's and
the Doctor's tables were in a rattle of cheerful talk:
Kettle's was in a state of boredom. In desperation
he brought out his sacred topic.

At once every car within range started to listen :
he saw that at once. But he mistook the motive.
The men around him—they were mostly Americans
—thought that the whole thing was an effort of
humor. It never occurred to them that this vine-
gary-faced little sailor actually himself made the sentimental rhymes he quoted to them ; and when it
dawned upon them that this was no joke, and the

man was speaking in sober, solemn earnest, the funniness of it swept over them like a wave. The table yelped with inextinguishable laughter.

Of a sudden **Captain** Kettle realised that he **was** his passengers' butt, and sat **back** in **his chair as** though he was getting ready for a **spring.**

In his **first** torrent of rage **he** could with gusto have shot the lot of them ; but to begin with he was unarmed, and, in the second place, passengers are not crew ; and moreover, after the first explosion, the laughter began to die away. One by one the diners looked at the grim, savage, little **face** glaring at them from the end of the table, and their mirth seemed to chill. The laughter ended, and **an** uncomfortable silence grew, and remained to the finish of the meal.

During the succeeding meals moreover up till **the** end of the voyage, that silence was very little **en-**croached upon **at the** Captain's end of the middle table. Any **one who** ventured to speak, had the benefit of Captain Kettle's full gaze, and found it disconcerting. Even to passengers **on a** modern steam ferry, the Captain is **a** person of some majesty, and this one had a look about him that **did not invite** further liberties.

That batch of passengers dispersed to the four corners of the earth from Queenstown and Liverpool, **and the** *Armenia* saw them no more ; but news of **the** fracas somehow or another reached the headquarters' office, and a kindly hint was given to Captain Kettle that such scenes would be **better** avoided for the future.

"I quite know that passengers are awkward cattle to deal **with,**" said the partner who put it **to him.**

"but you see, Captain, we make our living by carry-ing them, and we can't afford to have our boats made unpopular.   You should use more tact, my dear skipper.   Tact; that's what you want.   Stand 'em champagne out of your entertainment allowance, and they'll stand it back, and run up bigger bills with the wine steward.   It all means profit, Cap-tain, and those are the ways you must get it for us. We aren't asking you to drum round for cargo now. Your game is to make the boat cheery and comfort-able for passengers, so that they'll spend a lot of money on board, and like it and come again and spend some more.   Tumble?"

The Captain of the *Armenia* heard, and intended to conform.   But, admirer of his though I must con-scientiously write myself, I cannot even hope that in time he would have shaken down fitly into the berth; for to tell the truth, I do not think a more unsuitable man to govern one of these modern steam hotels could be found on the seas of either hemi-sphere.   However, as it happened, the concession was not demanded of him.   His luck, that cruel, evil fortune, got up and hit him again, and his ship was cast away, and he saw himself once more that painful thing, a shipmaster without employ.   More cruel still, he found himself at the same time in intimate touch with a great temptation.

The fatal voyage was from New York home, and it was in the cold, raw spring-time when passenger lists are thin.   The day before sailing a letter addressed "Captain Kettle, S.S. *Armenia*," made its appearance on the chart-house table.   How it got there no one seemed to know, but with the crowd of stevedores and others working cargo, it would have been very easy for a messenger from the wharf to slip it on board unobserved. The letter was typewritten, and carried the address of an obscure saloon in the Bowery. It said:

"There is a matter of $50,000 (£10,000) waiting for you to earn with a little pluck and exertion. You can either take the game or leave it, but if you conclude to hear more, come here and ask the barman for a five-dollar cocktail and he will show you right inside. If you are frightened, don't come. We got no use for frightened men, we can easy find a man with more sand in him somewhere else."

The little sailor considered over this precious document for the full of an hour. "Some smuggling lay," was his first conclusion, but the sum of money appeared too big for this; then he was half minded to put down the whole thing as a joke; then as a lure to rob him. The final paragraph and the address given, which was in the worst part of New York city, seemed to point shrewdly to this last. And I believe the prospect of a scrimmage was really the thing that in the end sent him off. But any way, that evening he went, and after some difficulty found the ruffianly drinking shop to which he had been directed.

He went inside and looked inquiringly across the bar.

The shirt-sleeved barman shifted his cigar. "Well, Mister, what can I set up for you?"

"You're a bit proud of your five-dollar cocktails here, aren't you?"

The man lowered his voice. "Say, are you Captain Cuttle?"

"Kettle! confound you."

"Same thing, I guess. Walk right through that door yonder and up the stair."

Captain Kettle patted a jacket pocket that bulged with the outline of a revolver. "If any one thinks they are going to play larks on me here, I pity 'em."

The barman shrugged his shoulders. "Don't blame you for coming 'heeled,' boss. Guess a gun sometimes chips in handy round here. But I think the gents upstairs mean square biz."

"Well," said Kettle. "I'm going to see;" and opened the door and stumped briskly up the stairway.

He stepped into a room, barely furnished, and lit by one grimy window. There was no one to receive him, so he drummed the table to make his presence known.

Promptly a voice said to him : " Howdy, Captain? "Will ye mind shuttin' the door?"

Now Kettle was not a man given to starting, but he started then. The place was in the worst slum in New York. Except for a flimsy table and two battered chairs, the room was stark empty, and this voice seemed to come from close beside him. Instinctively his fingers gripped on the weapon in his jacket pocket.

He slewed sharply round to make sure he was alone, and even kicked his foot under the table to see that there was no jugglery about that, and then the voice spoke to him again, with Irish brogue and Yankee idiom quaintly intermingled.

"Sure, Captain, I have to ask yer pardon for

keeping' a brick wall right here between us. But I've me health to consider, an' I reckon our biz will be safest done this way."

The little sailor's grim face relaxed into a smile. His eye had caught the end of a funnel which lay flush with the wall.

" Ho? " he said. " That's your game, is it? A speaking-tube. Then I suppose you've got something to say you are ashamed of?"

" Faith, I'm proud of it. A pathriot is never ashamed of his cause."

" Get to business," said Kettle. " My time's short, and this waiting-room of yours is not over savoury."

" It's just a little removal we wish you to undertake for us, Captain. You have gotten a Mr. Grimshaw on your passenger list for this run to Liverpool?"

" Have I?"

" It's so. He's one of the big bosses of your British Government."

" Well, supposing I have?"

" He's been out here as a sort of commission, and he's found out more than is good for him. He sails by the *Armenia* to-morrow, and if you can—well—so contrive that he doesn't land at the other side, it means you are set up for life."

Captain Kettle's face stiffened, and he was about to break out with something sharp. But he restrained himself and asked instead: " What's the figure?"

" $50,000—say 10,000 of your English sovereigns."

" And how do I know that I should get paid?"

The answer was somewhat astounding.

" You can pocket the money here, right now," said the voice.

" And once I got paid, what hold would you have on me? How do you know I'd shove this Grimshaw over the side? That I suppose is what you want?"

The voice chuckled. " We've agents everywhere, Captain. We'd have you removed pretty sharp if you tried to diddle us."

" Oh, would you?" snapped Kettle. " I've bucked against some tolerably ugly toughs in my time and come out top side, and shouldn't mind tackling your crowd for the sheer sport of the thing. But look here, Mr. Paddy Fenian, you've got hold of the wrong man when you came to me. By James, yes, you skulking, cowardly swine! You face behind a wall! Come out here and talk. I won't lift my hands. I'll use my feet to you and kick your backbone through your hat. You'd dare to ask me to murder a man, would you?"

Captain Kettle's eloquence had an unlooked for effect. The voice from the speaking tube laughed.

The sailor went on afresh, and spoke of the unseen one's ancestors on both sides of the house, his personal habits, and probable future. He had acquired a goodly flow of this kind of vituperation during his professional career, and had been compelled to keep it bottled up before the passengers on the liner. He felt a kind of gusto in letting his tongue run loose again, and had the proud consciousness that each of his phrases would cut like the lash of a whip.

But the unseen man apparently heard him unruffled. " Blow off steam, skipper," said he ; " don't mind me."

Kettle looked round the empty room dejectedly. " You thing ! " he said. " I could make a man with more spirit than you out of putty."

" Of course you could, skipper," said the voice with the brogue ; " of course you could. I don't really exist. I'm only a name, as your beastly Saxon papers say when they abuse me. But I can hit, as they know, and I can draw cheques as you can find out if you choose. You can have your pay yet if you see fit to change your mind, and ' remove ' spy Grimshaw between here and Liverpool. We've plenty of money, and you may as well have it as any one else. It's got to be spent somehow."

" I'd give a lot to wring your neck," said Kettle. He tapped the wall to test its thickness.

" You tire me," said the voice. " Why can't you drop that ? You can't get at me ; and if you go outside and set on all the police in New York city, you'll do no good. The police of this city know which side their bread's margarined. I'm the man with the cheque-book, sonny, and you bet they're not the sample of fools that'd go and try to snuff me out."

" This is no place for me," said Kettle. " It seems I can't lug you out of the drain where you live, and if I stay in touch of your breath any longer, I shall be poisoned. I've told you who I consider your mother to be. Don't forget."—And the little bearded sailor strode off down the stair again and into the street. He had no inclination to go to the police, having a pious horror of the law, and so he got a trolley car which took him down to the East River, and a ferry which carried him across to his SHIP.

The time was 2 a.m., and the glow of the arc lamps and the rattle of winch chains, and the roar of working cargo, went up far into the night. But noise made little difference to him, and even the episode he had just gone through was not sufficient to keep him awake.

The master of a Western Ocean ferry gets little enough of sleep when he is on the voyage, and so on the night before sailing he stores up as much as may be.

As it chanced Mr. Grimshaw took steps to impress himself on Captain Kettle's notice at an early stage of the next day's proceedings. The ship was warping out of dock with the help of a walking-beam tug, and a passenger attempted to pass the quartermaster at the foot of the upper bridge ladder. The sailor was stubborn, but the passenger was imperative, and at last pushed his way up, and was met by Kettle himself at the head of the ladder.

"Well, sir?" said that official.

"I've come to see you take your steamer out into New York Bay, Captain."

"Oh, have you?" said Kettle. "Are you the Emperor of Germany, by any chance?"

"I am Mr. Robert Grimshaw."

"Same thing. Neither you nor he is Captain here. I am. So I'll trouble you to get to Halifax out of this before you're put. Quarter-master, I'll log you for neglect of duty."

Grimshaw turned **and** went down the ladder with a flushed cheek. "Thank you, Captain," he said over his shoulder. "I've got influence with your owners. I'll not neglect to use it."

It chanced also that Captain Kettle had been cutting down his Purser's perquisites more ruthlessly than usual in New York, and that worthy man thirsted for revenge. He had taken Mr. Grimshaw's measure pretty accurately at first sight, and was tolerably sure that eight days of his conversation would irritate his skipper into a state approaching frenzy. So he portioned off the commissioner to the end right-hand chair at the Captain's table, **and** promised himself pleasant revenge in overlooking the result.

Captain Kettle worked the *Armenia* outside the bar and came down to dinner. Horrocks whispered in his ear as he came down the companion, "Mr. Grimshaw's the man on your right, sir. Had to give him to you. He's some sort of a big bug in the government at home ; been over in New York inquiring into the organization of those Pat-lander rebels."

Kettle nodded curtly and went on to his seat. The meal began, and went on. Mr. Grimshaw made no allusion to the previous encounter. He had made **up** his mind to exact retaliation in full, and started at once to procure it. He had the reputation in London of being a " most superior person," and he possessed in **a** high degree the art of being courteously offensive. He was a clever man with his tongue, and never overstepped the bounds of suavity.

How the wretched Kettle sat through that meal **he** did not know. Under this polished attack he was impotent of defence. Not a chance was given him for retort. And all the thrusts went home. He retired from the dinner-table with a moist per-spiration on his face, and an earnest prayer that the *Armenia* would carry foul weather with her all the way up to Prince's landing stage, so that he might be forced to spend the next seven or eight days on the chilly eminence of the upper bridge.

And now we come to the story of how Captain Owen Kettle's luck again buffeted him.

The *Armenia* was steaming along through the night, to the accompaniment of deep and dismal hootings from the syren. A fog spread over the Atlantic, and the bridge telegraph pointed to " Half speed ahead " as the Board of Trade directs. The engine-room, however, had private instructions as usual, and kept up the normal speed.

On the forecastle head four lookout men peered solemnly into the fog and knew that for all the prac-tical good they were doing they might just as well be in their bunks.

On the bridge, in glistening oilskins, Kettle and two mates stared before them into the thickness, but could not see as far as the foremast. And the *Armenia* surged along at her comfortable fourteen knots, with five hundred people asleep beneath her deck. The landsman fancies that on these occasions steamships slow down or stop; the liner captain knows that if once he did so, he would have little chance of taking his ship across the Atlantic again. A day lost to one of these ocean ferries means in coal, and food, and wages, and so on, a matter of £1,000 or so out of the pockets of her owners, and this is a little sum they do not care to forfeit without strong reason. They expect their captains to drive the boats along as usual, and make up for the added risk by increased watchfulness and precaution, and a keen noting of the thermometer for any sudden fall which should foretell the neighbourhood of ice.

Now the *Armenia* was skirting the edge of the Banks, on the recognized steam lane to the Eastward, which differs from that leading West ; and by all the laws of navigation there should have been nothing in the way. Nothing, that is, except fishing schooners, which do not matter, as they are the only sufferers if they haven't the sense to get out of the way.

But, suddenly, through the fog ahead there loomed out a vast shape, and almost before the telegraph rung its message to the engine-room, and certainly before steam could be shut off, the *Armenia's* bow was clashing and clanging and ripping and buckling as though it had charged full tilt against a solid cliff.

The engines stopped, and the awful tearing noises ceased, save for a tinkling rattle as of a cascade of glass, and, "There goes my blooming ticket," said Kettle bitterly. "Who'd have thought of an iceberg as far south as here this time of year." But he was prompt to act on the emergency.

"Now, Mr. Mate, away forward with you, and get the carpenter, and go down and find out how big the damage is." The crew were crowding out on deck. "All hands to boat stations. See all clear for lowering away, and then hold on all. Now

13

keep your heads, men. There's no damage, and if there was damage, there's no hurry. Put a couple of hands at each of the companion-ways, and keep all passengers **below**. We can't have them messing round here yet awhile."

The Purser was standing at the bottom of the upper bridge ladder half-clad, cool, and expectant. "Ah, **Mr.** Horrocks, come here."

The *Armenia* had slipped back from the berg by this time and lay still, with the fog dense all around her. "Now it's all up with the old *Atrocity*, Purser, look how she's by the head already. Get your crew of stewards together, and victual the boats. Keep 'em in hand well, or else we shall have a stampede **and a lot of drowning**. I'll **have** the boats in the water **by the time** you're ready, and then you must hand up **the** passengers, women first."

"Aye, aye, **sir**."

"Wait a minute. If any one won't do as he's bid, shoot. We must keep order."

The Purser showed a pistol. "I put that in my pocket," said he, "when I heard her hit. Good-bye, skipper, I'm sorry I haven't been a better shipmate to you."

"Good-bye, Purser," said Kettle, "you aren't a **bad sort**."

Mr. Horrocks ran off below, and the chief officer came back with his report, which he whispered quietly in the shipmaster's ear. "It's fairly scratched the bottom off her. There's sixty feet gone, clean. Collision bulkhead's nowhere. There's half the Atlantic on board already."

"How long will she swim?"

" The carpenter said twenty minutes, but I doubt it."

" Well, away with you, Mr. Mate, and stand by your boat. Take plenty of rockets and distress lights, and if the fog lifts we ought to get picked up by the *Georgic* before morning. She's close on our heels somewhere. If you miss her and get separated make for St. John's."

" Aye, aye, sir."

" So long, Mr. Mate. Good luck to you."

" Good-bye, skipper. Get to the inquiry if you can. I'll swear till all's blue that it wasn't your fault, and you may save your ticket yet."

" All right, Matey. I see what you mean. But I'll not going to shoot myself this journey. I've got the missis and the kids to think about."

The mate ran off down the ladder, and Kettle had the upper bridge to himself. The decks of the steamer glowed with flares and blue-lights. A continuous steam of rockets spouted from her superstructure, far into the inky sky. The main foredeck was already flush with the water, and on the hurricane deck aft, thrust up high into the air, frightened human beings bustled about like the inhabitants of some disturbed ant-hill.

Pair by pair the davit tackles screamed out, and the liner's boats kissed the water, rode there for a minute to their painters as they were loaded with the dense human freight, and then pushed off out of suction reach, and lay to. Dozen by dozen the passengers left the luxurious steam hotel, and got into the frail open craft which danced so dangerously in the clammy fog of that Atlantic night.

Deeper the *Armenia's* fore part sank beneath the cold waters as **her forward** compartments swamped.

From far beneath him in the hull, Kettle could hear the hum of the bilge pumps as they fought the incoming sluices; and then at last those stopped, and a gush of steam burred from the twin funnels to tell that the engineers had been forced to blow off their boilers to save an explosion.

A knot of three men stood at the head of the port gangway ladder shouting for Kettle. He went gloomily down and joined them. They were the Purser, the second mate, and Mr. Grimshaw.

Kettle turned with a blaze **of** fury on his suave tormenter. "Into the boat with you, sir. How do you dare to disobey my orders and stay behind when the passengers were ordered to go? Into the boat with you, **or by** James, I'll throw you there."

Mr. Robert Grimshaw opened his lips for speech.

"If you answer me back," said Kettle, "I'll shoot you dead."

Mr. Grimshaw went. He had a tolerable knowledge of men, and he understood that this ruined shipmaster would be as good as his word. He picked his way down the swaying ladder to where **the w**hite-painted lifeboat plunged beneath, finding footsteps with clumsy landsman's diffidence. He reached the grating at the foot **of** the ladder, and paused. The lifeboat surged up violently towards him over the sea, and then swooped down again in the trough.

"Jump, you blame' fool," the second mate yelled in his ear, "or the steamer will be down under us." And Grimshaw jumped, cannoned heavily against

the boat's white gunwale, and sank like a stone **into
the black water.**

At a gallop there flashed through Captain Kettle's
brain a string of facts.   He was offered £10,000 if
this man did not reach Liverpool; he himself would
be out of employ, **and** back on the streets again;
his wife and children would go hungry.   Moreover,
he had endured cruel humiliation from this man,
and hated him poisonously.   Even by letting him
passively drown **he** would procure revenge and
future financial easement.   But then the memory of
that Irish-American **at the** speaking-tube in the
Bowery came back to him, **and the** thought **of** oblig-
ing a cowardly assassin **like that drove** all other
thoughts from **his mind.**   He thrust Horrocks and
the second-mate aside, and dived into **the waters
after** this passenger.

It is no easy thing to find a man in a rough **sea**
and an inky night like that, and for long enough
neither returned to the **surface.**   The men in the
lifeboat, fearing that the *Armenia* would founder
and drag them down in her wash, **were** beginning to
shove off, when the **two** bodies showed on the
waves, and were dragged on **board** with boat-
hooks.

Both were insensible, and in the press **of** the moment **were** allowed to remain so on the bottom gratings of **the** boat.   Oars straggled out from her sides,
frantically labouring, and the boat fled over the seas
like some uncouth insect.

But they **were** not without **a** mark to steer for.
Rockets were streaming **up** out of another part of
the night, and presently, as they rowed on over that

bleak watery desert, the outline of a great steamer shone out, lit up like some vast stage picture. The other boats had delivered up their freights, and been sent adrift. The second mate's boat rowed to the foot of her gangway ladder.

" This is the *Georgic*," said a smart officer, who received them. " You are the last boat. We've got all your other people unless you've lost any."

" No," said the second mate. " We're all right. That's the Old Man down there with his fingers in that passenger's hair."

" Dead ? "

" No, I saw 'em both move as we came alongside."

" Well, pass 'em up and lets get 'em down to our doctor. Hurry now. We wanted to break the record this passage, and we've lost a lot of time already over you."

" Right-o," said the *Armenia's* second mate drearily, " though I don't suppose our poor old skipper will thank us for keeping him alive. After piling up the old *Atrocity*, he isn't likely to ever get another berth."

" Man has to take luck as he finds it at sea," said the *Georgic's* officer, and shouted to the rail above him, " All aboard, sir."

" Cast off that boat ! " " Up gangway," came the orders, and the *Georgic* continued her race to the East.

CHAPTER IX.

THE RAIDING OF DONNA CLOTILDE.

IF any one had announced in the Captains' Room
at Hallett's that a man could leave that sanctum
shortly before turning-out time, and be forthwith kidnapped in the open streets of South Shields, every
master-mariner within hearing would have put him
down contemptuously as a gratuitous liar. All
opinions in the Captains' Room were expressed
strongly, and with due maritime force of language.

The place seemed to its frequenters the embodi-
ment of homeliness and security. There was a
faint smell of varnish in the atmosphere, and always
had been within the memory of the oldest habitué
and shipmasters came back to the odour with a
sigh of pleasure, as men do return to the neighbourhood of an old and unobtrusive friend. Captains
met in that room who traded to all parts of the
globe, talked, and soon found acquaintances in common. It was a sort of informal club, with no sub-
scription, and an unlimited membership. The holding of a master's " ticket " was the only entrance
qualification, and it was not considered polite to ask
your neighbour whether he was at that moment in
or out of employment.

If you were a genuine master mariner, but of an unclubable disposition, you did not go to the Captains' Room at Hallett's a second time and always made a point of getting rather red and speaking of it contemptuously when the place was mentioned afterwards. If you did not hold a master's ticket, even if you were that dashing thing, a newly fledged mate, the barmaiden on guard spotted you on the instant, and said " that door was private," and directed you to the smoke-room down the passage.

Into this exclusive chamber Captain Owen Kettle had made his way that day after tea, and over two modest half pints of bitter beer had done his share in the talk and the listening, from 8 till 10.30 of the clock. He had exchanged views with other ship-masters on cargoes, crews, insurances, climates, and those other professional matters which the profane world (not in the shipping interest) finds so dreary ; and had been listened to with deference. He was a man who commanded attention, and though you might not like what he said, you would not dream of refusing to listen to it.

That special night, however, Captain Kettle's personal views on maritime affairs were listened to with even more deference than usual. A large red-haired man swung into the Captains' Room some few minutes after Kettle had seated himself, and after ordering his beverage and a cigar, nodded with a whimsical smile in Kettle's direction, and asked him how he liked the neighbourhood of Valparaiso as a residence.

"I forget," said the little sailor, drily enough.

"All right, Captain," said the red-haired man,

" don't you mind me.   I never remember too much myself either.   Only you did me a good turn out there, although you probably don't know it, and I'd be proud if you'd have a **drink or a smoke with me** now in remembrance."

" You're very polite, Captain."

" Don't mention it, Captain," said the red-haired man, and struck the bell.   " Same?   Half-a-pint of bitter, **please,** Miss, and one of your best fourpenny smokes."

The general talk of the Captains' Room, which had halted for the moment, went on again.   **One** worthy mariner had recently failed to **show** a clean bill of health in Barcelona, and had been sent to do twenty days penance at the quarantine station, which is in Port Mahon, Minorca.   As a natural consequence, he wanted to give his views on **Spain** and Spanish government with length and bitterness, but somehow the opportunity was denied him. The red-haired man put **in** a sentence or two, and a question, and it was Kettle's views on the matter to which the Captain's Room found itself listening.

A salvage point was brought up by a stout gentleman in the Baltic timber trade **who was** anxious to air his sentiments ; but the red-haired man skilfully intervened, and " Kettle on Salvage " was asked for and heard.   And so on all through the evening. The red-haired man did his work cleverly, and no one resented it.

Now, Kettle was a man who liked being listened to, and there **is** no doubt that his vanity was tickled by all this deference from his professional equals. There is no doubt also that the smug security of

Hallett's lulled his usual sense of wariness, which may in part account for what happened afterwards. And so, without further excuse for him, it is my painful duty to record that an hour after he left the Captains' Room, the little sailor was entrapped and kidnapped by what, to a man of his knowledge, was one of the most vulgar of artifices.

He emptied his tumbler, stood up, and said he must be going. The red-haired man looked at the round cabin clock on the wall and mentioned that it was his time also; and together they went outside into the damp, dark main street of South Shields.

"Going back to your ship, Captain?" asked the big stranger.

"Why, no, Captain," said Kettle. "I live here, and I'm off home."

"Then I suppose I must say good-night. Hope to meet you again, though. What boat are you on now, Captain?"

"Well, I'm putting in a bit of a spell ashore just now, Captain. Fact is, I haven't come across any employment quite to my taste lately. 'Tisn't every shipowner I care to serve under."

"No," said the red-haired man. "They are brutes, most of them. But look here, Captain, there'd be no offence in my getting you the refusal of a berth, would there?"

Kettle flushed. "Captain," he said, "you're very good. You see I'm married, with children, and I've never earned enough to put anything by. Between men, I don't mind telling you I'm on my beam ends. If I can't get hold of an advance note this week, it will mean going to the pawnshop for Mrs. Kettle's next Sunday's dinner."

The red-haired man sighed. " Well, Captain," he said, "you needn't thank me. It's just my duty to my employers to put this thing in your way. But we'll not speak of it here in the open. Come along off to my steamboat."

" Right," said Kettle. " Where have you got her?"

" She's lying at a buoy in the river. We can get a boat from the steps."

Nothing much more was said between them then. the big, red-haired man seemed indisposed for further talk, and Kettle was too proud to ask questions. Together they walked with their short seaman's stride down the wet, new streets of the seaport, and Captain Kettle made his brain ache by hoping that this would not be another item to add to his long list of disappointments. He had not earned a day's wage for six months, and he was in such straits for want of money that he was growing desperate.

They got down to the steps and took a waterman's boat, turned up the piece of plank which lay in the stern sheets, and sat on the dry side, and then pushed off into the dark river. The red-haired man picked up the yoke lines, and steered the boat amongst the dense shipping ; past tiers of coasting schooners, and timber droghers, and out-of-work clinker-built tugs ; past ungainly iron steam tramps, fishing craft, dredges, and the other resting traffic of the Tyne ; and finally rounded up under a frieze of sterns, and ran alongside the gangway of a 200-ton steam yacht.

" Hullo," said Kettle, "pleasure ? "

" Well, hardly that," said the red-haired man. "Step aboard, Captain, and I'll pay off the water-man."

" He'd better wait to take me ashore again."

" No, let him go. We may have a long talk. I'll put you ashore in one of my own boats when you go. Now, Captain, here we are. Come below to my room."

" You've got steam up, I see," said Kettle as they walked aft along the white, wet decks.

" My orders," said the red-haired man.

" Sail soon ? "

" May start any minute. We never know. My owner's a rare one for changing mind."

" Huh," said Kettle, " might be a woman."

" Devilish like a woman," said the red-haired man drily.   He opened a door at the foot of the companion-way, and turned an electric-light switch. This is my room, Captain. Step right in. A drop of whisky would be a good thing to keep out the cold whilst we talk. Excuse me a minute while I go get a couple of tumblers. I guess the steward's turned in."

Kettle seated himself on a velvet-covered sofa, and looked round at the elaborate fittings of the cabin. " Satin-wood panels," he commented, " nickel battens to put the charts on, glass backed book-case, and silk bunk-curtains ; no expense spared anywhere. Lord ! who wouldn't sell a farm and go to sea? But the old man said she wasn't pleasure ! I wonder what the game is? Contraband, I guess ; many a yacht's great on that. Well, anyway, I've got to hear."

The red-haired man came back with two half-filled tumblers and a water jug. "Here's the poison," said he; "mix it according to your own weight."

"That's rather more than **my** usual whack," said Kettle eyeing the tumbler; "but it's a cold, **wet** night, so here's—By the way, Captain, I'm afraid I've forgotten your name?"

"My name?" said the red-haired man. "**Oh, yes.** I'm Douglas, Captain Douglas."

"Captain Douglas," said Kettle thoughtfully. "No, I can't say I recall it at present. Well, sir, anyway, here's your very good health and prosperity."

"Same," said the red-haired man, and absorbed his whisky and **water** with the dexterity of **an artist.** Out of politeness Captain Kettle finished his tumbler also; there is **an** etiquette about these matters.

Silence filled the cabin for a minute or so, broken only by the distant clatter of a shovel on **a** firebar, and Kettle looked at **the** cabin clock. It was half-past eleven, and Mrs. Kettle would be expecting him home. "Hullo," he said, "firing **up?** Oh, I suppose you've got to keep steam in the donkey boiler, whilst you're in harbour, to run your dynamo. By the way, you were talking about some employment **you** could put in my way, Captain?" he added suggestively.

"Employment!" said Douglas uneasily. "Oh, was **I?** Employment! Yes, to be sure. Well, you see, Captain, it was my owner I was speaking for, and I've been thinking it over, and perhaps on the whole you'd better see her for yourself."

"Her!" said Kettle. "Is there a woman at the head of this concern?"

"A lady, call her. But look here, Captain, you're getting sleepy. Why not turn in here for the night, and see her yourself in the morning?"

Kettle yawned, and his head nodded. "I am sleepy and that's a fact, though I don't know why I should be. But it wouldn't do for me to turn in here for the night. Mrs. Kettle's expecting me at home, and I've never broken word to her since I was married. I should take it as kind, Captain, if you could give me some notion about this piece of employment now, so that I could see whether it's worth——" He yawned again, and struggled with his heavy eyelids—"You must understand, please, Captain, that time is scarce with me; I must get em. ployment at once. I can't stand by and see my missus and youngsters hungry."

Captain Douglas swore, and hit the table with his fist. "It's beastly hard," he said, "and I hate myself for bringing you here."

"What's that noise overhead?" said Kettle. "What are your crew doing on deck?" He tried to rise, but fell back stupidly on the sofa. A harsh bell clanged from somewhere beneath, and the *slop-slop* of water came to him through the yacht's side.

"She's swinging round in the stream, and some-one's rung 'stand-by' to the engine room."

"Sounds like it," the red-haired man admitted.

Again Kettle tried to rise, and with an immense effort tottered to his feet; but he had been given a drug too powerful for even his iron will to fight against; and he swayed, and then pitched helplessly sideways on to the carpet.

The last flickering gleams of consciousness were

passing away from him, but the truth of what had happened had flashed upon him at last. "Shanghaied," he murmured; "by James, yes, Shanghaied, that's what this means.   Well, I pity the man—that Shanghaied me.   By—James—yes."   He breathed stertorously a time or two more, as though trying to get out other words, and then dropped off into a deathly stupor.

Then the door of the state-room creaked slyly open, and the red-haired man started violently. He turned and saw a tall, dark woman just crossing the threshold. "Donna Clotilde!" he said nervously.   "I thought you were ashore.   Then it was by your orders——"

"That the yacht was got under way! *Si, Señor.* I saw you coming on board with the man we have been hunting for these last two years, and as soon as the pair of you got below, I sent word to the mate to call all hands, and get out of the Tyne as soon as the pilot could manage it."   She knelt beside Kettle's prostrate body, and passed her hand caressingly over his damp forehead.   "You are sure you have not overdone it?" she asked.

"I am sure of nothing like that," he answered grimly.   "But I gave him the dose you measured out yourself, so what's done is your own affair.   I only added enough whisky to drown the taste, and the poor little beggar drank it all down at one mouthful."

"I don't see that you need pity him much.   He will be all right when he wakes."

"When he wakes it will be at sea, and I have heard him speak of his wife and kids.   That's why

I pity him, Donna Clotilde. Incidentally I'm a bit sorry for myself." He stooped over the prostrate man, and took a **revolver** from the back pocket of his trousers. "Look there! You see the fellow took a gun with him even to Hallett's. It's grown to be a habit with him. **He's** a dead shot, too, and doesn't mind shooting."

"I didn't think you were **a** coward."

"You know quite well I'm not, Señorita. But this Captain Kettle will remember that I was the fellow that decoyed him on board, and he'll be pretty anxious to square up the account when he wakes."

"You are well paid on purpose to cover all risks," said the woman with some contempt.

"And I shall be earning my pay," **said** the red-haired man doggedly. "This small person here's a holy terror. Well, I must be getting on deck to see the pilot take her down **the** river. Here, I'll put him on the bed before I go. He'll sleep it off more comfortably there."

"You shall not touch him," said Donna Clotilde. "I will do all that's needful. I have waited for this moment for three long years."

"You must be pretty keen on him if **you** can sit by him when he does not know you."

"I have loved him since the first moment we met, and he knows it; and I do not mind who else knows it also. I am entirely without shame in the matter: I glory in it. **I am not** one of your cold-blooded European women."

"Well," he said, "you're paying me to run this yacht, and I must be off up to see the pilot take her out of the river without losing us any paint." And he went out of his room, and left Donna Clotilde La Touche alone with this man by whom she was so fiercely attracted.

The yacht steamed out between Tyne pier heads, and the pilot left her in the coble which had been towing stern-first alongside. Her destination was the Mediterranean, but she did not port her helm at once. Instead, she held on straight out into the North Sea, and then turned off to make the Mediterranean, north about; that is, through the Pentland, and round Scotland. She kept clear of Ireland also, making a course for herself through the deeper wildernesses of the North Atlantic, avoiding the north-and-south traffic of the Bay, and in fact sighting scarcely a single vessel till the red-haired man at last starboarded his helm and put her east for the Straits.

The voyage was not one of monotony. Captain Kettle lay for the first twenty-four hours in a state of snoring unconsciousness, and when he did come to his wits again, found himself in a cabin alone. He got up and stretched. His limbs were heavy and languid, but he was not conscious of having received any hurt. He clapped a hand to the region of his loins and nodded his grim head significantly. His pistol was missing.

He looked in the glass and saw that his face above the red torpedo beard was drawn and white, and that his eyes were framed in black, dissipated-looking rings. There was an evil taste in his mouth, too, which even a bottleful of water did not allay. However, all of these were minor details; they might

14

be repaired afterwards. His first requirement was revenge on the man who had lured him aboard.

His natural instincts of tidiness made him go through the ceremony of toilette, and then he put on his cap, and, spruce and pale, went out through the luxurious cabin and passageways of the yacht, and found his way on deck.

The time was night; the cold air was full of moonshine; and fortune favoured him insomuch that the red-haired man whom he sought was himself standing a watch. He walked up to him without any concealment, and then, swift as light, slung out his right fist, sending every ounce of his weight after it, and caught the red-haired man squarely on the peak of the jaw.

The fellow went down as if he had been pole-axed, and Kettle was promptly on top of him. The three other hands of the watch on deck were coming fast to their big captain's assistance, and Kettle made the most of his time. He had been brought up in a school where he was taught to hit hard, and hit first, and keep on hitting, and moreover he was anatomically skilled enough to know where to hit with most effect. He had no time then for punctilious fighting; he intended to mark his man in return for value received; and he did it. Then the three lusty deck hands of the watch came up and wrenched him off, and held him for their officer in turn to take vengeance on.

Kettle stood in their grip, panting, and pale, and exultant.

"You great ugly red-polled beggar!" he said, "I've made your face match your head, but you needn't thank me for **it**. **You**'d dare to Shanghai me, would you? By James, I'll make your ship a perfect hell till I'm off it."

"**You** hit **a man** when he's not looking."

"**Liar!**" said Kettle. "**You saw** me plain enough. If you were half a sailor you'd never have been hit."

"You're half my size. I couldn't fight you."

"Tell your hands to set me adrift, and try."

The big man was tempted, but he swallowed down his inclination. He ordered the men who were holding Captain Kettle to set him **free and go** away **forward** again, and then he thrust **his own fists** res-olutely in his pockets.

"Now," he said, when they were alone, "**I own** up to having **earned** what you've given me, and I hope that'll suit you, for if it is doesn't, I'll shoot you like a rat with your own gun. You've handled me in a way no other man has done before, and so you can tickle your pride with that, and simmer down. If you **want** to know, I was a man like yourself, hard up; and I was paid to kidnap you, and I'd have kidnapped the devil for money **just** then."

"I know nothing about **the** devil," **said** Kettle acidly; "but you've got me, **and** you couldn't very well find a worse bargain. If you are not a fool, you will set me ashore at once."

"**I** shall act entirely by my owner's orders."

"Then trot out your owner, and I'll pass the time of day with him next. I'm not particular. I'll kill the whole blooming ship's company if I don't get my own way."

"Man, don't you be a fool. You can't hit a woman."

" A woman ?"

"Yes, I told you before—Donna Clotilde. You know her well enough."

" Donna Clotilde, who?"

" La Touche."

The stiffening seemed suddenly to go out of the little man. He stepped wearily across the deck, and leant his elbows on the yacht's polished topgallant rail. " By James!" he murmured to the purple arch of the night. " By James! that—that woman. What a ruddy mess." And then he broke off into dreary musing. He had known this Donna Clotilde La Touche before ; had entered her employ in Valparaiso ; had helped her revolutionary schemes by capturing a warship for her. In return she had conceived a mad infatuation for him. But all the while he regarded her merely as his employer. In the end he had been practically set adrift at sea in an open boat as a penance for not divorcing his own wife and marrying her. And now she was come to add to his other troubles by beginning to persecute him again. It was hard, bitterly hard.

By some subtle transference of thought, the woman in her berth below became conscious of his regard, grew restless, woke, got more restless, dressed, came on deck, and saw this man with whom she was so fiercely enamoured, staring gloomily over the bulwarks. With her lithe, silent walk she stepped across the dewy decks under the moonlight, and without his hearing her, leant on the rail at his side and flung an arm across his shoulders.

Captain Kettle woke from his musing with a start, stepped coldly aside, and saluted formally. He had an eye for a good-looking woman, and this one was deliciously handsome.   He was always chivalrous toward the **other sex**, whatever might be their characters; **but** the fact of his own kidnapping at the moment of Mrs. Kettle's pressing need, made **him** almost as hard as though a man stood before him **as** his enemy.

"Miss La Touche," he said, "do you wish **me to** remember you with hatred?"

"I do not wish you to have need to remember me at all. As you know, I wish you to stay with me always."

"That, as I have told you before, Miss, is impossible for more reasons **than** one. **You have done me** infinite mischief already. I might **have** found employment by this time had I stayed in South Shields, and meanwhile my wife and children are hungry. Be content with that, and set me ashore."

"I repeat the offer I made you in South America. Come with me, get a divorce, and your wife shall have an income such as she never dreamed of, and such as you never could have got her in all your life otherwise. You know I am not boasting. As you must know by this, I am one of the richest women in the world."

"Thank you, but I do not accept the terms. Money is not everything."

"And meanwhile, remember, I keep you on board **here,** whether you like it or not; and, until you give way to what I want, your wife may starve. So if she and your children are in painful straits, you must recollect that it is entirely your fault."

"Quite so," said Kettle. "She will be content to starve when she knows the reason."

Donna Clotilde's eyes began to glitter.

"There are not many men who would refuse if I offered them myself."

"Then, Miss, I must remain curious."

She stamped her foot. "I have hungered for you all this time, and I will not give you up for mere words. You will come to love me in time as I love you. I tell you you will, you must, you shall. I have got you now, and I will not let you go again."

"Then, Miss," said Kettle grimly, "I shall have to show you that I am too hot to hold."

She faced him with heaving breast. "We will see who wins," she cried.

"Probably," said Captain Kettle, and took off his cap. "Good-night, Miss, for the present. We know how we stand : the game appears to begin between us from now." He turned deliberately away from her, walked forward, and went below ; and, after a little waiting, Donna Clotilde shivered and went back to her own luxurious state-room.

But if she was content to spend the rest of the night in mere empty longing, Captain Kettle was putting his time to more practical use. He was essentially a man of action.

Cautiously, he found his way to the steward's store-room, filled a case with meat tins and biscuit, and then coming on deck again, stowed it away in the lifeboat, which hung in davits out-board, without being noticed. With equal success he took the boat's breaker forward, filled it from a water tank, and got it fixed on its chocks again, still without being seen. The moon was behind clouds, and the darkness favoured him. He threw down the

coils of the davit falls on deck, cast off one from
where it was belayed, took a turn and carried the
bight to the other davit so that he could lower away
both tackles at once.

But he was not allowed to get much further.   The
disused blocks screamed like a parcel of cats as the
ropes rended through them ; there was a shrill
whistle from the officer of the watch ; and half-a-
dozen men from various parts of the deck came
bounding along to interfere.

Captain Kettle let go both falls to overhaul as
they chose, picked up a greenheart belaying-pin out
of the pin rail, and stood on the defensive.   But the
forward fall kinked and jammed, and though the
little man fought like a demon to keep off the watch
till he got it clear, they were too many for him, and
drove him to the deck by sheer weight of numbers.
He had cracked one man's forearm in the scuffle,
laid open another's face, and smashed in the front
teeth of a third, and they were rather inclined to
treat him roughly, but the red-haired skipper came
up, and by sheer superior strength picked him up,
kicking and struggling, and hustled him off below
whether he liked it or no.

The lifeboat dangled half-swamped from the forward davit tackle, and all hands had to be piped before they could get her on board again ; and by the
time they had completed this job, there was another
matter handy to occupy their attention.   A fireman
came up from below, white-faced and trembling :

" The yacht's half full of water," he said.

Now that their attention was called to it, they
noticed the sluggish way she rode the water.

"She must **have** started a plate or something," **the** fireman went on excitedly. "We've got both bilge pumps running, and they won't look at it." The water's coming in like **a** sluice."

"Carpenter," sang out the red-haired man, "come below with me and see if **we can** find anything," and he led the way to the companion. Between decks they could hear the water slopping about under the flooring. It seemed a bad, almost a hopeless case.

Instinctively the red-haired man went to his own **room** to pocket his valuables, and by a chance he **was** moved to lift up the door in the floor which covered the bath beneath it. Ah, there was the mischief. The sea cock which filled the bath was turned on to the full, and the iron tub was gushing water on every side. **The next** state-room was empty, but the bath cock there was also turned on to the full; and after going round the ship, and finally entering Kettle's room (and covering him with a revolver), and turning off his water supply, he found that **the** sea had been pouring inboard from no fewer than eight separate apertures.

"And this is your work, you little fiend, I suppose?" said the red-haired man savagely.

"Certainly," said Captain Kettle. "Shoot me if **you** like, **put me** ashore if you choose, but don't grumble **if you** find **me** a deuced ugly passenger. I'm not in the habit of being made to travel where I don't wish."

That afternoon Kettle contrived to set the **yacht** afire in three separate places, and a good deal of damage was done (and night had fallen again) before **the** scared crew managed to extinguish the flames;

and this time Donna Clotilde intervened. She asked
for Kettle's parole that he would attempt no further
mischief; and when this was flatly refused, incontinently put him in irons. **The** lady was somewhat
tigerish in her affections.

A second time Captain Kettle managed to get the
yacht in a blaze, at the imminent peril of immolat-
ing himself, and then, from lack **of** further opportunity to make himself obnoxious, lay quiet in his
lair till such time as the yacht would of necessity go
into harbour to coal. The exasperated **crew** would
cheerfully have murdered him if they had been given
the chance, but Donna Clotilde would not permit
him to be harmed. She was a young woman who,
up to this, had always contrived to have her **own**
way, and she firmly believed that she **would tame**
Kettle in time.

When the yacht passed the Straits she had only
four days' more coal on board, and the executive
(and Kettle) expected that she would go into Gibraltar and lay alongside a hulk to rebunker. But
Donna Clotilde had other notions. She had the
yacht run down the Morrocco coast, and brought **to**
an anchor. So long as she had Captain Kettle **in**
her company upon the waters, she did not vastly
care whether she was moving or at a standstill.

"You cannot escape me here," she said to him
when the cable had roared from the hawse pipe, and
the dandy steamer had swung to a rest. "The yacht
is victualled for a year, and I can stay here as long as
you choose. You had far better be philosophical
and give in. Marry me now, and liking will come
afterwards."

Kettle looked at the tigerish love and resentment which blazed from her black eyes, and answered with cold politeness that time would show what happened; though, to tell the truth, indomitable though he was as a general thing, he was at that time feeling that escape was almost impossible. And so for the while he more or less resigned himself to captivity.

Under the baking blue of a Mediterranean sky this one-sided courtship progressed, Donna Clotilde alternating her ecstasies of fierce endearment by paroxysms of invective, and Kettle enduring both in equal coldness and immobility. The crew of the yacht looked on, stolidly non-interferent, and were kept by their officers at cleaning and painting, as necessary occupiers to the mind. But one or other of them, of their own free will, always kept an eye on their guest, whether he was on deck or below. He had given them a wholesome taste of his quality, and they had an abject dread of what he might be up to next if he was left alone. They quite understood that he would destroy the yacht and all hands if, by doing so, he could regain his personal liberty.

But others, it seems, besides those already mentioned in this narrative, were taking a lively interest in the smart yacht and her people. She was at anchor in the bay of the Riff coast, and the gentry who inhabited the beach villages, and the villages in the hills behind the beach, had always looked upon anybody and anything they could grab as their just and lawful prey. The Sultan of Morocco, the war ships of France, Spain, and elsewhere, and the emissaries of other powers had time after time endeavoured to school them in the science of civilization without effect, and so they still remain to-day, the only regularly practising pirates in the Western World.

The yacht was sighted first from the hills; was reported to the beach villages; and was reconnoitred under cover of night by a tiny fishing-boat. The report was pleasing, and word went round. Bearded brown men collected at an appointed spot, each with the arms to which he was best accustomed; and when darkness fell, four large boats were run down to the feather edge of the surf. There was no indecent hurry. They did their work with method and carefulness, like men who are used to it; and they arrived alongside the yacht at 3 A. M., confidently expecting to take her by surprise.

But the crew of the yacht, thanks to Captain Kettle's vagaries, were not in the habit of sleeping over soundly; they never knew what piece of dangerous mischief their little captive might turn his willing hand to next; and, as a consequence, when the anchor watch sang out his first alarm, not many seconds elapsed before every hand aboard was on deck. The yacht was well supplied with revolvers and cutlasses, and half a minute sufficed to get these up from below and distributed, so that when the Riffians attempted to board, the defenders were quite ready to do them battle.

Be this how it may, however, there is no doubt as to which side got the first advantage. The yacht's low freeboard made but a small obstacle to a climber from the large boats alongside, and neither the deckhands, nor the stockhold crew, were any of them trained fighting men. In their 'prentice hands the kicking revolvers threw high, and were only useful as knuckledusters, and till they had thrown them down, and got their cutlasses into play, they did hardly any execution to speak about. The Riff men, on the other hand, had been bred and born in an atmosphere of skirmish, and made ground steadily.

At an early point of the scuffle, Captain Kettle came on deck with a cigar in his mouth, and hands in his pockets, and looked on upon matters with a critical interest, but did not offer to interfere one way or the other. It was quite a new sensation to him, to watch an active fight without being called upon to assist or arbitrate.

And then up came from below Donna Clotilde La Touche, dressed and weaponed, and, without a bit of hesitation, flung herself into the turmoil. She saw Kettle standing on one side, but neither besought nor commanded him. She would have died sooner than ask for his help then, and be met with a refusal.

Into the mêlée she went, knife and pistol, and there is no doubt that her example, and the fury of her rush, animated the yacht's crew, and made them stronger to drive the wall of their assailants back. To give Donna Clotilde her due, she was as brave as the bravest man, and, moreover, she was a certain shot at moderate range. But, after her revolver was empty and the press closed round her, it was not long before an expert hand twisted the knife from her grasp, and then the end came quickly. An evil-smelling man noted her glorious beauty, and marked her out as his special loot. He clapped a couple of sinewy arms around her, **and bore her** away towards the bulwarks, and his **boat.**

Some one had switched on the electric deck lights, and the fight was in a glow **of** radiance. Everything was to be clearly seen. Donna Clotilde was being dragged resisting along **the** decks, and Kettle looked on placidly smoking his cigar. She **was** heaved up on the bulwarks ; in another moment she would be gone from his path **forever.**

Still her lips made no sound, though her great, black eyes were full of wild **entreaty. But the eyes were** more than Kettle could **stand.** He stooped and picked up **a** weapon from amongst the litter on **deck,** and rushed forward and **gave** a blow, and the Riffian dropped limply, and Donna Clotilde stood by the yacht's bulwark, breathless and gasping.

"Now you get away below," he ordered curtly. "I'll soon clear this rabble over the side."

He watched to see her obey him, **and** she did it meekly. Then he gave his attention to the fight. He broke a packet of cartridges **which lay** on the deck planks, picked up and loaded a revolver, and commenced to make himself useful to the yacht's **crew ;** and from that moment the fortune of the battle turned.

Captain Owen Kettle was (and is) a beautiful fighter, and this was just his fight. Against his cool-headed ferocity the Riffians gave way like sand before waves. **He** did **not** miss a blow, he did not waste a shot ; all his efforts went home with the deadliest effect. His voice, too, was a splendid ally. The yacht's crew had been doing their utmost already : they had been fighting for their bare lives.

But with Kettle's poisonous tongue to lash them they did far more; they raged like wild beasts at the brown men who had invaded their sacred decking, and drove them back with resistless fury.

"Hump yourselves, you lazy dogs!" Kettle shouted. "Keep them on the move. Drive them over the bows. Murder those you can reach. Am I to do all this job myself? Come on, you mongrels."

The red cutlasses stabbed and hacked, and the shrieks and yells and curses of the fight grew to a climax; and then the Riffians with a sudden panic gave way, and ran for the side, and tumbled over into their boats. There was no quarter asked or given. The exasperated yachtsmen cut down all they could reach even whilst they were escaping; and when the sound had gone, they threw after them the killed and wounded, to be rescued or lost as they chose. Afterwards, having a moment's respite, they picked up their revolvers again, loaded them, and kept up a spattering, ill-aimed fire till the boats were out of reach. Then when they turned to look to their own killed and hurt, they found a new crisis awaiting them.

Captain Kettle was on the top of the deck house which served as a navigating bridge, ostentatiously closing up the breech of the revolver after reloading it. He wished for a hearing, and after what they had seen of his deadly marksmanship, they gave it to him without demur. His needs were simple. He wanted steam as soon as the engineers could give it him, and he intended to take the yacht into Gibraltar right away. Had anybody an objection to raise?

The red-haired man made himself spokesman. "We should have to go to Gib anyway," said he, "Some of us want a doctor badly, and three of us want a parson to read the funeral service. Whether you can get ashore once we do run into Gib, Captain, is your own concern."

"You can leave that to me safely," said Captain Kettle. "It will be something big that stops me from having my own way now."

The men dispersed about their duties, the decks were hosed down, and the deck lights switched off. After awhile Donna Clotilde came gliding up out of the darkness, and stepped up the ladder to the top of the deck house. Kettle regarded her uneasily.

To his surprise she knelt down, took his hand, and smothered it with burning kisses. Then she went back to the head of the ladder. "My dear," she said, "I will never see you again. I made you hate me, and yet you saved my life. I wish I thought I could ever forget you."

"Miss La Touche," said Kettle, "you will find a man in your own station one of these days to make you a proper husband, and then you will look back at this cruise and think how lucky it was you so soon sickened, and kicked me away from you."

She shook her head and smiled through her tears.

"You are generous," she said. "Good-by. Good-bye, my darling. Good-bye." Then she went down the ladder, and Kettle never saw her again.

A quartermaster came up and took the wheel. The windlass engine had been clacking, and the red-haired man called out from forward, "All gone."

"Quartermaster," said Kettle.

"Yessir," said the quartermaster.

" Nor' nor' west and by west."

" Nor' no' west n'b' west it is, sir," said the quartermaster briskly.

CHAPTER X.

MR. GEDGE'S CATSPAW.

CAPTAIN OWEN KETTLE folded the letter-card, put it in his pocket, and relit his cigar. He drew paper towards him, and took out a stub of pencil and tried to make verse, which was his habit when things were shaping themselves awry, but the rhymes refused to come. He changed the metre: he gave up labouring to fit the words to the air of "Swanee River," and started fresh lines which would go to the tune of "Greenland's Icy Mountains," a metre with which at other times he had been notoriously successful. But it failed him now. He could not get the jingle; spare feet bristled at every turn; and the field of poppies, on which his muse was engaged, became every moment more and more elusive.

It was no use. He put down the pencil and sighed, and then, frowning at himself for his indecision, took out the letter-card again, and deliberately re-read it, front and back.

Captain Kettle was a man who made up his mind over most matters with the quickness of a pistol-shot; and once settled, rightly or wrongly, he always stuck to his decision. But here, on the letter-card, was a matter he could not get the balance of at all; it refused to be dismissed, even temporarily, from his mind; it involved interests far too large to be hazarded by a hasty verdict either **one** way or the other; and the difficulty in coming **to** any satisfactory conclusion irritated him heavily.

The **letter-card was** anonymous, **and** seemed to present **no clue** to its authorship. It was typewritten; it was posted, **as** the stamp showed, **in** Newcastle; it committed its writer in no **degree** whatever. But it made statements which, if true, **ought** to have sent somebody to penal servitude; and it **threw out** hints, which, true or untrue, made Captain Kettle heir to a whole world of anxiety and trouble.

It is an excellent academic rule to entirely disregard anonymous letters, but it is by no means always an easy **rule to** follow. **And** there are times when a friendly warning must be conveyed anonymously or not at all. But Kettle did not worry his head about the ethics of anonymous letter-writing as **a** profession; his **attention** was taken up by this typewritten card **from** "Well-wisher," which he held in his hand:

" Your ship goes to sea never to reach port. There is an insurance robbery cleverly **rigged.** *You think yourself very smart, I know, but this time you are being made a common gull of."*

And the **writer wound** up by saying: "*I can't give you any hint of how it's going to be done. Only I know the game's fixed. So keep your weather eye skinned, and take the* Sultan of Labuan *safely out and back, and maybe you'll get something more solid than a drink.*

" From
" Your Well-wisher."

Captain Kettle was torn, as he read, by many conflicting sentiments. Loyalty to Mr. Gedge, his owner, was one of them. Gedge had sold him before, but that was in a way condoned by this present appointment to the *Sultan of Labuan*. And he wanted very much to know what were Mr. Gedge's wishes over the matter.

His own code of morality on this subject was peculiar. Ashore in South Shields he was as honest as a bishop ; he was a strict chapel member ; he did not even steal matches from the Captains' Room at Hallett's, his house of call, which has always been a recognised peculation. At sea he conceived himself to be bought, body and soul, by his owner for the time being, and was perfectly ready to risk body and soul in earning his pay.

But the question was, how was this pay to be earned?

Up till then he would have said : " By driving the *Sultan of Labuan* over the seas as fast as could be done on a given coal consumption ; by ruthlessly keeping down expense ; and, in fact, by making the steamer earn the largest possible dividend in the ordinary way of commerce." But this typewritten letter-card hinted at other purposes, which he knew were quite within the bounds of possibility, and if he was being made into a catspaw——

He hit the unfinished poems on the table a blow with his fist. " By James ! " he muttered, " a catspaw ? I didn't think of it in that light before. Well, we'd better have a clear understanding about the matter."

He got up, crammed the blue letter-card into his pocket, and took his cap.

"My dear," he called down to Mrs. Kettle, who was engaged on the family wash in the kitchen below, "I've got to run up to the office to see Mr. Gedge. I don't think I quite understand his wishes about running the boat. Get your tea when it's ready. I don't want to keep you and the youngsters waiting."

Captain Kettle thought out many things as he journeyed from South Shields to the grimy office of his employer in Newcastle, but his data were insufficient, and he was unable to get hold of any scheme by which he could safely approach what was, to say the very least of it, a very delicate subject. Mr. Gedge had hired him as captain of the *Sultan of Labuan*, had said no word about losing her, and how was he to force the man's confidence? It looked the most unpromising enterprise in the world. Moreover, although in the outer world he was as brave a fellow as ever lived, he had all a shipmaster's timidity at tackling a ship-owner in his lair, and this, of course, handicapped him.

In this mood, then, he was ushered upon Gedge in his office, and saw him signing letters and casting occasional sentences to a young woman who flicked them down in shorthand.

The ship-owner frowned. He was very busy. "Well, Captain," he said, "what is it? Talk ahead. I can listen whilst I sign these letters."

"It's a private question I'd like to ask you about running the boat."

"Want Miss Payne to go out?"

"If I might trouble her so far."

Gedge jerked his head towards the door, "Type out what you've got," he said. The shorthand writer went out and closed the glass door after her. "Now, Kettle."

Captain Kettle hesitated. It was an awkward subject to begin upon.

"Now then, Captain, out with it quick. I'm in the dickens of a hurry."

" I wish you'd let me know a little more exactly —in confidence, of course—how you wish me to run this steamboat. Do you want me to—I mean——"

"Well, get on, get on."

"When do you want her back?"

Gedge leant back in his chair, tapped his teeth with the end of his pen. "Look here, Captain," he said, "you didn't come here to talk rot like this. You've had your orders already. You aren't a drinking man, or I'd say you were screwed. So there's something else behind. Come, out with it."

"I hardly know how to begin."

"I don't want rhetoric. If you've got a tale tell it, if not——" Mr. Gedge leant over his desk again and went on signing his letters.

Captain Kettle stood the rudeness without so much as a flush. He sighed a little, and then, after another few moments' thought, took the letter-card from his pocket and laid it on his employer's table. After Gedge had conned through and signed a couple more sheets, he took the card up in his fingers and skimmed it over.

As he read the color deepened in his face, and Kettle saw that he was moved, but said nothing.

For a moment there was silence between them, and Gedge tapped at his teeth and was apparently lost in thought. Then he said : " Where did you get this ? "

" Through the post."

" And why did you bring it to me ? "

"I thought you might have something to say about it."

"Shown it to any one else ? "

" No, sir ; I'm in your service, and earning your pay."

"Yes ; I pulled you out of the gutter again quite recently, and you said you'd be able to get your wife's clothes out of pawn with your advance note."

" I'm very grateful to you for giving me the berth, sir, and I shall be a faithful servant to you as long as I'm in your employ. But if there's anything on, I'd like to be in your confidence. I know she isn't an old ship, but——"

" But what ? "

"She's uneconomical. Her engines are old-fashioned. It wouldn't pay to fit her with triple expansions and new boilers."

"I see. You appear to know a lot about the ship, Captain—more than I do myself, in fact. I know you're a small tin saint when you're within hail of that Ebenezer, or Bethel, or whatever you call it here ashore, but at sea you've got the name for not being over particular."

" At sea," said the little sailor with a sigh, "I am what I have to be. But I couldn't do that. I'm a poor man, sir ; I'm pretty nearly a desperate man ; but there are some kinds of things that are beyond me. I know it's done often enough, but—you'll have to excuse me. I can't lose her for you."

"Who's asking you?" said Gedge cheerily. " I'm not. Don't jump at conclusions, man. I don't want the *Sultan of Labuan* lost. She's not my best ship, I'll grant; but I can run her at a profit for all that; and even if I couldn't I am not the sort of man to try and make my dividends out of Lloyd's. No, not by any means, Captain; I've got my name to keep up."

Captain Kettle brought up a sigh of relief. "Glad to hear it, sir; I'm glad to hear it. But I thought it best to have it out with you. That beastly letter upset me."

Gedge laughed slily. " Well, if you want to know who wrote the letter, I did myself."

Kettle started. He was obviously incredulous.

"Well, to be accurate, I did it by deputy. You hae yer doots, eh? Hang it, man; what an un-believing Jew you are." He pressed one of the electric pushes by the side of his desk, and the shorthand writer came in and stood at the doorway.

" Miss Payne, you typed this letter-card, didn't you?" he asked, and Miss Payne dutifully answered: " Yes."

" Thank you. That'll do. Well, Kettle, I hope you're satisfied now? I sent this blessed card be-cause I wanted to see how deep this shore-going honesty of yours went, which I've heard so much about and now I know, and you may take it from me that you'll profit by it financially in the very near future. The shipmasters I've had to do with have been mostly rogues, and when I get hold of a straight man I know how to appreciate him. Now, good-by, Captain, and a prosperous voyage to you. If you **catch** the midnight mail to-night from here, you'll **just** get down to Newport to-morrow in time to see **her** come into dock. Take her over at once, you know ; **we** can't have any time wasted. Here good-bye. I'm frantically busy."

But busy though he might be, Mr. Gedge did **not** immediately return to signing his letters after Captain Kettle's departure. Instead, he took out a handkerchief and wiped his forehead and wiped his hands, which for some reason seemed to have grown unaccountably clammy ; and for awhile he lay back **in his** writing-chair **like a man** who feels physically sick.

Captain **Kettle**, however, went his ways humming a cheerful air, and as the twelve o'clock mail roared out that night across the high-level bridge, he settled himself to sleep in his corner of a third-class carriage and to dream the dreams of a man who, after many vicissitudes, has **at** last found righteous employment. It was a new experience **for** him, and he permitted himself the luxury of enjoying **it to** the full.

A train clattered him into Monmouthshire some **twelve hours later,** and he stepped out on Newport **platform into a fog raw** and fresh from the Bristol Channel. **His small,** worn portmanteau he could easily **have** carried **in** his hand, but there is an etiquette **about these** matters which even hard-up ship-masters, **to** whom a shilling is **a** financial rarity, **must** observe ; **and so** he took a four-wheeler down to the agent's office, and made himself known. The *Sultan of Labuan*, it seemed, had come up the Usk and gone into dock barely an hour before, and so Kettle, obedient to his **orders, went down at once** to take her over.

It was not **a pleasant** operation, this ousting another man **from his** livelihood, **and as Kettle had** been supplanted **a weary number of times himself,** he thought **he knew pretty well the** feelings of the man **whom** he had come to replace. **His** reception, **however,** surprised him. Williams, the former master **of the** *Sultan of Labuan,* **handed over his** charge with an air of obvious and sincere relief, and Kettle felt that he was **being eyed with a certain** embarrassing curiosity. **The man was not** disposed **to be** verbally communicative.

" **Y**ou look knocked up," said **Kettle.**

" Might well **be,"** retorted Captain Williams. " **I** haven't had a blessed wink of sleep since I **pulled** my anchors out of Thames **mud."**

" Not had bad **weather, have** you ? "

" No, weather's **been right** enough. Bit thickish, that's all."

" What's kept **you** from **having a** watch below, then ? "

" 'Fraid of losing the ship, Captain. I never been **up** before the Board **of Trade yet, and** don't want **to try** what it feels like.'

" Oh ! " said Kettle with a sigh, " it's horrible ; they're brutes. I know. I have been there."

" So I might have guessed," said Williams drily.

" Look **here," said Kettle,** " what are you driving at ? "

" No offence, Captain, no offence. I'll just shut my head now. Guess I've been talking too much already. Result of being over-tired, I suppose. Let's get on with the ship's papers. They are all in this tin box."

" But I'd rather you said out what you got to say."

" Thanks, Captain, but no. This is the first time we've met, I think?"

" So far as I remember."

" Well, there you are then; personally you no doubt are a very nice pleasant gentleman, but still there's no getting over the fact that you're a stranger to me; and anyway, you're in Gedge's employ, and I'm not; and there's a law of libel in this country which gets up and hits you whether you are talking truth or lies."

" English laws are beastly, and that's a fact."

" Reading about them in the paper's quite enough for me. Now, Captain, suppose we go ashore with these papers and I can sign off and you can sign on. Afterwards we'll have a drop of whisky together if you like just to show there's no ill-will."

"You are very polite, Captain," said Kettle. " I'm sure I don't like the notion of stepping in to take away your employment. But if it hadn't been me, he'd have got some one else."

The other turned on him quickly.

" Don't think you're doing me a bad turn, Captain because you aren't. I was never so pleased to step out of a chart-house in my life. Only thing is, I hope I aren't doing you a bad turn by letting you step in."

" By James," said Kettle, " do speak plain, Captain ; don't go on hinting like this."

" I am maundering on too much, Captain, and that's a fact. Result of being about tired-out, I suppose. But you must excuse me speaking fur- ther: there's that confounded libel law to think about. Now, Captain, here's the key of the chart- house door, and if you'll let me, I'll go out first and you can lock it behind you. You'll find one of the tumblers beside the water-bottle broken; it fell out of my hand this morning just after I'd docked her ; but all the rest is according to the inventory ; and I'll knock off threepence for the tumbler when we square up."

They plunged straightway into the aridities of business, and kept at it till the captaincy had been formally laid down and handed over, and then the opportunity for further revelations was gone.

Captain Williams was clearly worn out with weariness; responsibility had kept him going till then, but now that responsibility had ended he was like a man in a trance. His eyes drooped, his knees failed drunkenly ; he was past speech ; and if Kettle had not by main force dragged him off to a bed at a temperance hotel, he would have toppled down incontinently and slept in the gutter like one dead. As it was he lay on the counterpane in the heaviest of sleep, the picture of a strong man worn out with watching and labour, and for a minute or so Kettle stood beside the bed and gazed upon him thoughtfully.

" By James," he muttered, " if I could make you speak, Captain, I believe you could tell a queerish tale."

But Kettle did not loiter by this taciturn bedside. He had signed on as master of the *Sultan of Labuan;* he was in Mr. Gedge's employ, and earning Mr. Gedge's pay ; and every minute wasted on a steamer means money lost. He went briskly across to the South dock **and set** the machinery of business to work without **delay.** There was **grumbling** from mates, engineers, and crew that they had been given leisure for scarcely a breath of shore air, but Kettle was not a man who courted popularity from his underlings by offering them indulgences. **He** stated that their duty was to get the water ballast out and the coal under hatches in the shortest time on record, and mentioned that he was the man who would **see it done.**

The men grumbled of **course** ; behind their driver's back they swore ; **two deck** hands and three of the stokehold **crew** deserted, leaving their wages, and were replaced by others from the shipping office ; **and** still the **work** went remorselessly on under the grey glow of the fog so long as daylight lasted, and then under the glare of raw electric arc lamps. The air was full of gritty dust and **the** roar of falling **coal.** A waggon was shunted up, dangled aloft in hydraulic arms, ignominiously emptied end first, and then **put** to ground again and petulantly sent away to find a fresh load, whilst its successor was being nursed **and** relieved. Two hundred tons to the hour was what that hydraulic staith could handle, but for all that it **did** not break the coal unduly.

In the forehold the trimmers gasped and choked as they steered the black avalanches into place ; and presently another of the huge staithes crawled up along the dock wall, with a gasping tank-loco and a train of waggons in attendance, and then the *Sultan of Labuan* was being loaded through the after hatch also. It was a triumph of machinery and organisation, and tired men in a dozen departments cursed Kettle for keeping them at such a remorseless pressure over their tasks.

Down to her fresh-water plimsol the steamer was sunk, and then the loading ceased. Even Kettle did not dare to overload. He knew quite well that there were the jealous eyes of a Seamen and Firemen's Union official watching him from somewhere on the quays, and if she was trimmed an inch above her marks the *Sultan of Labuan* would never be let go through the outer dock-gate. So the burden was limited to its legal bounds, and Kettle got his clearance papers with the same fierce, business-like bustle ; and came back and stepped lightly up on to the tramp's upper bridge.

The pilot was there waiting for him, half admiring, half repelled : the old blue-faced mate and the carpenter were on the forecastle-head ; the second mate was aft ; the chief himself and the third engineer were at the throttle and the reversing gear below. The ship's entire complement had quite surrendered to the sway of this new task-master, and stood in their coal-grime and their tiredness ready to jump at his bidding.

Bristol Channel tides are high, and the current of the Usk is swift. It was going to be quick work if they did not miss the tide, and the pilot, who had no special stake in the matter, said it could not be done. Kettle, however, thought otherwise, and the pilot in consequence saw some seamanship which gave him chills down the back.

"By gum, Captain," he said, when they were fairly out of the river, "you can handle her."

"Wait till I know her, pilot, and then I'll show you."

"Haven't got nerves enough. Look you, Captain, you'll be having a bad crumple-up if you bustle a big loaded steamboat about docks at that rate."

"Never bent a plate in my life."

"Well, I hope you never will. Look you, now, you're a little tin wonder in the way of seamanship."

"Quartermaster," said Kettle, "tell my steward to bring two goes of whisky up here on the bridge. Pilot, if you say such things to me, you make me feel like a girl with a new dress, and I want a drop of Dutch courage to keep my blushes back."

"Well," said the pilot when the whisky came, "here's lots of cargo, Captain, and good bonuses."

"Here's deep-draught steamers for you, pilot, and plenty of water under 'em."

The whisky drained down its appointed channels, and the pilot said: "By the by, I've this for you, Captain," and brought out a letter-card.

"Typewritten address," said Kettle. "No postmark on the stamp. Who's it from?"

"Man I came across. Look you, though, I didn't know him ; but he said there was a useful tip in the letter which it would please you to have after you sailed."

Kettle tore off the perforated edges, and looked inside the card. Here was another anonymous com-

munication, also from "Well-wisher," and, as before
warning him against **the** machinations of Gedge.
"Got no idea who the man was who gave it you?"
he asked.

"Well, I **did have a bit of** talk with him **and a**
drink, and I rather gathered he might have had
something to do with insurance; but he didn't say
his name. Why, isn't he a friend of yours?"

"I rather think he is," said **Kettle**; "but I can't
be quite sure yet." He did not add that the anonymous writer guaranteed him **a present of** £50 if the
Sultan of Labuan drew **no** insurance money till he
had moored her in Port Said.

From the very outset, the **voyage of** the *Sultan
of Labuan* was unpropitious. Before she **was clear**
of the Usk it was found that three more of her crew
had managed to slip away ashore, and so were gone
beyond replacement. Whilst she was still **in the**
brown, muddy waters of the Bristol Channel, there
were two several breakdowns **in** the engine-room
which necessitated stoppages and anxious repairs.
The engines of the *Sultan of Labuan* were her weak
spot, for otherwise her hull was sound enough. But
these machines were old, and wasteful in steam, and
made all the difference in economy which divides a
profit from a loss in these modern **days of** fierce sea
competition."

With Murgatroyd, the old blue-face mate, Kettle
had been shipmates before, and there **existed**
between the two men a strong dislike and a certain
mutual esteem. They interviewed over duty matters
when the pilot left. "Mr. Murgatroyd," said the
little skipper, "you'll keep hatches off, and do every

thing for ventilation. This Welsh coal's as gassy as petroleum."

" Aye, aye," rumbled the mate ; " but how about when **heavy weather comes,** and the decks are full of water ? "

" You'll have fresh **orders** from me before then. Get hoses to work now and sluice down. The ship's **a** pig-stye."

" Aye, aye ; but the hands are dog-tired."

" Then it's your place to drive them. I should **have** thought you'd been long enough at sea to know that. But if you aren't up to your business, **just say, and** I'll swop you over with **the** second mate **right now.**"

The old mate's face grew purpler. " If you want a driver," he said, " you shall have one ; " and with that he went his ways and roused the tired deck-hands to **work,** after the time-honoured methods.

But if Captain Kettle did not spare his crew, he was equally hard on himself. He was at sea now and wearing his sea-going conscience, which was an entirely different piece of mental mechanism to that which regulated his actions ashore. He had re-ceived Mr. Gedge's precise instructions to run the coal boat in the ordinary method, and he intended to do it relentlessly and to the letter.

He had had his doubts about **Mr.** Gedge's real wishes before, and even the episode of Miss Payne, the typewriter, had not altogether deceived him ; but the second letter from " Well-wisher," which the pilot brought on board, cleared the matter up beyond a doubt. There was not the faintest chance that Gedge had written that ; there was not the faintest reason to disbelieve now that Gedge wished his uneconomical steamboat off his hands, and had arranged for her never again to come into port.

Now, properly approached—say with sealed orders to be opened only at sea—I think there is very little doubt but what Captain Kettle would have undertaken to carry out this piece of nefarious business himself. The average mariner thinks no more of "making the insurance pay" than the average traveller does of robbing his fellow countrymen by the importation of Belgian cigars and Tauchnitz novels from a Channel packet. And with Kettle, too, loyalty to an employer, so long as that employer treated him squarely, ranked high. But for a second time "Well-wisher" had repeated the word "catspaw," and for his purpose he could not have used a better spur.

The little captain's face grew grim as he read it. "By James!" he muttered, "if that's the game he's trying to play, I'll make him rue it."

However, though at the beginning of a voyage it may be easy to make a resolve like this, it is not so easy to carry it into practical effect. If the machinery was on board, human or otherwise, for making the *Sultan of Labuan* fail to reach port, it was not at all probable that Kettle would find it before he saw it in working order. When arrangements for a bit of barratry of this kind are gone about nowadays, they are performed with shrewdness. Your ingenious gentlemen, who makes a devil of clockwork and guncotton to blow out a steamer's bottom, or makes a compact with one of her crew to open the bilge-cocks, is dexterous enough to cover up his trail very completely, having a wholesome awe of the law of the land, and a large distaste for penal servitude.

Moreover, Captain Owen Kettle was not the man to receive gratuitous information on such a point from his underlings. To begin with, he was the *Sultan of Labuan's* captain, and, by the immemorial etiquette on the sea, a ship's captain is always a man socially apart. He is a dictator for the time being, with supreme power of life and death ; is addressed as " Sir "; and would be regarded with social awe and coldness by his own brother, if the said brother were on board as one of the mates or one of the assistant engineers.

With the chief engineer alone, although he does not sit at meat with him, may a merchant captain unbend, and with the chief of the *Sultan of Labuan* Kettle had picked a difference over a commission on bunkering not ten minutes after he had first stepped on board. He had the undoubted knack of commanding men ; he could look exactly after his employer's property ; but he had an unfortunate habit of making himself hated in the process.

Over that initial episode of washing the coal-grime from the ship's outer fabric, he had already come into intimate contact with his crew. The tired deck-hands had refused duty : clumsy old Murgatroyd had endeavoured to force them into it by the time-honoured methods, and had been knocked down in the scuffle and trampled on ; when up came Kettle, already spruce and clean, and laid impartially into the whole grimy gang of them with a deck-scrubber. They were new to their little skipper's virtues, and thought at first that they would treat him as they

had already treated the fat old mate, and as a consequence bleeding faces and cracked heads were plentiful, and curses went up, bitter and deep, in half the
tongues of Europe. But Kettle still remained spruce
and clean, and aggressive and untouched.

It takes some art to thoroughly thrash a dozen
savage, full-grown men with a light broom without
breaking the stick or knocking off the head, and the
crew of the *Sultan of Labuan* were not slow to recognise their Captain's ability. But at the same
time they were not inspired with any overpowering
love for him.

In the course of that night an iron belaying-pin
whisked up out of the darkness, and knocked off his
cap as he stood on the upper bridge, and just before
the dawn a chunk of coal whizzed up and smashed
itself into splinters on the wheelhouse wall, not an
inch from his ear. But as Kettle replied to the first
of these compliments by three prompt revolver
shots almost before the thrower had time to think,
and rushed out and caught the second assailant by
the neck-scruff and forced him to eat up every scrap
of coal that had been thrown, the all-nation crew decided that he was too ugly to tackle usefully, and
tacitly agreed to let him alone for the future, and to
do their lawful work. The which, of course, was exactly what Kettle desired.

By this time the *Sultan of Labuan* had run down
the Cornish coast, had rounded Land's End, and was
standing off on a course which would make Finis-
terre her next landfall. The glass was sinking
steadily; the sea-scape was made up of blacks and
whites and lurid greys; but though the air was cold

and raw, the weather was not any worse than need have been expected for the time of year. The hatches were off, and a good strong smell of coal-gas billowed up from below and mingled with the sea scents.

With all a northern sailor's distrust for a "Dago," Kettle had spotted his spruce young Italian second mate as Gedge's probable tool, and watched him like the apple of his eye. No man's actions could have been more innocent and normal, and this of course, made things all the more suspicious. The engineer staff, who had access to the bilge-cocks, and could arrange disasters to machinery, were likewise, *ex officio*, suspicious persons, but as it was quite impossible to overlook them at all hours and on all occasions, he had regretfully to take them very largely on trust.

Blundering, incompetent old Murgatroyd, the mate, was the only man on board in whose honesty Kettle had the least faith, simply because he considered him too stupid to be intrusted with any operation so delicate as barratry, and to Murgatroyd he more or less confided his intentions.

"I hear there's a scheme on board to scuttle this steamboat," he said, "because she's too expensive to run. Well, Mr. Gedge, the owner, gave me orders to run her, and he told me he made a profit on her. I'm going by Mr. Gedge's words, and I'm going to take her to Port Saïd. And let me tell you this, if she stops anywhere on the road, and goes down, all hands go down with her, even if I have to shoot them my-self. So they'd better hear what's in the wind, and

have a chance to save their own skins. You understand what I mean?"

" Aye," grunted the mate.

" Well, just let word of it slip out—in the right
way, you understand."

" Aye, aye. Hadn't we better get the hatches on
and battened down? She's shipping in green pretty
often now, and the weather's worsening. There's a
good slop of water getting down below, and they
say it's all the bilge pumps can do to keep it under."

" Mr. Meddle Murgatroyd," Kettle snapped, "are
you master of this blamed ship, or am I? You
leave me to give my orders when I think fit, and get
down off this bridge."

" Aye," grunted the mate, and waddled clumsily
down below.

The old man's suggestion about the hatches had
touched upon a sore point. Kettle knew quite well
that it was dangerous to leave the great gaps in the
decks undefended by planking and tarpaulin. A
high sea was running, and the heavy-laden coal-boat
rode both deep and sodden. Already he had put
her a point and a half to westward of her course, so
as to take the oncoming seas more fairly on the
bow.

But still he hung on to the open hatches. The coal
below was gassy to a degree, and if the ventilation
was stopped it would be terribly liable to explosion.
The engine and boiler rooms were bulkheaded off,
and there was no danger from these; but the subtle
coal-gas would spread over all the rest of the vessel's
living quarters—as the smell hinted—and a carelessly
lit match might very comfortably send the whole of

her decks hurtling into the air.   Kettle had no wish to meet Mr. Gedge's unspoken wishes by an accident of this sort.

However, it began to be plain that as they drew nearer to the Bay the weather worsened steadily, and at last it came to be a choice between battening down the hatches both forward and aft, or being incontinently swamped.   Hour after hour Kettle in his glistening oilskins had been stumping backwards and forwards across the upper bridge, watching his steamboat like a cat, and holding on with his order to the very furthest moment.   But at last he gave the command to batten down, and both watches rushed to help the carpenter carry it out.   The men were horribly frightened.   It seemed to them that in that gale, and with that sea running, it was insane not to have battened her down long before.

The hands clustered on the lurching iron decks with the water swirling against them waist-high, and shipped the heavy hatch covers, and got the tarpaulins over; and then the Norwegian carpenter keyed all fast with the wedges, working like some amphibious animal half his time under water.

The *Sultan of Labuan* was fitted with no cowl ventilators to her holds, and even if these had been fitted they would have been carried away.   So from the moment of battening down, the gas which oozed from the coal mixed with the air till the whole ship became one huge explosive bomb, which the merest spark would touch off.   Captain Kettle called his mate to him and gave explicit orders.

"You know what a powder hulk is like, Mr. Mate?"

" Aye," said Murgatroyd.

" Well, this ship is a sight more dangerous, and we have got to take care if we do not want to go to Heaven quick. It's got to be ' all lights out ' aboard this ship till the weather eases and we can get hatches off again. Go round now and see it done yourself, Mr. Murgatroyd, please. Watch the doctor dowse the galley fire, and then go and take away all the forecastle matches so the men can't smoke. Put out the side lights, the masthead light, and the binnacle lamps. Quartermasters must steer as best they can from the unlit card."

" Aye, aye. But you don't mean the side lights too, do ye? There's a big lot of shipping here in the Bay, and we might easy get run down—" The old man caught an ugly look from Kettle's face and broke off. And grumbling some ancient saw about " obeying orders if you break owners," he shuffled off down the ladder.

Heavier and heavier grew the squalls, carrying with them spindrift which beat like gravel against the two oilskinned tenants of the collier's upper bridge ; worse and worse grew the sea. Great, green waves reared up like walls, crashed on board, and filled the lower decks with boiling, yeasty surge. The funnel-stays and the scanty rigging hummed like harp strings to the gale.

Deep though she was in the water, there were times when her stern heaved up clear, and the propeller raced in a noisy catherine-wheel of fire and foam. On every side, ahead, abeam, and astern, were nodding yellow lights, jerked about by unseen ships over thunderous, unseen waves. It was a regular Biscay gale, such as all vessels may count on in that corner of the seas one voyage out of eight, a gale with **heavy** seas in the midst of a dense crowd of shipping. But there was nothing in it which seamanship under ordinary circumstances could not meet.

Captain Kettle hung on hour after **hour under shelter of** the dodgers on the upper bridge, a small, wind-brushed figure in yellow oilskins and black rubber thigh-boots. About such a "breeze" in an ordinary way he would have thought little. Taking **his** vessel through it with the minimum of danger was only part of the daily mechanical routine. But **he stood there a prey to** the liveliest anxiety.

The thousand-and-one dangers in the Bay appeared before **him** magnified. If the ship for any sudden and unavoidable reason went down, the odds were that he himself and all hands would be drowned ; but at the same time Gedge would be gratified in so easily touching the coveted insurance money. The fear of death did not worry the little skipper in **the** very least degree whatever, but he had a most thorough objection to being in any way Mr. Gedge's catspaw.

Twice they had near escapes from being run down. The first time was from a sodden blundering Cardiff ore steamer, which was driving north through **the** thick of it, with very little of herself showing except two stumpy masts and a brine-washed smokestack. She would have obviously drowned out **any** lookout on her fore deck, and the bridge officers got too much spindrift in their eyes **to** see with any clearness. But time is money, and even Cardiff ore steamers must make passages, and so her master drove **her** blindly ahead full steam, slap-slop-wallow, **and** trusted that other people would get out of his way.

Kettle's keen eyes picked **her** up out of the sea mists just in time, and ported his own helm, and missed her sheering bow with the *Sultan of Labuan's* quarter by a short two fathoms. A touch in that insane turmoil of sea would have sent both steamers down to the shells and the flickering weed below; but there was no touch, and so each went her way **with** merely a perfunctory interchange of curses, which were blown into nothingness by **the** gale. Escapes on these occasions didn't count, and **it is** etiquette not to speak about them ashore afterwards.

The second shave came from a big white-painted Cape liner, which came up from astern, lit like a theatre, and almost defying the very gale itself. Her lookouts and officers were on the watch for lights. But the unlit collier, which was half her time masked by the seas like a half-tide rock, never struck their notice.

Kettle, with all a shipmaster's sturdy dislike for shifting his helm when he legally had the right of the road, held on till the great knife-like bow was **not a** score of yards from his taffrail. But then he gave way, roared out an order to the quartermaster at the wheel, and the *Sultan of Labuan* fell away to starboard. As if the coal-boat had been a magnet, the Cape liner followed, drawing nearer hand over fist.

Changing direction further was as dangerous as keeping on **as** he was, so Kettle bawled to the quartermaster to " Steady on that," and then the great, white steam-hotel suddenly seemed to wake to her danger, and swerved off on her old course again. **So close** were they, that Kettle fancied he could **hear** the quick, agitated rattle of her wheel engines **as** they gave her a "hard down" helm. **And he** certainly saw officers on her high upper-**bridge** peering at him through the drifting **sea**-smoke with a curiosity that was more than pleasant.

"Trying to pick out the old tub's name," he mused grimly, "so as to report me for carrying no lights. By James, I wish some of those dandy pas-senger-boat officers could try this low-down end of the tramping trade for a bit."

Night went and day came, gray, and wet, and desolate. The heavier squalls had passed away, but a whole gale still remained, and the sea was, if anything, heavier. The coal-boat rarely showed all of herself at once above the waters. Her progress was a succession of dives, her decoration (when she was visible) a fringe of spouting scuppers. Watch **had** succeeded watch with the dogged patience of sailor men ; but watch after watch Kettle hung on behind the canvas dodgers at the weather end of **the** bridge. He was red-eyed and white-cheeked, **his** torpedo beard was foul with sea salt, he was un-pleasant to look upon, but he was undeniably very much awake, and when the accident came (which he concluded was **Mr.** Gedge's effort to realise the coal-boat's insurance), he was quite ready to cope **with** emergencies.

From somewhere in the bowels of the ship there came the muffled boom of an explosion ; the bridge buckled up beneath his feet, so that he was very nearly wrenched from his hold; and the iron main deck, which at that moment happened to be free of water, rippled and heaved like a tin biscuit-box moves when it is kicked. There was a tinkle of broken glass as some blown-out skylights crashed back upon the deck.

He looked forward and he looked aft, and to his surprise saw that both hatches were still in place and that very little actual damage was visible, and then he had his attention occupied by another matter. From the stoke-hold, from the forecastle, and from the engine-room the frightened crew poured out into the open, and some scared wretch cried out to "lower away zem boats."

Here was a situation that needed dealing with at once, and Kettle was the man to do it. From beneath his oilskins he lugged out the revolver which they knew so painfully already, and showed it with ostentation. "By James," he shouted, "do you want to be taught who's captain here? I'll give cheap lessons if you ask."

His words reached them above the hooting and brawl of the gale, and they were cowed into sullen obedience.

"Carpenter, take a couple of men and away below with you and see what's broke. You blessed, split-trousered mechanics, away down to your engine-room or I'll come and kick you there. The second mate and his watch get tarpaulins over those broken skylights. Where's Mr. Murgatroyd? In his bunk, I suppose, as usual; not his watch: no affair of his if the ship's blown to Heaven when he's off duty. Here, you steward, go and turn out Mr. Murgatroyd."

The men bustled about after their errands, and the engines which had stopped for a minute, began to rumble on again. Captain Kettle paraded the swaying bridge and awaited developments.

Presently the bareheaded steward fought his way up the bridge-ladder against the tearing wind, and bawled out some startling news. "It's Mr. Murgatroyd's room that's been blown up, sir, made a 'orrid mess of. Chips says 'e picked up 'is lighted pipe in the alleyway, sir, an' it must a' been that that fired the gas."

"The blamed old thickhead," said Kettle savagely.

"'E was arskin' for you, sir, was the mate, though we couldn't rightly make out what 'e said."

"He won't be pleased to see me. Smoking, by James, was he?"

"The mate's burnt up like a piece of coke," said the steward persuasively. "'E cawn't last long."

The carpenter came up on the bridge. "Dose blow-up vas not so bad for der ole ship, sir. She nod got any plates started dot I can see. Dey have der bilge-pumps running, but der's nod much water. Und der mate, sir. He say he vould like to see you. He's in ver' bad way."

"All right," said Kettle, "I'll go and see him." He called up the Italian second mate on to the bridge and gave over charge of the ship to him, and then went below.

The author of all the mischief, the stupid old man who, through sheer crass ignorance, had gone to bed and smoked a pipe in this powder mine, lay horribly injured in the littered alleyway, with a burst straw cushion under the shocking remnants of his head. Most of his injuries were plain to the eye, and it was a marvel that he lingered on at all. It was very evident that he could not live for long, and it was clear, too, that he wanted to speak.

Kettle's resenment died at the sight of this poor charred cinder of humanity, and he knelt in the litter and listened. The sea noises and the ship noises without almost drowned the words, and the old mate's voice was very weak. It was only here and there he could pick up a sentence.

"*Nearly got to wind'ard of you, skipper. . . . It was me. . . . Gedge paid me fifty pound for the job . . . scuttle her . . . after Gib . . . would 'a done it, too . . . in spite of your blooming teeth.*"

The old fellow broke off, and Kettle leant near to him. "How were you going to scuttle her?" he asked.

There was no answer. A second time he repeated the question, and then again a third time. The mate heard him. The sea roared outside, the wind boomed overhead, the cluttered wreckage clanged about the alleyway. The old man was past speech but he opened an eye, his one remaining eye, and slowly and solemnly winked.

It was his one recorded attempt at humour during a lifetime, and the effort was his last. His jaw dropped, wagging to the thud of the ship, his eye opened in a glassy, unseeing stare, and he was as dead a thing as the iron deck he lay upon.

"Well, matey," said Kettle, apostrophising the poor charred form, "we've been shipmates before, but I never liked you. But, by James, you had your points.   You shall be buried by a *pukka* parson in Gib, and have a stone put over your ugly old head, if I have to pay for it **myself**.   I think I **can** hammer out a **bit of** verse, too, **which**'ll make **that** stone a thing **people** will remember.

"By James, though, won't Gedge be **mad over this**! Gedge will think I spotted the game you were playing for him, and murdered you out of hand.   Well, that's all right, and **it** won't hurt you, matey.   I want Gedge to understand I'm a man that's got to be dealt straight with.   I want Mr. Blessed Gedge **to** understand that **I'm** not the kind of lamb to make into a catspaw by any manner **of means**.   I bet he does tumble to that, too.   But I bet also that he sacks me from this berth before I've got the coals over **into** the lighters at Port Saïd.   By James, yes, Gedge is a man that sticks **to** his plans, and as he can't lose the *Sultan of Labuan* with me as her skipper, he'll jerk another old man **into** the chart-house on the end of a wire, who'll do the job more to his satisfaction."

The Norwegian carpenter came up, and **asked a** question.

"**No, no, Chips;** put **the** canvas away.   I want you to knock **up some** sort of a box for the poor old mate, and **we'll** take him to Gib, and plant him there in style.   I owe **him a bit.**   We'll all get safe enough to Port **Saïd now.**"

CHAPTER XI.

THE SALVING OF THE DUNCANSBY HEAD.

" THE boat's an old P. and O. lifeboat," said Mr.
McTodd, " diagonal-built of teak, and quite big
enough for the purpose. Of course, something
with steam in her would be better, because we're
both steamer-men ; but that's out of the question.
That would mean too many to share. So the thing
is, can you buy this lifeboat and victual her for the
trip ? I'm no' what ye might call a capitalist myself, just for the moment."

Captain Kettle eyed the grimy serge of his companion with disfavour. " You don't look it," he
said. " That last engine-room you got sacked from
must have been a mighty filthy place."

" 'Twas," said McTodd. " But as it happened, I
didn't get the sack. I ran from her here in Gib because I'd no wish to get back to England and have
this news useless in my pocket. And, of course, I
had to let slide the eight pound in wages that was
due to me."

" By James, it's beginning to look like business
when a Scottie runs away from siller that he's righte-
ously earned."

" Well, I'm no' denying it was a speculation. It's
a bit of a speculation, if ye come to reckon up, ask-

ing a newly-sacked sea captain to join in such a venture."

Kettle's face hardened. "See here," he said, "keep a civil tongue in your head, or go out of this lodging. I'm to be treated with respect, or I don't deal with you."

"Then let my clothes alone and be civil yourself. It's a mighty dry shop this, Captain."

"I've no whisky in the place nor spare money to buy it. If we're to go on with this plan of yours, we shall want every dollar that can be raised."

"That's true, and neither me nor 'Tonio have ten shillings between us."

Kettle gave up pacing the room and sat himself on the edge of the table and frowned. "I don't see the use of taking either Antonio, if that's his name, or your other Dago. I don't like the breed of them. You and I would be quite enough to handle an open boat, and quite able to take care of ourselves. If the wreck's got the money on her, and we finger it, we'll promise to bring them back their share all right; and if the thing's a fizzle, as it's very likely to be, well, they'll be saved a very unpleasant boat-cruise."

"It's no go," said the engineer, "and you may make up your mind to have them as shipmates, Captain, or sit here on your tail where you are. D'ye think I've any appetite for Dagos myself? No, sir, no more than you. I don't trust them no more than a stripped thread. And they don't trust me. They wouldn't trust you. They would no' trust the Provost of Edinboro' if he was to make similar proposals to them."

"Then have you no idea where this steamboat was put on the ground?"

"Man, I've telled ye 'no' already."

"Seems to me you don't know much, Mr. Mc-Todd."

"I don't. What I know is this: I came ashore here after a vera exhausting trip down the Mediterranean, just for a drink to fortify the system against the chills on the run home. I went to a little dark shebeen, where I kenned the cut-throat in charge, and gave the name of the ship I wanted sending back to, in case sleep overcame me, and settled down for an afternoon's enjoyment. Ye'll ken what I mean?"

"I know you're a drunken beast when you get the chance for an orgie."

"I have my weaknesses, Captain, or maybe I'd no' have left Ballindrochater, where my father was Free Kirk Meenister. We both have our weaknesses, Captain Owen Kettle, and it's they that have brought us to what we are."

"If you don't leave me alone and get on with your yarn," said Kettle acidly, "you'll find yourself in the street."

"Oh, I like your hospitality fine, and I'll stay, thanks. Weel, I'd just settled myself down to a good square drink at this Spaniard's shebeen, when out of a dark corner comes 'Tonio and the other Dago, bowing and taking off their hats as polite as though I'd been an archbishop at the very least.

"I'd met 'Tonio in Lagos. He was greaser on a branch boat there, and I was her second engineer. He's some English, and he did the talking. The

17

other Dago knew nothing but his **own** unrighteous tongue, and just said *see-see* when 'Tonio explained to him **what** was going on, and grinned like a bagful of monkeys. I give **'Tonio** credit: **he** spat out his tale like a man.   **He and his** mate were **in** the stoke-hold of a **Dago** steamboat coming from **the River** Plate to Genoa, and calling at some of the Western Islands *en route.*

"One night they were just going off watch, and **were** leaning over the rail to get a breath of cool **air** before turning in. They were steaming past some rocky islands, and there in plain sight of them was a vessel hard and fast ashore. There was no mistake about it: they both saw her: a steamboat of some **fifteen** hundred tons. And what was more, the **other Portugee, 'Tonio's** friend, **said** he knew her. According to him she was the *Duncansby Head.* He'd served in her stokehold three voyages, and he said he'd know her anywhere."

"**A** Dago's word isn't worth much for a thing like that," said Kettle.

"Wait a **bit.** The **pair of them** stayed where they were and looked at the rest of the watch on **deck.** The second **mate on the** bridge was staring **ahead** sleepily; the quartermaster at the wheel was nodding and blinking at the binnacle; the lookout on the forecastle was seated on a fife-rail, snoring; **no one of** these had seen **the** wreck. And so they themselves didn't talk. Their boat was running short of coal, and so she put into Gib here to re-bunker; and from another Dago on the coal-hulk, who came aboard to help trim, they got some news. The *Duncansby Head* had shifted her cargo at sea, had picked up heavy weather and got unmanageable, and had been left by her crew in the boats. The mate's boat and the second mate's boat were picked up; the old man's boat had not been heard of. It was supposed that the *Duncansby Head* herself had foundered immediately after she was deserted."

"Yes, all that's common gossip on the Rock. Mulready was her skipper: J. R. Mulready: I'd known him years."

"Weel, poor deevil, it's perhaps good for him he's drowned."

"Yes, I suppose it is. He's saved a sight of trouble. D'ye know, Mac, Jimmy Mulready and I passed for mate the same day, and went to sea with our bran-new tickets in the same ship, him as mate, me as second."

"The sea's an awful poor profession for all, except a shipowner that lives ashore."

"'Tis. Yes, that's a true word. It is. And so Antonio and his mate told the other Dago that they'd seen the wreck?"

"Not much. They kept their heads shut. There was money in the idea if it could only be worked, and a Portugee likes dollars as much as a white man. So there you have the whole yarn, except that they got to know that the *Duncansby* was on her way home after a long spell at tramping when she got into trouble, and carried all the money she'd earned in good solid gold in the chart-house drawer."

"It sounds a soft thing, I'll not deny," said Kettle. "But why should Mr. Antonio and his friend come to you?"

"They ran from their ship here in Gib, and laid

low till she had sailed.   It was the natural thing for them to do.   But when they began to look round them in cold blood, they found themselves a bit on the beach.   They'd no money ; there's such a shady crowd here in Gib that everything's well watched, and they couldn't steal ; and so there was nothing for it but to take a partner into the concern.   Of course being Dagos, they weren't likely to trust one of their own sort."

"Not much.   And so they came to you?"

"They knew me," said the engineer.   "And I came to you because I knew you, Captain.   I'm no navigator myself, though I can make shift to handle a sail boat, so a navigator was wanted.   I said to myself the man, in all creation for this job is Captain Kettle, and then what should I do but run right up against you."

"Thank you, Mac."

"But there's one other thing you'll have to do, and that's buy, beg, borrow or steal the ship to carry the expedition, because the rest of us can't raise a blessed shilling amongst us.   It needn't be a big outlay.   That old P. and O. lifeboat which I was talking about would carry us fine, and I think three five-pound notes would buy her."

"Very well," said Kettle.   "And now let's get a move on us.   There's been enough time spent in talk, and the sooner we're on that wreck the less chance there is of any one else getting there to over-haul her before us."

It would be unprofitable to follow in detail the fitting out of this wrecking expedition upon insufficient capital, and so be it briefly stated that the old lifeboat (which had passed through many hands since she was cast from the P. and O. service) was purchased by dint of haggling for an absurdly small sum, and victualled and watered for eighteen days. The Portuguese, who still refused to disclose the precise location of the wreck, said that it might take a fortnight to reach her, and prudence would have suggested that it was advisable to take at least a month's provisions. But the meagreness of their capital flatly forbade this, and they were only able to furnish the boat with what would spin out to eighteen days on an uncomfortably short ration. They trusted that what pickings they might find in the storerooms of the wreck herself would provide them for the return voyage.

With this slender equipment then, they sailed forth from Gibraltar Bay, an obvious party of adventurers. They were bombarded by the questions and the curious stares of all the shipping interest on the Rock; they were flatly given to understand by a naval busybody (who had been bidden carry his inquisitiveness to the deuce) that they had earned official suspicion, and would be watched accordingly: and if ever ill-wishes could sink a craft, that ancient P. and O. lifeboat was full to her marks.

The voyage did not begin with prosperity. There is always a strong surface current running in through the Straits, and just then the breezes were light. The lifeboat was a dull sailer, and her people in consequence had the mortification of keeping Carnero Point and the frowning Rock behind in sight for three baking days. The two Portuguese were

first profane, then sullen, then frightened ; some
saint's day, it appeared, had been violated by the
start ; and they began first to hint at, and then to
insist on a return.   To which Kettle retorted that
he was going to see the matter through now, if he
had to hang in the Straits for the whole eighteen
days, and subsist for the rest of the trip upon dew
and their belts ; and in this McTodd backed him up.

Once started and away from the whisky bottle,
there was nothing very yielding about Mr. McTodd.
Only one compromise did Kettle offer to make.   He
would stand across and drop his Portuguese partners
on the African shore if they on their part would disclose the whereabouts of the wreck ; and in due
time, when the dividends were gathered, he faith-
fully promised them their share.   But to this they
would not consent.   In fact, there was a good deal
of mutual distrust between the two parties.

At last, however, a kindly slant of wind took the
lifeboat in charge, and hustled her wetly out into
broad Atlantic ; and when they had run the shores
of Europe and Africa out of sight, and there was
nothing round them but the blue heaving water, with
here and there a sail and a steamer's smoke, then
Senhor Antonio saw fit to give Captain Kettle a
course.

" We was steamin' from a Teneriffe to Madeira when
we saw those a rocks with *Duncansby Head* asho'."

" H'm," said Kettle.   " Those'll be the Salvage
Islands."

" Steamah was pile up on de first.   'Nother island
we pass after."

" That's Piton Island if I remember.   Let's have

a look at the chart."   He handed over the tiller to McTodd, took a tattered Admiralty chart from one of the lockers, and spread it on the damp floor gratings.   The two Portuguese helped with their brown paws to keep it from fluttering away.   "Yes, either Little Piton or Great Piton.   Which side did you pass it on?"

Antonio thumped a gunwale of the lifeboat.

"Kept it on the port hand going North, did you? Then that'll be Great Piton, and a sweet shop it is for reefs according to this chart.   I wish I'd a Directory.   It will be a regular cat's dance getting in. But I say, young man, isn't there a light there?"

"Lighta?   I not understand."

"You savvy—lighthouse—*faro*—show-mark-light in dark?"

"Oh, yes, lighta-house.   I got there.   No, no lighta-house."

"Well, there's one marked here as 'projected,' and I was afraid it might have come.   I forgot the Canaries were Spanish, and Madeira was Portugee, and that these rocks which lie halfway would be a sort of slack cross between the pair of them. *Mañana's* the motto, isn't it, Tonio?   Never do to-day what you hope another flat will do for you to-morrow."

"*Si, si, mañana*," said the Portuguese, who had not understood one word in ten of all this.   "*Mañana* we find rich, plenty too-much rich.   God sava Queen!"

"Those Canary fishing schooners land on the Salvages sometimes," said McTodd, "so I heard once in Las Palmas."

"I guess we got to take our chances, Mac.   If

the old wreck's been overhauled before we get there, it's our back luck; if she hasn't been skimmed clean, we'll take what there is, and I fancy **we** shall be men enough to stick to it.   It isn't as if she was piled up on some civilised beach, with coastguards to take possession and all the rest of it.   The islands **are either** Spanish or Portugee.   They belong to a pack **of** thieves anyway; and we've just as much right **to** help ourselves as anyone else has.   What we've got **to do** at present is to shove this old ruin of a life-boat along as though she were a racing yacht.   At the shortest we've got seven hundred miles of blue water ahead of us."

Open-boat voyaging in the broad Atlantic may have **its pleasures, b**ut these, such as they were, did not appeal **to** either Kettle or his companions. They were thoroughgoing steamer sailors; they despised sails; and the smallness of their craft gave them qualms both mental and physical.   **By day the** sun scorched them with intolerable glare and violence; by night the clammy sea mists drenched them **to** the bone.

For a larger vessel the weather would have been accounted favourable; for their cockle-shell it was **once** or twice terrific.   **In two** squalls **that** they ran **into,** breaking combers filled the lifeboat to the thwarts, and they had to bale for their bare lives. They were cramped and sore from their constrained position and want of exercise; they got sea-sores on their wrists and salt-grime on every inch of their persons; they **were** growing gaunt on the scanty **rations;** and, in fact, a better presentation of a boat full of desperate castaways it would be hard to hit upon. Flotillas of iridescent, pink-sailed nautilus scudded constantly beside them, dropping as constantly astern; and these made their only company. Except for the nautilus, the sea seemed desolate.

In this guise then they ended their voyage, which had spun out to nigh upon a thousand miles through **contrary winds** and the necessity for incessant tacking; and in the height of one blazing afternoon they **rose** to the tops of the islands out of **a** twinkling turquoise sea.

These appeared first as mere dusty black rocks sticking up out of the calm blue—Great Salvage Island to the northward, and Great Piton to the south and beyond—but they grew as the boat neared them, and presently appeared to be built upon a frieze of dazzling feathery whiteness. The lifeboat swept on to reach them, climbing and diving over the rollers. She had canvas decks, quartermast high, contrived to throw off the sprays; and over these the faces of her people peered ahead, wild and gaunt, salt-crusted and desperate.

Great Salvage Island drew abeam and passed away astern; Great Piton lay close ahead now, fringed with a thousand reefs, each with its spouting break**ers.** The din of the surf came to them loudly up the wind. A flock of seafowl, screaming and circling, **sailed** out **to** escort them in; and ahead, behind the banks of breakers, drawing them on as water will draw a choking man, was the rusted smokestack **and** stripped masts of a derelict merchant steamer.

There is a yarn about an open boat which had voyaged twelve hundred miles over the lonely Pacific, coming upon a green atoll, and being sailed reck-lessly in through the surf, and drowning every soul on board ; and the yarn is easily believable.   Captain Kettle and his companions had undergone horrible privations ; here, at last, was the isle of their hopes, and the treasure (as it seemed) in full view ; but, by some intolerable fate, they were barred from it by relentless walls of surf.   Kettle ran in as close as he dared, and then flattened in his sheets, and sailed the lifeboat close-hauled along the noisy line of the breakers to the Norrard, looking for an opening.

The two Portuguese grumbled openly, and when not a ghost of a landing-place showed, and Kettle put her about to sail back again, even the cautious McTodd put up his word to " run in, and risk it."

But Kettle, though equally sick as they were of the boat and her voyage, had all a sailor's dislike for losing his ship whatever she might be, and cowed them all with voice and threats ; and at last his for-bearance was rewarded. A slim passage through the reef showed itself at the southern end of the island ; and down it they dodged, trimming their sheets six times a minute, with an escort of dangers always close on either hand ; and finally ran into a rocky bay which held comparatively smooth water.

There was no place to beach the boat ; they had to anchor her off ; but with a whip on the cable they were able to step ashore on a ledge of stone, and then haul the boat off again out of harm's way.

It may be thought that they capered with delight at treading on dry land again ; but there was nothing of this. With their cramped limbs and disused joints, it was as much as they could do to hobble, and every step was a wrench. But the lure ahead of them was great enough to triumph over minor difficulties. Half a mile away **along** the rocks was the *Duncansby Head*, and for her **they raced at** the top of their crippled gait. And the seafowl screamed curiously above their heads.

They scratched and tore themselves in this fran- **tic** progress over the sharp volcanic rocks, they **choked** with thirst, they panted with their labor ; but none of these things mattered.

The deserted steamer, when they came to her, was lying off from the **shore at** the other side of a lake of deep water. But they were fit for no more waiting, and each, as he came opposite her, waded in out of his depth, and swam off with eager strokes. Davit-falls trailing in the water gave them an en- trance way, **and up** these they climbed with the quickness of apes ; and then, with one accord, they made for the pantry and **the** steward's storeroom. The gold which had lured them was forgotten ; the immediate needs of their famished bodies were the only things they remembered. They found a cheese, a box of musty biscuits, and a filter full of stale and tepid water; and **they** gorged till they were filled, and swore they had never sat to so deli- cious a meal.

With repletion came the thoughts of fortune again, and off they went to the charthouse to finger the coveted gold. But here was a disappointment ready and waiting for them. They had gone up in a body, neither nationality trusting the other, and together they ransacked the place with thorough- **ness.** There were papers in abundance, there were clothes furry with mildew, there was a broken box of cheap cigars; but of money there was not so much as a bronze piece.

"Eh, well," said Kettle, sitting back on the musty bedclothes, "we have had our trouble for nothing. Some one's been here first, and skimmed the place clean. By James, yes. And look on the floor there. See those cigarette ends? They're new and dry. If the old man had been a cigarette smoker he wouldn't have chucked his butts on his charthouse deck, and, even if he had done, they'd have been washed to bits when she was hove down on her beam ends. You can see by the decks outside that she's been pretty clean swept. No, it's those fishermen, as you say, who have been here before us."

"Well," said McTodd, "if I were a swearer, I could say a deal."

"The Dagos are swearing enough for the whole crowd of us, to judge by the splutter of them. The money's gone clean. It's vexing, but that's a fact. Still, I don't like to go back empty-handed."

"I'm as keen as yoursel'. There's that eight pound of my wages I left when I ran in Gib, that's got to be made up somehow. What's wrong with getting off the hatches, and seeing how her cargo's made up?"

"She's loaded with hides. I saw it on the manifest. There was Jimmy Mulready's scrawl at the foot of it. That photo there above the bed-foot will be his wife. Poor old Jimmy. He got religion before I did, and started his insurance, too, and, if he's kept them both up, he and his widow ought to be all right— By James, did you feel that ?"

McTodd stared round him.

"What ?" he asked.

"She moved.

"I took it for sure she was on the ground."

"So did I. But she isn't. There, you can feel her lift again."

They went **out** on deck. The sun was already dipping in the western sea behind **the** central hill of the island, and in another few minutes it would be **dark.** There is little twilight so far south. So they took cross bearings on the shore, and watched intently. Yes, there was not **a** doubt about it. The *Duncansby Head* floated, and she was moving across the deep water lake that held her.

"Mon !" said the engineer enthusiastically, "ye've a great head, and a great future before you. I'd never have guessed **it.**"

"I took it for granted she'd beaten her bottom out in getting here ; but she's blundered in through the reefs without touching ; and if she's come in, she can get out again, and we're the fellows to take her."

"With engines."

"With engines, yes. If she's badly broken down in the hardware shop, **we're done.** I'd forgotten the machinery, and that's a fact. We'll find a lantern, and I'll go down with you, Mac, and give them an inspect."

The two Portuguese had already sworn themselves to a standstill, and had gone below and found bunks; but the men from the little islands in the North had more energy in their systems, and they expanded it tirelessly. McTodd overhauled every nut, every bearing, every valve, every rod of the engines with an expert's criticism, and found nothing that would prevent active working; Kettle rummaged the rest of the ship; and far into the morning they foregathered again in the charthouse, and compared results.

She had been swept, badly swept; everything movable on deck was gone; cargo had shifted, and then shifted back again till she had lost all her list and was in proper trim; the engines were still workable if carefully nursed; and, in fact, though battered, she was entirely seaworthy. And while with tired gusto they were comparing these things, weariness at last got the better of them, and first one and then the other incontinently dropped off into the deadest of sleep.

That the *Duncansby Head* had come in unsteered and unscathed through the reefs, and therefore under steam and control could go out again, was on the face of it a very simple and obvious theory to propound; but to discover a passage through the rocks to make this practicable was quite another matter. For three days the old P. and O. lifeboat plied up and down from outside the reefs and had twenty narrow escapes from being smashed into staves. It looked as if Nature had performed a miracle, and taken the steamer bodily in her arms, and lifted her over at least a dozen black walls of stone.

The two Portuguese were already sick to death of

the whole business, but for their feelings neither Kettle nor McTodd had any concern whatever. They were useful in the working of the boat, and therefore they **were taken** along, **and** when they refused duty or did it with too much listlessness to please, they were cuffed into activity again. There was no verbal argument about the matter, "Work or Suffer" was the simple motto the **two** islanders went upon, **and it** answered admirably. They knew the breed of the Portuguese of old.

At last, by dint of daring and toil, the secret of the pass through the noisy spouting reefs was won; it was sounded carefully and methodically for sunken rocks, and noted in all possible ways; and **the** P. and O. lifeboat was hoisted on the *Duncansby's* davits. The Portuguese were driven down into the stokehold to represent double watches of a dozen men and make the requisite steam; McTodd fingered the rusted engines like **an** artist; and Kettle took his stand alone with the steam wheel on the upper bridge.

They had formally signed articles, and apportioned themselves pay, Kettle **as** Master, McTodd **as** Chief Engineer, and the Portuguese as firemen, because salvage is apportioned *pro rata*, and the more pay a man is getting the larger is his bonus. **On** which account (at McTodd's suggestion) they awarded themselves paper stipends which they could **feel** proud of, and put down the Portuguese for the ordinary fireman's wages then paid out of Gibraltar, neither more nor less. For, as the engineer said: "There **was** a fortune to be divided up somehow, and it would be a pity for a pair of unclean Dagos to have more than was absolutely necessary, seeing that they would not know what to do with it."

Captain Kettle felt it to be one of the supreme moments of his life when he rang on the *Duncansby's* bridge telegraph to " Half-speed ahead." Here was a bid for fortune such as very rarely came in any shipmaster's way ; not getting salvage, the larger part of which an owner would finger, for mere assistance, but taking to port a vessel which was derelict and deserted—the greatest and the rarest plum that the seas could offer. It was a thought that thrilled him.

But he had not much time for sentimental musings in this strain. A terribly nervous bit of pilotage lay ahead of him ; the motive power of his steamer was feeble and uncertain ; and it would require all his skill and resourcefulness to bring her out into deep blue water. Slowly she backed or went ahead, dodging round to get a square entrance to the fairway, and then with a slam Kettle rang on his telegraph to " Full speed ahead," so as to get her under the fullest possible command.

She darted out into the narrow, winding lane between the walls of broken water, and the roar of the surf closed round her. Rocks sprang up out of the deep—hungry black rocks, as deadly as explosive torpedoes. With a full complement of hands, and with a pilot for years acquainted with the place, it would have been an infinitely dangerous piece of navigation ; with a half-power steamer which had only one man all told upon her decks, and he almost a stranger to the place, it was a miracle how she got out unscathed. But it was a miracle assisted by the most brilliant skill. Kettle had surveyed the channel in the lifeboat, and mapped every rock in his head, and when the test came he was equal to it. It would be hard to come across a man of more iron nerve.

Backing, and going ahead, to get round right-angled turns of the fairway, shaving reefs so closely that the wash from them creamed over her rail, the battered old tramp steamer faced a million dangers for every fathom of her onward way ; but never once did she actually touch, and in the end she shot out into the clear, deep water, and gaily hit diamonds from the wavetops into the sunshine.

It is possible for a man to concentrate himself so deeply upon one thing that he is deaf to all else in the world ; and until he had worked the *Duncansby Head* out into the open, Captain Kettle was in this condition. He was dimly conscious of voices hailing him, but he had no leisure to give them heed. But when the strain was taken off, then there was no more disregarding the cries. He turned his head, and saw a half-sunk raft, which seven men with clumsy paddles were frantically labouring towards him along the outer edge of the reefs.

Without a second thought he rang off engines, and the steamer lost her way and fell into the trough and waited for them. From the first he had a fore-boding as to who they were ; but the men were obvi-ously castaway ; and by all the laws of the sea and humanity he was bound to rescue them.

Ponderously the raft paddled up and got under

the steamer's lee.   Kettle came down off the bridge
and threw them the end of a halliard, and eagerly
enough they scrambled up the rusted plating, and
clambered over the rail.   They looked around them
with curiosity, but with an obvious familiarity.

"I left my pipe stuck behind that stanchion," said
one, "and, by gum, it's there still."

"Fo'c's'le door's stove in," said another; "I
wonder if they've scoffed my chest."

"You Robinson Crusoes seem to be making yourselves at home," said Kettle.

One of the men knuckled his shock of hair.   "We
was on her, sir, when she happened her accident.
We got off in the Captain's boat, and she was
smashed to bits landing on great Salvage yonder.
We've been living there ever since on rabbits and
gulls and cockles till we built that raft and ferried
over here.   It was tough living, but I guess we were
better off than the poor beggars that were swamped
in the other boats."

"The other two boats got picked up."

"Did they though?   Then I call it beastly hard
luck on us."

"Captain Mulready was master, wasn't he?   Did
he get drowned when your boat went ashore?"

The sailor shrugged his shoulders.   "No, sir.
Captain Mulready's on the raft down yonder.   He
feels all crumpled up to find the old ship's afloat,
and you've got her out.   She'd a list on when we
left her that would have scared Beresford, but she's
chucked that straight again ; and who's to believe
it was ever there?"

Kettle grated his teeth.   "Thank, you, my lad,"

he said. " I quite see. Now get below and find
yourself something to eat, and then you go forrard
and turn too." Then, leaning his head over the
bulwark, he called down: " Jimmy !"

The broken man on the raft looked up. " Hullo,
Kettle, that you ? "

" Yes. Come aboard."

" No, thanks. I'm off back to the island. I'll
start a picnic there of my own. Good luck, old man."

" If you don't come aboard willingly, I'll send and
have you fetched. Quit fooling."

" Oh, if you're set on it," said the other tiredly,
and scrambled up the rope. He looked around with
a drawn face. " To think she should have lost that
list, and righted herself like this. I thought she
might turn turtle any minute when we quitted her ;
and I'm not a scary man either."

" I know you aren't. Come into the charthouse
and have a drop of whisky. There's your missus'
photo stuck up over the bed-foot. How's she ? "

" Dead, I hope. It will save her going to the
workhouse."

" Oh, rats. It's not as bad as that."

" If you'll tell me why not ? I shall lose my ticket
over this job, sure, when it comes before the Board
of Trade, and what owner's likely to give me another
ship ? "

" Well, Jimmy, you'll have to sail small, and live
on your insurance."

" I dropped that years ago, and drew out what
there was. Had to—with eight kids, you know.
They take a lot of feeding."

" Eight kids, by James !"

"Yes, eight kids, poor little beggars, and the missus and me all to go hungry from now onwards. But they do say workhouses are very comfortable nowadays. You'll look in and see us sometimes— won't you, Kettle?" He lifted the glass which had been handed to him. "Here's luck to you, old man, and you deserve it. I bought that whisky from a chandler in Rio. It's a drop of right, isn't it?"

"Here, chuck it," said Kettle.

"I'm sorry," said Captain Mulready, "but you shouldn't have had me on board. I should have been better picknicking by myself on Great Piton yonder. I can't make a cheerful shipmate for you, old man."

"Brace up," said Kettle.

"By the Lord, if I'd only been a day earlier with that raft," said the other musingly, "I could have taken her out, as you have done, and brought her home and I believe the firm would have kept me on. There need have been no inquiry; only 'delayed,' that's all; no one cares so long as a ship turns up sometime."

"It wouldn't have made any difference," said Kettle, frowning. "Some of those lousy Portuguese have been on board and scoffed all the money."

"What money?"

"Why, what she'd earned. What there was in the charthouse drawer."

The dishevelled man gave a tired chuckle. "Oh, that's all right. I put in at Las Palmas, and transferred it to the bank there, and sent home the receipt by the B. and A. mail boat to Liverpool. No, I'm pleased enough about the money. But it's this other thing I made the bungle of, just being **a day too** late with **that raft.**"

Kettle heard a sound and sharply turned his head. He saw a grimy man in **the** doorway. " Mr. Mc-Todd," he said, " who the mischief gave you leave to quit your engine-room ? Am I to understand you've been standing there in that doorway to listen ? "

" Her own engineer's come back, so I handed her **over** to him and came on deck for a spell. As for listening, I've heard every word that's been said. **Captain** Mulready, you have my vera **deepest** condolences."

" Mr. McTodd," said Kettle, with **a** sudden blaze **of** fury, " I'm captain of this ship, and you're intruding.   Get to Hamlet out of here."   He got up and strode furiously out of the door, and Mr. McTodd retreated before **him.**

" Now keep your hands off me," said the engineer. " I'm **as mad** about the thing **as** yourself, and I don't mind blowing off **a** few pounds of temper.   I don't know Captain Mulready, and you do, but I'd hate to see **any** man all crumpled **up** like that if **I** could help it."

" He could be helped by giving him back his ship, **and** I'd do **it** if **I** was by myself.   But I've got a Scotch partner, **and I'm not going to try** for the impossible."

" Dinna abuse Scotland," said McTodd, wagging a grimy forefinger. ^ It's your ain wife and bairns ye're thinking about."

" I ought to be, Mac, but, God help me ! I'm not."

" Varra weel," said McTodd ; " then, if that's the

case, skipper, just set ye doon here and we'll have a palaver."

"I'll hear what you've got to say," said Kettle more civilly, and for the next half-hour the pair of them talked as earnestly as only poor men can talk when they are deliberately making up their minds to resign a solid fortune which is already within their reach. And at the end of that talk Captain Kettle put out his hand and took the engineer's in a heavy grip. "Mac," he said, "you're Scotch, but you're a gentleman right through under your clothes."

"I was born to that estate, skipper, and I no more wanted to see yon puir deevil pulled down to our level than you do. Better go and give him the news, and I'll get our boat in the water again, and revictualled."

"No," said Kettle, "I can't stand by and be thanked. You go. I'll see to the boat."

"Be hanged if I do!" said the engineer. "Write the man a letter. You're great on the writing line: I've seen you at it."

And so in the tramp's main cabin below Captain Kettle penned this epistle:

To CAPTAIN J. R. MULREADY.

DEAR JIMMY,

Having concluded not to take trouble to work *Duncansby Head* home, have pleasure in leaving her to your charge. We, having other game on hand, have now taken French leave, and shall now bear up for Western Islands. You've no call to say anything about our being on board at all. Spin your own yarn, it will never be contradicted.—Yours truly,

O. KETTLE (Master),

p. p. N. A. McTODD (Chief Engineer), O. K.

P.S.—We taken along these two Dagos. If you had them they might talk when you got them home. We having them, they will not talk. So you've only your own crowd to keep from talking. Good luck, old tintacks.

Which letter was sealed and nailed up in a conspicuous place before the lifeboat left *en route* for Grand Canary.

It was the two Portuguese who felt themselves principally aggrieved men. They had been made to undergo a great deal of work and hardship; they had been defrauded of much plunder which they quite considered was theirs, for the benefit of an absolute stranger in whom they took not the slightest interest; and, finally, they were induced " not to talk " by processes which jarred upon them most unpleasantly.

They did not talk, and in the fulness of time they returned to the avocation of shovelling coal on steam vessels. But when they sit down to think, neither Antonio nor his friend (whose honoured name I never learned) regard with affection those little islands in the Northern Sea, which produced Captain Owen Kettle and his sometime partner, Mr. Neil Angus McTodd.

CHAPTER XII.

THE WRECK OF THE CATTLE-BOAT.

THERE was considerable trouble and risk in bringing the lifeboat up alongside, but it must be granted
that she was very unhandy.

The gale that had blown them out into the Atlantic had moderated, certainly, though there was
still a considerable breeze blowing, but the sea was
running as high as ever, and all Captain Kettle's skill
was required to prevent the boat from being incontinently swamped. McTodd and the two Portuguese baled incessantly, but the boat was always
half waterlogged. In fact, from constitutional
defects, she had made very wet weather of it all
through the blow.

It was the part of the steamer to have borne down
and given the lifeboat a lee in which she could have
been more readily handled, and three times the
larger vessel made an attempt to do this, but without
avail. Three times she worked round in a wallowing circle, got to windward, and distributed a smell
of farmyard over the rugged furrows of ocean, and
then lost her place again before she could drift down
and give the smaller craft shelter. Three times did
the crew of the lifeboat, with maritime point and
fluency, curse the incompetence of the rust-streaked
steamer and all her complement.

" By James," said Kettle savagely, after the third attempt, "are **they all farmers on** that ship? I've **had** a nigger **steward that** knew more about handling a vessel."

" She's **an** English ship," **said McTodd, "and** delicate. They're nursing her in the engine-room. **Look at** the **way** they throttle her down when she races."

" **The fools on her** upper bridge are enough for me too look at," Kettle **retorted. "Why** didn't they **put a sailorman** aboard of her **before she was** kicked out **of port? By James, if** we'd **a** week's water and victual with **us** in the lifeboat **here, I'd** beat back for **the** Canaries as we are, and keep clear of that tin farmyard for bare safety's sake."

" We haven't a crumb nor a drink left," said the engineer, "and **I'd not** recommend this present form **of** conveyance to the insurance companies." A wave-top came up from **the** tireless grey sea, and slapped green and cold about his neck and shoulders —"Gosh ! **There** comes more of the Atlantic to bale back into place. Mon, **this** is no' the kind of navigation I admire."

Meanwhile **the** clumsy tramp-steamer had gone round in a jagged circle of a mile's diameter, and was climbing back to position again over **the** hills and dales **of** ocean. She rolled, and she pitched, and she wallowed amongst the seas, and to the lay mind she would **have** seemed helplessness personified. **But to** the expert eye she showed defects in her handling with every sheer she took amongst the angry waste of waters.

" Old man and the mates must be staying down

below out of the wet," said Kettle contemptuously as he gazed. " Looks as if they've left some sort of a cheap Dutch quartermaster on the upper bridge to run her. Don't tell me there's an officer holding an English ticket in command of that steamer. They aren't going to miss us this time though if they know it."

" Looks like as if they were going to soss down slap on top of us," said McTodd, and set to taking off his coat and boots.

But the cattle steamer, if not skilfully handled, at any rate this time had more luck. She worked her way up to windward again, and then fell off into the trough, squattering down almost out of sight one minute, and, in fact, showing little of herself except a couple of stumpy, untidy masts and a brine-washed smoke stack above the seascape, and being heaved up almost clear the next second, a picture of rust-streaks and yellow spouting scuppers.

Both craft drifted to leeward before the wind, but the steamer offered most surface, and moved the quicker, which was the object of the manœuvre. It seemed to those in the lifeboat that they were not going to be missed this time, and so they lowered away their sodden canvas, shipped tholepins, and got out their oars. The two Portuguese firemen did not assist at first, preferring to sit in a semi-dazed condition on the wet floor gratings ; but McTodd and Kettle thumped them about the head, after the time-honoured custom, till they turned to, and so presently the lifeboat, under three straining oars, was holding up towards her would-be deliverer.

A man on the cattle boat's upper bridge was ex-

hibiting himself as **a very** model of nervous inca-
pacity, and two at any rate of the castaways in the
lifeboat were watching him with grim scorn.

" Keeping them on the dance in **the** engine-room,
isn't he ? " said McTodd.   " He's rung that telegraph
bell fifteen different ways this last minute."

" That man **isn't** fit to skipper anything that hasn't
got a tow-rope made fast ahead," said Kettle contemptuously.   " He hasn't the nerve of a pound of
putty."

" I'm thinking we shall **lose the boat.** They'll
never get her aboard in one **piece."**

" If we get amongst their cow **pens with** our bare
lives we shall be lucky.   They're going to heave us
a line.   Stand by to catch it, quick."

The line was thrown and caught. The cattle-
steamer surged up over a huge rolling sea, showing her jagged bilge-chocks clear ; and then she
squelched down again, dragging the lifeboat close
in a murderous cuddle, which smashed in one of her
sides as though it had been made from egg-shell.
Other lines were thrown by the hands who stood
against the rail above, and the four men in the
swamping boat each seized an end.

Half climbing, half hoisted from above, **they** made
their way up the rusted plating, and the greedy
waves from underneath sucked and clamoured at
their heels.   It was quite a toss-up even then
whether they would be dragged from their hold ; but
human muscles can put forth desperate efforts in
these moments of desperate stress ; and they reached
the swaying deck planks, bruised, and **breathless**
and gasping, **but** for the time being safe.

The cattle-boat's mate who had been assisting their arrival, sorted them into castes with ready perception. " Now, you two Dagos," he said to the Portuguese, "get away forrard—port side—and bid some of our firemen to give you a bunk. I'll tell the steward to bring you along a tot of rum directly." He clapped a friendly hand on McTodd's shoulder. " Bo's'n," he said, "take this gentleman down to the mess-room, and pass the word to one of the engineers to come and give him a welcome." And then he turned as to an equal, and shook Kettle by the hand. "Very glad to welcome you aboard, old fellow—beg pardon, 'Captain' I should have said ; didn't see the lace on your sleeve before. Come below with me, Captain, and I'll fix you up with some dry things outside, and some wet things in, before we have any further chatter."

" Mr. Mate," said Kettle, "you're very polite, but hadn't I better go up on to the bridge and say ' howdy ' to the skipper first ? "

The mate of the cattle-boat grinned and tucked his arm inside Captain Kettle's, and dragged him off with kindly force towards the companion-way. "Take the synch from me, Captain, and don't The old man's in such a mortal fear for the ship, that he's fair crying with it. If he'd had his way, I don't fancy he'd have seen your boat at all. He said it was suicide to try and pick you up with such a sea running. But the second mate and I put in some ugly talk, and so he just had to do it. Here's the companion. Step inside, and I'll shut the door."

" Pretty sort of captain to let his mates boss him."

"Quite agree with you, Captain: quite agree with you all the way. But that's what's done on this ship, and there's no getting over it. It's not to my liking either—I'm an old *Conway* boy, and was brought up to respect discipline. However, I daresay you'll see for yourself how things run before we dump you back on dry mud again. Now. here we are at my room, and there's a change of clothes in that drawer beneath the bed, and underwear below the settee here. You and I are much of a build, and the kit's quite at your service till your own is dry again."

The mate was back again in ten minutes—dripping, cheerful, hospitable. "Holy tailors!" said he, "how you do set off clothes! Those old duds came out of a slop-chest once, and I've been ashamed of their shabbiness more years than I care to think about; but you've a way of carrying them that makes them look well-fitting and quite new. Well, I tell you I'm pleased to see a spruce man on this ship. Come into the cabin now and peck a bit. I ordered you a meal, and I saw the steward as I came past the door trying to hold it down in the fiddles. The old girl can roll a bit, can't she?"

"I should say your farmyard's getting well churned up."

"You should just go into those cattle decks and see. It's just Hades for the poor brutes. We're out of the River Plate, you know, and we've carried bad weather with us ever since we got our anchors. The beasts were badly stowed, and there were too many of them put aboard. The Old Man grumbled, but the shippers didn't take any notice of him.

They'd **signed for** the whole ship, and they just crammed as many sheep and cows into her as she'd hold."

" **You'll have** the Cruelty to Animals people on board of you before you're docked, and then your skipper had better look out."

" He knows that, Captain, quite as well **as you do,** and there isn't a man more sorry for himself in all the Western Ocean. He'll be fined heavily, and have his name dirtied, so sure as ever he sets a foot **ashore.** Legally, I suppose, he's responsible; but really **he's no more to** blame than you. He is part **of the** ship, just as the engines, or the mates, or the tablespoons are; and the whole bags o' tricks was let by **wire from** Liverpool to a South American Dago. If he'd talked, he'd have got **the** straight kick-out from the owners, and no further argument. You see they are little bits of owners."

" They're the worst sort."

" It doesn't matter who they are. A skipper has got to do as he's told."

" Yes," said Kettle with a sigh, " I know that."

" Well," said the **mate,** "you may thank **your best** little star that you're only here as a passenger. The grub's beastly, **the ship** stinks, the cook's a fool, and everthing's as uncomfortable as can be. But there's one fine amusement ahead of you, and that's try and cheer up the other passenger."

" Stowaway ?"

" No, *bonâ fide* passenger, if you can imagine **any**one being mug enough to book a room **on a foul** cattle-loaded tramp like this. But I guess it **was** because she was **hard up.** She was a governess, or something of that sort, in Buenos Ayres, lost her berth, and wanted to get back again cheap. I guess we could afford to cut rates and make a profit there."

" Poor lady."

" I've not seen much of her myself. The second mate and I are most of the crew of this ship (as the Old Man objects to our driving the regular deck-hands), and when we're not at work, we're asleep. I can't stop and introduce you. You must chum on. Her name's Carnegie."

" Miss Carnegie," Kettle repeated, "that sounds familiar. Does she write poetry ?"

The mate yawned. "Don't know. Never asked her. But perhaps she does. She looks ill enough."

The mate went off to his room then, turned in, all standing, and was promptly asleep. Kettle, with memories of the past refreshed, took paper and a scratchy pen, and fell to concocting verse.

He wondered, and at the same time he half dreaded, whether this was the same Miss Carnegie whom he had known before. In days past she had given him a commission to liberate her lover from the French penal settlement of Cayenne. With in-finite danger and difficulty he had wrenched the man free from his warders, and then, finding him a worthless fellow, had by force married him to an old Jamaican negress, and sent the girl their mar-riage lines as a token of her release. He had had no word or sign from her since, and was in some dread now lest she might bitterly resent the liberty he had taken in meddling so far with her affairs.

However, like it or not, there was no avoiding the

meeting now, and so he went on—somewhat fever-
ishly—with his writing.

The squalid meal entitled tea came on, and he
had to move his papers. A grimy steward spread a
dirty cloth, wetted it liberally with water, and
shipped fiddles to try and induce the tableware to
keep in place despite the rolling. The steward
mentioned that none of the officers would be down,
that the two passengers would meal together, and in
fact did his best to be affable ; but Kettle listened
with cold inattention, and the steward began to wish
him over the side whence he had come.

The laying of the table was ended at last. The
steward put on his jacket, clanged a bell in the alley
way, and then came back and stood swaying in the
middle of the cabin, armed with a large tin teapot,
all ready to commence business. So heavy was the
roll, that **at** times he had to put his hand on the
floor for support.

Captain Kettle watched the door with a haggard
face. He was beginning to realise that an emotion
was stirred within him that should have no place in
his system. He told himself sternly that he was a
married man with a family ; that he had a deep affection for both his wife and children ; that, in cold
fact, he had seen Miss Carnegie in **the** flesh but
once before. But there was no getting over the
memory that she made poetry, a craft that he adored ;
and he could not forget that she had already lived
in his mind for more months than he dared count.

His conscience took him by the ear, **and** sighed
out the word Love. On **the** instant, all his pride
of manhood was up in arms, and he rejected the

imputation with scorn ; and then, after some thought, formulated his liking for the girl in the term Interest. But he knew full well that his sentiment was something deeper than that.   His chest heaved when he thought of her.

Then, in the distance he heard **her** approaching. He wiped the moisture from his face with the mate's pocket-handkerchief. Above the din of the seas **and the noises** from the crowded cattle-pens outside, he could make **out** the faint rustle of draperies, and the uncertain footsteps of someone painfully making a way along, hand over hand **against** the bulkheads. A bunch of fingers appeared round the jamb **of a** door, slender white fingers, one of them decked with a queer old ring, which he had seen just once before, and had pictured a thousand times since. And then the girl herself stepped out into the cabin, swaying to the roll of the ship.

She nodded to him with instant recognition.   "It was you they picked up out of the boat?   Oh I am so glad you are safe."

Kettle strode out towards **her** on his steady sea legs, and stood before her, still not daring to take her hand. "You have forgiven me?" he murmured. "What I did was a liberty, I know, but if I had not liked you so well, I should not have dared to do it."

She cast down her eyes and flushed. "You are the kindest man I ever met," she said. "The very kindest." She took his hand in both hers, and gripped it with nervous force. "I shall never forget what you did for me, Captain."

The grimy steward behind them coughed and

rattled the teapot lid, and so they sat themselves at the table and the business of tea began. All of the ship's officers were either looking after the work entailed by the heavy weather on deck, **or** sleeping the sleep of utter exhaustion in their bunks ; and so none joined them at the meal. But the steward incessantly hovered at their elbows, and it was only during his fitful absences that their talk was anything like unrestrained.

"You said you liked poetry," the girl whispered shyly when the first of these opportunities came. "I wrote the most heartfelt verses that ever came **from me, over** that noble thing you tried to do for **a** poor stranger like me."

Captain Kettle blushed like a maid. "For one of the magazines ?" he asked.

She shook her head sadly. "It was not published when I left England, and it had been sent back **to** me from four magazine offices. That was **noth**ing new. They never would take any of my stuff."

Kettle's fingers twitched suggestively. "I'd like **to** talk a minute or so with some of those editors. I'd make them sit up."

"That wouldn't make them print my poems."

"Wouldn't it, Miss? **Well,** perhaps you know best there. But I'd guarantee it'd hinder them **from** printing anything **else for** awhile, the inky-fingered brutes. The twaddling stories those editors set up **type,** about low-down pirates and **de**tective **bugs are** enough to make one sick."

It appeared that Miss Carnegie's father **had** died since **she and** Kettle had last met, **and** the girl **had** found herself left almost destitute. She had been lured out to Buenos Ayres by an advertisement, but without finding employment, and, sick at heart, had bought with the last of her scanty store of money a cheap passage home in this cattle-boat.

She would land in England entirely destitute; and although she did not say this, spoke cheerfully of the future, in fact, Kettle was torn with pity for her state. But what, he asked himself with fierce scorn, could he do? He was penniless himself; he had a wife and family depending on him; and who was he to take this young unmarried girl under his charge?

They talked long on that and other days, always avoiding vital questions; and, meanwhile, the reeking cattle-boat wallowed north, carrying with her, as it seemed, a little charmed circle of evil weather as her constant accompaniment.

Between times, when he was not in attendance on Miss Carnegie, Kettle watched the life of the steamer with professional interest, and all a strong man's contempt for a weak commander. The 'tween decks was an Aceldama. In the heavy weather the cattle-pens smashed, the poor beasts broke their legs, gored one another, and were surged about in horrible *mêlées*. The cattle-men were half incapable, wholly mutinous. They dealt out compressed hay and water when the gangways were cleared, and held to it that this was the beginning and end of their duty. To pass down the winch chain, and haul out the dead and wounded, was a piece of employment that they flatly refused to tamper with. They said the deck hands could do it.

The deck hands, scenting a weak commander, said

they had been hired as sailor-men, and also declined to meddle, and, as a consequence, this necessary sepulture business was done by the mates.

In Kettle's first and only interview with the cattle-boat's captain he saw this operation going on through a hatchway before his very face. The mate and the second mate clambered down by the battens, and went along the filthy gangway below, dragging the winch chain after them. The place was cluttered with carcases and jammed with broken pens, all surging together to the roll of the ship. The lowings and the groans of the cattle were awful. But at last a bight of rope was made fast round a dead beast's horns, and the word was given to haul. The winch chattered and the chain drew. The two men below, jumping to this side and that for their lives, handspiked the carcase free of obstacles, and at last it came up the hatch, a battered shapeless rag, almost unrecognisable.

A mob of men, sulky, sullen, and afraid, stood round the hatch, and one of these, when the poor remains came up, and swung to the roll of the ship over the side, cut the bowline with his knife, and let the carcase *plop* into the racing seas. The chain clashed back again down between the iron coamings of the hatch, and the two mates below went on with their work. No one offered to help them. No one, as Kettle grimly noted, was made to do so.

"Do your three mates run this ship, Captain?" asked Kettle at last.

"They are handy fellows."

"If you ask me, I should call them poor drivers. What for do they put in all the work themselves when there are that mob of deck hands and cattle-hands standing round doing the gentleman as though they were in the gallery of a theatre?"

"There was some misunderstanding when the crew were shipped. They say they never signed on to handle dead cattle."

"I've seen those kind of misunderstandings before, Captain, and I've started in to smooth them away."

"Well?" said the captain of the cattle-boat.

"Oh! with me!" said Kettle truculently, "they straightened out so soon as ever I began to hit. If your mates know their business, they'd soon have that crew in hand again."

"I don't allow my mates to knock the men about. To give them their due, they wanted to; they were brought up in a school which would probably suit you, Captain, all three of them; but I don't permit that sort of thing. I am a Christian man, and I will not order my fellow-men to be struck. If the fellows refuse their duty, it lies between them and their consciences."

"As if an old sailor had a conscience!" murmured Kettle to himself. "Well, Captain, I'm no small piece of a Christian myself, but I was taught that whatever my hand findeth to do, to do it with all my might, and I guess bashing a lazy crew comes under that head."

"I don't want either your advice or your theology."

"If I wasn't a passenger here," said Kettle, "I'd like to tell you what I thought of your seamanship and your notion of making a master's ticket re-spected. But I'll hold my tongue on that. As it is,

I think I ought just to say I don't consider this ship's safe, run the way she is."

The captain of the cattle-boat flushed darkly. He jerked his head towards the ladder. "Get down off this bridge," he said.

"What!"

"You hear me. Geddown off my bridge. If you've learnt anything about your profession you must know this is private up here, and no place for blooming passengers."

Kettle glared and hesitated. He was not used to receiving orders of this description, and the innovation did not please him. But for once in his life he submitted. Miss Carnegie was sitting under the lee of the deckhouse aft, watching him, and somehow or other he did not choose to have a scene before her. It was all part of this strange new feeling which had come over him.

He gripped his other impulses tight, and went and sat beside her. She welcomed him cordially. She made no secret of her pleasure at his presence. But her talk just now jarred upon him. Like other people who see the ocean and its traffic merely from the amateur's view, she was able to detect romance beneath her present discomforts, and she was pouring into his ear her scheme for making it the foundation of her most ambitious **poem.**

In Kettle's mind, to build an epic on such a groundwork, was nothing short of profanation. He viewed the sea, seamen, and sea duties with an intimate eye; to him they were common and unclean **to the** furthest degree : no trick of language could elevate their meannesses. He pointed out how she would

prostitute her talent by laying hold of such an unsavoury subject, and extolled the beauty of his own
ideal.

" Tackle a cornfield, Miss," he would say again and
again, " with its butter-yellow colour, and its blobs
of red poppies, and the green hedges all round.
You write poetry such as I know you can about a cornfield, and farmers, and farm buildings with thatched
roofs, and you'll wake one of these mornings (like
all poets hope to do some day) and find yourself
famous.   And because why, you want to know?
Well, Miss, it's because cornfields and the country
and all that are what people want to hear about,
and dream they've got handy to their own back
doorstep. They're so peaceful, so restful. You
take it from me, no one would even want to read
four words about this beastly cruel sea, and the brutes
of men who make their living by driving ships across
it. No, by Ja—No, Miss, you take it from a man
who knows, they'd just despise it." And so they
argued endlessly at the point, each keeping an un-
changed opinion.

Perhaps of all the human freight that the cattle-
boat carried, Mr. McTodd was the only one person
entirely happy. He had no watch to keep, no work
to do ; the mess-room was warm, stuffy, and entirely
to his taste ; liquor was plentiful ; and the official
engineers of the ship were Scotch and argumenta-
tive. He never came on deck for a whiff of fresh
air, never knew a moment's tedium ; he lived in a
pleasant atmosphere of broad dialect, strong tobacco,
and toasting oil and thoroughly enjoyed himself ;
though when the moment of trial came, and his

thews and energies were wanted for the saving of human life, he quickly showed that this Capua had in no way sapped his efficiency.

The steamer had, as has been said, carried foul weather with her all the way across the Atlantic from the River Plate, as though it were a curse inflicted for the cruelty of her stevedores. The crew forgot what it was like to wear dry clothes, the afterguard lived in a state of bone-weariness. A harder captain would have still contrived to keep them up to the mark; but the man who was in supreme command was feeble and undecided, and there is no doubt that vigilance was dangerously slackened.

A fog, too, which came down to cover the sea, stopped out all view of the sun, and compelled them for three days to depend on a dead reckoning; and (after the event) it was said a strong current set the steamer unduly to the westward.

Anyway, be the cause what it may, Kettle was pitched violently out of his bunk in the deep of one night, just after two bells, and from the symptoms which loudly advertised themselves, it required no expert knowledge to tell that the vessel was beating her bottom out on rocks, to the accompaniment of a murderously heavy sea. The engines stopped, steam began to blow off noisily from the escapes, and what with that, and the cries of men, and the crashing of seas, and the beating of iron, and the beast cries from the cattledecks, the din was almost enough to split the ear. And then the steam syren burst out into one vast bellow of pain, which drowned all the other noises as though they had been children's whispers.

Kettle slid on coat and trousers over his pyjamas, and went and thumped at a door at the other side of the alleyway.

"Miss Carnegie?"

"Yes."

"Dress quickly."

"I am dressing, Captain."

"Get finished with it, and then wait. I'll come for you when it's time."

It is all very well to be cool on these occasions, but sometimes the race is to the prompt. Captain Kettle made his way up on deck against a green avalanche of water which was cascading down the companionway. No shore was in sight. The ship had backed off after she had struck, and was now rolling heavily in the deep trough. She was low in the water, and every second wave swept her.

No one seemed to be in command. The dim light showed Kettle one lifeboat wrecked in davits, and a disorderly mob of men trying to lower the other. But some one let go the stern fall so that the boat shot down perpendicularly, and the next wave smashed the lower half of it into splinters. The frenzied crowd left it to try the port quarter-boat, and Kettle raced them across the streaming decks, and got first to the davits. He plucked a greenheart belaying pin from the rail, and laid about him viciously. "Back, you scum!" he shouted; "get back, or I'll smash in every face amongst you. Good Lord, isn't there a mate or a man left on this stinking farmyard? Am I to keep off all this two-legged cattle by myself?"

They fought on, the black water swirling waist

deep amongst them with every roll, the syren bellowing for help overhead, and the ship sinking under their feet; and gradually, with the frenzy of despair, the men drove Kettle back against the rail, whilst others of them cast off the falls of the quarter-boat's tackles preparatory to letting her drop. But then, out of the darkness, up came McTodd and the steamer's mate, both shrewd hitters, and men not afraid to use their skill, and once more the tables were turned.

The other quarter-boat had been lowered and swamped; this boat was the only one remaining.

"Now, Mac," said Kettle, "help the mate take charge, and murder every one that interferes. Get the boat in the water, and fend off. I'll be off below and fetch up Miss Carnegie. We must put some hurry in it. The old box hasn't much longer to swim. Take the lady ashore, and see she comes to no harm."

"Oh, aye," said McTodd, "and we'll keep a seat for yerself, skipper."

"You needn't bother," said Kettle. "I take no man's place in this sort of tea-party." He splashed off across the streaming decks, and found the cattle-boat's captain sheltering under the lee of the companion, wringing his hands. "Out, you blitherer," he shouted, "and save your mangy life. Your ship's gone now: you can't play hash with her any more." After which pleasant speech he worked his way below, half swimming, half wading, and once more beat against Miss Carnegie's door. Even in this moment of extremity he did not dream of going in unasked.

She came out to him in the half-swamped alley-way, fully dressed. "Is there any hope?" she asked.

"We'll get you ashore, don't you fear." He clapped an arm round her waist, and drew her strongly on through the dark and the swirling water towards the foot of the companion. "Excuse me, Miss," he said. "This is not familiarity. But I have got the firmer sea-legs, and we must hurry."

They pressed up the stair, battling with great green cascades of water, and gained the dreadful turmoil on deck. A few weak stars gleamed out above the wind, and showed the black wave tops dimly. Already some of the cattle had been swept overboard, and were swimming about like the horned beasts of a nightmare. The din of surf came to them amongst the other noises, but no shore was visible. The steamer had backed off the reef on which she had struck, and was foundering in deep water. It was indeed a time for hurry. It was plain she had very few more minutes to swim.

Each sea now made a clean breach over her, and a passage about the decks was a thing of infinite danger. But Kettle was resourceful and strong, and he had a grip round Miss Carnegie and a hold on something solid when the waters drenched on him, and he contrived never to be wrenched entirely from his hold.

But when he had worked his way aft, a disappointment was there ready for him. The quarterboat was gone. McTodd stood against one of the davits, cool and philosophical as ever.

"You infernal Scotchman, you've let them take

away the boat from you," Kettle snarled. " I should thought you could have kept your end up with a mangy crowd like that."

" Use your eyes," said the engineer. " The boat's in the wash below there at the end of the tackles with her side stove in. She drowned the three men that were lowered in her because they'd no' sense enough to fend her off."

" That comes of setting a lot of farmers to work a steamboat."

" Awell," said McTodd, " steamers have been lost before, and I have it in mind, Captain, that you've helped."

" By James, if you don't carry a civil tongue, you drunken Geordie, I'll knock you some teeth down to cover it."

" Oh, I owe, you that," said McTodd, " but now we're quits. I bided here, Captain Kettle, because I thought you'd maybe like to swim the leddy off to the shore, and at that I can bear a useful hand."

" Mac," said Kettle, " I take back what I said about your being Scotch. You're a good soul." He turned to the girl, still shouting to make his voice carry above the clash of the seas and the bellow of the syren, and the noises of the dying ship : " It's our only chance, Miss—swimming. The life-buoys from the bridge are all gone—I looked. The hands will have taken them. There'll be a lot of timber floating about when she goes down, and we'll be best clear of that. Will you trust to us ? "

" I trust you in everything," she said.

Deeper and deeper the steamer sank in her wallow. The lower decks were swamped by this, and the miserable cattle were either drowned in their stalls or washed out of her. There was no need for the three to jump—they just let go their hold, and the next incoming wave swept them clear of the steamer's spar deck, and spurned them a hundred yards from her side.

They found themselves amongst a herd of floating cattle, some drowned, some swimming frenziedly; and with the inspiration of the moment laid hold of a couple of the beasts which were tangled together by a halter, and so supported themselves without further exertion. It was no use swimming for the present. They could not tell which way the shore lay. And it behoved them to reserve all their energies for the morning, so well as the numbing, cold of the water would let them.

Of a sudden the bellow of the steamer's syren ceased, and a pang went through them as though they had lost a friend. Then came a dull, muffled explosion. And then, a huge ragged shape loomed up through the night like some vast monument, and sank swiftly straight downwards out of sight beneath the black, tumbled sea.

"Poor old girl!" said McTodd, spitting out the sea water, "they'd a fine keg of whisky down in her mess-room."

"Poor devil of a skipper!" said Kettle; "it's to be hoped he's drowned out of harm's way, or it'll take lying to keep him any rags of his ticket."

The talk died out of them after that, and the miseries of the situation closed in. The water was cold, but the air was piercing, and so they kept their bodies submerged, each holding on to the bovine raft, and each man sparing a few fingers to keep a grip on the girl. One of the beasts they clung to quickly drowned; the other, strange to say, kept its nostrils above water, swimming strongly, and in the end came alive to the shore, the only four-footed occupant of the steamer to be saved.

At the end of each minute it seemed to them that they were too bruised and numbed to hang on another sixty seconds; and yet the next minute found them still alive and dreading its successor. The sea moaned around them, mourning the dead; the fleet of drowned cattle surged helplessly to this way and to that, bruising them with rude collisions; and the chill bit them to the bone, mercifully numbing their pain and anxiety. Long before the dawn the girl had sunk into a stupor, and was only held from sinking by the nervous fingers of the men; and the men themselves were merely automata, completing their task with a legacy of will.

When from somewhere out of the morning mists a fisher boat sailed up, manned by ragged, kindly Irish, all three were equally lost to consciousness, and all three were hauled over the gunwale in one continuous dripping string. The grip of the men's fingers had endured too long to be loosened for a sudden call such as that.

They were taken ashore and tended with all the care poor homes could give; and the men, used to hardships, recovered with a dose of warmth and sleep.

Miss Carnegie took longer to recover, and, in fact, for a week lay very near to death. Kettle stayed on in the village making almost hourly inquiries for her. He ought to have gone away to seek fresh employment. He ought to have gone back to his wife and children, and he upbraided himself bitterly for his neglect of these duties. But still he could not tear himself away. For the future—— Well, he dreaded to think what might happen in the future.

But at last the girl was able to sit up and see him, and he visited her, showing all the deference an ambassador might offer to a queen. I may go so far as to say that he went into the cottage quite infatuated. He came out of it disillusioned.

She listened to his tale of the wreck with interest and surprise, She was almost startled to hear that others, including the captain and two of the mates, were saved from the disaster besides themselves, but at the same time unfeignedly pleased. And she was pleased also to hear that Kettle was subpœnaed to give evidence before the forthcoming inquiry.

"I am glad of that," she said, "because I know you will speak with a free mind. You have told me so many times how incompetent the captain was, and now you will be able to tell it to the proper authorities."

Kettle looked at her blankly. "But that was different," he said. "I can't say to them what I said to you."

"Why not? Look what misery and suffering and loss of life the man has caused. He isn't fit to command a ship."

"But, Miss," said Kettle, "it's his living. He's been brought up to seafaring, and he isn't fit for anything else.   You wouldn't have me send out the man to starve?   Besides, I'm a shipmaster myself, and you wouldn't have me try to take away another master's ticket?   The cleverest captain afloat might meet with misfortune, and he's always got to think of that when he's put up to give evidence against his fellows."

"Well, what are you going to do, then?"

"Oh, we've got together a tale, and when the old man is put up on his trial, the mates and I will stick to it through thick and thin.   You can bet that we are not going to swear away his ticket."

"His ticket?"

"Yes; his master's certificate—his means of liveli-hood."

"I think it's wrong," she said excitedly; "crimi-nally wrong.   And, besides, you said you didn't like the man."

"I don't; I dislike him cordially.   But that's nothing to do with the case.   I've my own honour to think of, Miss.   How'd I feel if I went about knowing I'd done my best to ruin a brother captain for good and always?"

"You are wrong," she repeated vehemently.

"The man is incompetent by your own saying, and therefore he should suffer."

Kettle's heart chilled.

"Miss Carnegie," he said, "I am disappointed in you.   I thought from your poetry that you had feelings; I thought you had charity; but I find you are cold.

"And you!" she retorted, "you that I have set up for myself as an ideal of most of the manly virtues, do you think I feel no disappointment when I hear that you are deliberately proposing to be a liar?"

"I am no liar," he said sullenly. "I have most faults, but not that. This is different; you do not understand. It is not lying to defend one's fellow ship-master before an Inquiry Board."

The girl turned to the pillow in her chair, and hid her face. "Oh, go!" she said, "go! I wish I had never met you. I thought you were so good, and so brave and so honest, and when it comes to the pinch, you are just like the rest! Go, go! I wish I thought I could ever forget you."

"You say you don't understand," said Kettle. "I think you deliberately won't understand, Miss. You remember that I said I was disappointed in you, and I stick to that now. You make me remember that I have got a wife and family I am fond of. You make me ashamed I have not gone to them before."

He went to the door and opened it. "But I do not think I shall ever forget," he said, "how much I cared for you once. Good-bye, Miss."

"Good-bye" she sobbed from her pillow, "I wish I could think you are right, but perhaps it is best as it is."

In the village street outside, was Mr. McTodd clothed in rasping serge, and inclined to be sententious. "They've whisky here," he said with a jerk of the thumb, "Irish whisky, that's got a smoky taste that's rather alluring when you've got over the first dislike. I'm out o' siller mysel' or I'd stand ye a glass, but if ye're in funds, I could guide ye to the place?"

Kettle was half tempted. But with a wrench he said " No," adding that if he once started, he might not know when to stop.

"Quite right," said the engineer, "you're quite (hic) right, skipper. A man with an inclination to level himself with the beasts that perish, should always be abstemious." He sat against a wayside fence and prepared for sleep.

" Like me," he added solemnly, and shut his eyes.

" No," said Kettle to himself ; " I won't forget it that way. I guess I can manage without. She pretty well cured me herself. But a sight of the Missis will do the rest."

And so Captain Owen Kettle went home to where Mrs. Kettle kept house in the by-street in South Shields, that unlovely town on Tyneside ; and a worrying time he had of it with that estimable woman, his wife, before the explanations which he saw fit to give were passed as entirely satisfactory. In fact he was not quite forgiven for his escapade with Miss Carnegie or for that other involuntary excursion with Donna Clotilde La Touche till such time as he had acquired fortune from adventure on the seas and was able to take Mrs. Kettle away from her unsavoury surroundings, and settle down in comfort in a small farmstead on the Yorkshire moors with a hired maid to assist at the housework. But that was not until some considerable time after he was wrecked with Mr. McTodd on the Irish Coast ; and between the two dates he assisted to make a good deal more history which is (or will be) else-where related.

THE END.